CW00407422

M.J. WHITE

Faze The City of Addicts

Dear Kate and Wendy

Thank you for all your

Support.

love

X

First published by Jillion Realms Publishing 2021

Copyright © 2021 by M.J. White

All rights reserved. No part of this publication may be reproduced, stored or transmitted in any form or by any means, electronic, mechanical, photocopying, recording, scanning, or otherwise without written permission from the publisher. It is illegal to copy this book, post it to a website, or distribute it by any other means without permission.

This novel is entirely a work of fiction. The names, characters and incidents portrayed in it are the work of the author's imagination. Any resemblance to actual persons, living or dead, events or localities is entirely coincidental.

M.J. White asserts the moral right to be identified as the author of this work.

First edition

This book was professionally typeset on Reedsy.
Find out more at reedsy.com

For Lyndsay,
and in memory of all the friends and family, I have lost along the way

Contents

Acknowledgement

Undoubtedly, I need to acknowledge Catherine Tully, who's creative writing class I attended in the Wirral in 2017. I wrote a short story titled 'A Leap of Faith.' Ironically, this is what I did. Catherine encouraged me to write and think about re-educating myself, without her, this journey would never have started, and I thank you so much.

A huge thank you to Emma Wallace, who allowed me to stay at her retreat in south-west France for a few weeks back in 2018 where the backbone of *Faze* was conceived.

I thank all the staff at Andover college who supported me in my first steps to becoming a writer and a special mention to Ryan Taylor, Carol Shepperd, and Susannah Putigny. Also, thank you to all the gang at the Andover Writers Circle, especially Sharon Vennall, and Norman Townsend for their support.

To all those that took time to read Faze in its early stages and encouraged me to continue in the pursuit of publishing, I am genuinely grateful to my siblings, Chris, Sarrah, and Sophie. Also, Alison (Mama) Ballantyne, my old friend Simon Hunter and new friend Jayne Peach. I give a huge thank you to Charlotte Popplee for the original edit of Faze. And to all my followers on social media and my website, I thank your continuing support and encouragement.

Faze would not have been possible if it were not for the

professional support I have received from John Dyson and Dr Ruth Verrier Jones. I also must thank all the staff at the University of Winchester Creative Writing Department and the Hampshire Writers Society's ongoing support.

To Erin Kaye and all the team and Jillion Realms Publishing I am so grateful you have taken me on board and believe in me and my work.

Most importantly, I would not be here, never-mind this book, if it were not for the constant support and love I receive from my Mum, my daughter Bethany and my partner Lyndsay, I am so grateful and lucky to have you in my life.

CHAPTER ONE

Red skies were slashed with wisps of white cloud, resembling a canvas which had been ripped through with giant claws. The setting sun gave a welcomed reprieve to the scorched earth and the desert-dwelling insects that were just emerging from under rocks. They lived in a vast canyon which had been gouged out by an ancient river leaving caucus fangs of stone, towering over the dry landscape.

Six-legged beasts, with four savage tusks, were migrating from their breeding grounds, heading south to meet the monsoon rains. In vast numbers, they marched over the dry earth, surrounded by the rocky peninsula.

The sheer number of them crashing over the desert plain, caused rocks to become detached from their mountain cradles, rolling into the valley, creating clouds of sand which mingled with the acrid air. At the head of the herd with a plated, boned frill protruding from his neck was a huge bull. Despite appearances, the Vinayaki were giant, docile beasts.

The cows in the herd had bulging udders which trailed in the sand as they struggled onward. Their massive tails swatted at the persistently biting flies, which sucked blood from their leathered rumps.

Huge, cloudy yellow pupils, squinted in the dry air. The

small trunk hanging from the middle of their faces tested the ground for moisture.

The herd began to grunt warnings to each other, and rearing up, the bull roared, signalling the alarm. The Vinayaki cows began to stampede, passing the bull, they engulfed him in a cloud of dust. The male Vinayaki turned about; a low rumble sounded from his throat.

A figure laid in cover, observing the herd moving away from the solitary bull, from the top of a mountain. Standing tall, with two piercing red eyes, he watched the scene below. He removed a flare gun from a holster on his hip. He fired a rocket, into the sky, and watched as it burst into a fountain of red, fiery smoke. The response to the flare was immediate.

The sound of roaring engines echoed in the canyon. The bull reared up again, bellowing towards the oncoming sound. He thrashed his huge six-foot tusks in the sand, rocking his head side to side, as he prepared to defend himself.

On the horizon, dozens of objects came into view, motors roared, tearing towards the bull. The predators were customised armoured dune buggies, with heavy machine guns attached to the roof. The drivers' red eyes were not affected by the sand blowing into their gormless faces. On the rear of the buggies, stood five more of the red-eyed Klóns. They all looked identical. Their beady eyes stared vacantly out towards the beast, no sign of fear or emotion in them. The buggies began to spread out as they approached their prey.

The bull held his ground, pawing the sand with his front legs. He helplessly watched as the vehicles surrounded him. The Klóns at the rear of the buggies leapt out onto the dense sand. Militarily, they spread out around the bull, which eyed them with fearful curiosity.

The buggies pulled away, falling into an arrow-shaped formation, giving chase to the fleeing herd. The bull shifted his vast bulk, roaring a warning to the herd, as the vehicles sped off into the distance.

The Klóns, with stabbing, cold, emotionless eyes, stared at the solitary bull. In unison, they took small, one-handed crossbows from their belts. A long cable trailed from the preloaded bolt in the shaft. The cable trailed under their arms creating a ringed bundle upon their backs, which was joined to a battery.

They pointed their crossbows upward and fired them into the sky, more than a hundred bolts with their trailing cables whipped through the air, falling around the bull, who twisted and turned, terrified. The bolts pierced the sand releasing a mechanism, which made the sharp arrowhead go deep into the ground, locking them in place. The cables crisscrossed each other, forming a net over the stranded beast.

The Klóns pressed a button on their belts, releasing an electrical current through the cables. They buzzed and glowed a turquoise blue. The bull, startled, bowed his head and began to charge toward the Klóns. Roaring, exposing huge teeth, the bull stomped madly forward. He was snagged on the electrical cables. They hissed and sizzled, as they burned deep into the flesh he roared in pain. He continued to charge ahead; his six legs became tangled up in the electrical web. His body jolted and spasmed.

The red eyes watched as the beast stumbled, crumbling to his knees. After several minutes, they released the cables from their belts. A magnet which resembled the head of a viper was attached to this end. The cables whizzed towards the bull, and the sad beast could only watch, as he was tied up unable to move. Death came quickly, and the aroma of burning meat wafted across the plain, as the bull gave out a final low purr. The electric cables faded to a dark grey, and loosening their tight grip, they slithered off the bull's burnt remains, retracted through the sand, back to their masters.

The buggies had since caught up with the stampeding Vinayaki. The roof-mounted automatic machine guns had movement sensors attached to them, firing huge bullets into the fleeing beasts. The Vinayaki were panic-stricken, grunting warning cries, they tripped and collided with each other in their haste to escape. Hundreds had fallen, hindering their stampede to safety. The matriarch at the head of the herd was lost and confused. The loud retorts from the machine guns panicked her. The dust and sand which was being whipped up by the heavy stampeding hoofs clouded her senses. Running at full speed, she did not see the ravine ahead until it was too late. She tried to halt, but the herd bundled into her rear, pushing her over the edge.

A mile away from the scene, more of the Klóns watched. One of them stood on top of an armoured truck. The sun shone down on the massive Klón, an air of authority about him. Stór was the largest, most powerful of his kind. He watched the herd fall to their deaths through a pair of binoculars. He tapped on the roof of the truck. Below his feet, was a heatproof volt, inside sat a man with a huge red beard.

He picked up a radio. "We have got them, hundreds of them, send out the bulldozers."

"Yes, sir," came a docile answer.

Back at the site of the bull's death, a grinding shuddering noise resounded through the canyon as a giant bulldozer rolled towards the dead creature. Sitting in the cab on top of the large vehicle were two Klóns. Ploughing forward, they scooped up the bull, who lay still, smoking from numerous open wounds.

The bulldozer followed the path of the herd until it reached the gorge — depositing the mighty bull over the edge of the vast ravine. The Vinayaki male rolled down into the gorge, bouncing from rock to rock, bones cracked and snapped upon the jagged boulders until he lay with the mangled herd at the bottom.

Stór watched, as more bulldozers pushed the broken carcases away, depositing their remains onto a giant metal platform, which protruded from the sand. This platform was hundreds of feet in diameter, almost hidden by the desert floor.

Several hours passed, and the platform was piled high with the dead Vinayaki. The Klón commander did not move a muscle, remaining still he observed the operation.

There was a grinding sound, an eruption of sand; dust billowed from around the edge of the metal circle. Steam shot out into the air, and the grinding and vibration of metal cogs was deafening. The metal plate began to descend into the ground, a giant elevator loaded with dead meat. The lift descended into a cutting room. Huge four-foot hooks hung from cast-iron rails, bolted to the rocky ceiling.

Dozens of butchers' slabs underneath followed the rails around the room. Stationed at each tabletop, a dozen slaves who appeared to be human. Their faces gaunt, their eyes heavy, their bodies were just skin and bone. One man's collar bone poked through the tethered T-shirt he wore under a butcher's apron, screaming of malnutrition. Sharp knives and saws lay ready on the blocks.

No one spoke as the massacred pile began to reveal itself. Blood poured over the platform edge, washing over the floor. The butchers waded into the blood, showing no concern that their bare feet were now wet and warm.

The sun above the ground had set, the heat which still crept in now bearable. Joined by a plague of flies and other parasites, they eagerly sucked the blood from the dead beasts, lapping from the vast pool which soon flooded the slaughterhouse floor.

The platform came to a grinding halt in the blood vat. Several of the Vinayaki still twitched, maybe the odd echo of life remained in some, but as soon as the lift came to a standstill, hundreds of the mindless humans went about them with roaring chainsaws.

Within seconds the cold bare concrete walls were being sprayed red, the great beasts were sawn and hacked into pieces.

Around two dozen individuals carried angle grinders; their task was to cut off the tusks, for the valuable chemical which laid within the ivory. Big chunks of flesh were carved up, and it took several people to lift the Vinayaki meat onto the large hooks. The meat was subsequently pushed around the rail to the furthest butcher's slab, where the humans scraped off the skin and took the flesh from the bone. The undesirable cuts went into a cart next to their bloody worktop; another cart sat next to this one, where more delicate cuts of meat were placed.

Around the edge of the vast hall, watching the slaves do their work, the red-eyed Klóns followed the slaves' every move as they went about their carnage.

Twenty metres up, between the opening of the lift and the lake of blood, a long black tinted window looked down on the scene. Standing behind the glass, monitoring the bloodshed, was the red-bearded man, Major Bliksem.

"They will be happy in Iris?" the vacant red-eyed Klón said.

The bearded man, Major Bliksem, whose face was claret, looked at Stór, the commander of the Klóns and spoke, "you would like to think so; this is the best hunt we have had all season put together."

From behind, it would be difficult to spot the difference between the two figures. Both stood six and a half feet tall, broad and muscular. Stór's width just inched past Bliksem's. The human's fiery, curly, red hair, would be the only defining difference. Bliksem played with his beard; he watched the slaves, sawing at the tusks. Major Bliksem had a keen eye and from his vantage point he spotted one of the slaves hiding a handful of the valuable ivory in his filthy trousers.

The Major spat on the floor, "fucking, thieving scum."

Stór, looked in the same direction as Bliksem, his scarlet eyes searched the area gormlessly.

"What good are you lot? You have over two hundred guards down there, not one of your dopey freaks can see a rat from ten yards away."

Bliksem studied Stór's face; emotionless, vacant with huge features. Stór had a broad nose, large mouth and a massive, round, bald head. They could almost pass for being human, the red staring eyes and their sheer size, was the only real difference. Also, they were not particularly bright. Bliksem had often thought that was just as well, or they would rule the world.

"Come on; I see I have to do everything my bloody self."

Stór almost looked hurt, as he followed Bliksem out of the small monitoring office.

$

The slave cried out in pain as Bliksem put more weight on the frail man's back. The slaughter hall had come to a halt. The hacking of ivory and meat had ceased. All eyes were upon the slave. He was face down in the Vinayaki blood, which was slowly draining away into the gutters surrounding the slaughterhouse floor. The man knew his fate; pleading for mercy would make things worse. He could only hope for a quick death.

Bliksem sneered, looking around the hall, a wild look in his deep black eyes. "I guess I must remind you dirty addicts, stealing is a crime. I am a generous man, am I not? I freely give you Faze for your hard work. I feed you, house you. Is this how you repay me?" his gruff voice bellowed so all could hear.

The slaves were addicts to the ivory. Just as gormless as the Klóns. Both were nothing more than expendable merchandise as far as Bliksem was concerned.

An evil grin twisted across his face. Hanging from his belt was a large machete. He pulled the blade free from the sheath and yanked the man's head up by his hair. The slave's face was stained crimson. He spat warm blood from a rotten mouth, groaning in pain. The Major pressed his boot harder into the slave's back. He screamed out as his ribs began to crack. Bliksem was laughing, menacingly. He brought down the machete. Blood-splattered into his face as he hacked off the man's right hand.

"Stop fucking sobbing," Bliksem screamed at him.

He brought the blade down again, taking the slave's left hand this time. Bliksem let go of the man's hair, his body dropping to the floor, wriggling in agony. His bloody stumps skidded and slipped in his blood, as he attempted to rise to his feet. Bliksem kicked him hard in the face with a heavy boot. The man's nose exploded; he collapsed forward and lost consciousness.

Bliksem looked around the hall, he signalled to the Klón who had been standing closest to the thief to step forward. The Klón obeyed. The Major pointed to the floor, and the Klón went to his knees like an obedient dog.

Red-faced, Bliksem pulled a revolver from his holster. At point-blank range, he shot the Klón in the face. The synthetic human fell backwards, his back arched, bright red eyes faded to black and slick silver fluid leaked like treacle from the exit wound.

"Everybody, get back to fucking work," he roared.

CHAPTER TWO

Now

Thousands of bats hung from the cavern ceiling, whispering to each other in their high-frequency chirps. Hundreds of feet below the black winged mass stood the underground metropolis of Aris. Referred to in other parts of the world as The City of Addicts.

The city sprawled out on the cavern floor for miles in every direction. The bats congregated above the western side of the town as there was less light there. To the south, the lab sector lit up the giant cavern walls. At the far northern end, was the cave's entrance, where the road from the outside world snaked into the city. The straight line of the road cut through the dismal ghetto. It passed a stagnant lake, which spread out to the east, leading up to a steel gate. This was the only entrance to the lab sector and was overlooked by the city's jail.

A dim torchlight could be made out moving down the street. Two figures huddled together, walking in the shadows of the high-rise buildings towering over them. Miles upon miles of decaying purpose-built tower blocks stretched out in every direction; no life seemed to come from within them.

The torchlight suddenly vanished as the two figures disappeared into a doorway. A humming noise grew louder and lights in the darkness hovered over the road. Two drones zigzagged through the air, scanning the streets. Regular patrols of the ghetto took place day and night. One of the drones hovered slowly over the place where the torchlight was only minutes ago. Hanging in the air, cameras on board searched the alleyways, lighting up the doorways, beaming live feedback to their headquarters. Satisfied the area was clear, the machines circled off westward.

Moments later, the two figures crawled out from their hiding place and chose to leave the torch switched off.

The Golden Goose sat centrally in the ghetto square, lighting up the street and the surrounding, dilapidated buildings. Once a thriving part of the city, the shops and tower blocks that surrounded the pub were now derelict and empty, with shattered glass fronts. Signage hung, rocking in the gentle breeze, which filtered through the cavern. In the shadows, Faze addicts huddled in groups, taking shelter from the cold which added gloom to their meaningless lives.

The night air was damp; condensation which gathered on the cave ceiling in the hot daytime formed a drizzle at night. The bar sign swung gently to-and-fro causing the rusted hinges to screech — the only sound in the dark, apart from the drizzle and the pitter-patter of bat guano, which showered more despair on the wretched inhabitants of Aris. The precarious swinging bar sign created playful shadows which shifted on the cracked, unkempt pavement.

Sophia was wrapped up, her neck invisible under several layers of clothes. She bowed her head as she walked out of the apartment doorway, she made sure the drones had gone before putting the torch into her pocket. The second figure emerged huddled under a blanket. They carried on their route, past the graffitied walls and the working girls who touted for business. The groans of the addicts who wandered the streets like zombies sent chills down Sophia's back. The night smelled of human excrement. The very air stuck to your skin like an invisible layer of filth.

Sophia brushed her dreadlocked fringe off her forehead, and they continued their hurried path towards The Golden Goose. Beside her, the figure, covered with a blanket, held the fabric sheet around their face with thin, pale hands.

She held out her arms, pulling the huddled figure closer to her. The person under the cloak struggled to walk in a straight line, trembling from cold and fear. Sophia's deep brown eyes scoured the skies and darted from dark alleys to the shady doorways. She was certain they were being followed.

She spoke softly to the burdened figure, "we are almost there now; you can rest soon, you'll be safe."

The person under the cape just nodded.

Every hundred feet, large screens were attached to the walls where broadcasts were played out by the state-run media. So far, the two figures had passed dozens of them. They all broadcasted a curfew warning. Being out late without a permit was prohibited. Tannoy speakers adorned every corner, but for now they were silent. Cameras scanned the streets twenty-four hours a day.

Finally reaching the town square, Sophia pushed her way through the main doors to the bar. Her right arm was still holding up the staggering, hunched form. The doors closed behind them.

From the darkness of a derelict building opposite, two small drones appeared. Lights flashed on the top of their mechanical shell, sending images back to headquarters.

$

The bar was packed out with people, hazy smoke laid across the room. The people in the bar watched the screen on the wall. The curfew warning had been replaced with a bright red screen, signalling Major Bliksem was about to make an announcement.

Sophia scanned the number of people in the room. She was pleased, many more had come than she had hoped—even some Oddities had come out of hiding. A group of men playing cards around a table looked up at Sophia, and gave her a nod. She winked back with a smile. Behind the bar was Ratty, a scrawny looking young man with sporadic fluff for a beard. Sophia waved at him to open the hatch at the end of the small bar.

"Where have you been? What's happening?" Ratty whispered, looking down his sharp nose at her. His face showed concern.

"It's a long story. Is my dad back yet?"

Ratty shook his head.

She half dragged her accomplice, who seemed to be slumping even more under an invisible weight. Behind the bar was a small cellar door which Ratty pulled open. Sophia, motioned for the blanketed figure to go down the ladder. Golden locks of hair were visible from under the blanket as they both moved down the ladder. Ratty closed the hatch behind them.

The bar was alive with chatter; old friends embraced each other and shared stories. The bar itself was dingy, cold and dark, but the people brought some warmth. There wasn't much of that in this part of Aris.

Resurfacing from behind the bar, Sophia hastily poured herself a drink. She surveyed the room again. There were some good people here; brave men and women, fighters, survivors, all giving her hope. But her father, One-Eyed Alan, was not here. Nor were her close friends, the twins, Hanisi and Marica. They should have been here by now. She tried to hide her concern. All eyes were on her now; time was running out.

The sound of drums blasted from the screen. The bar came to a standstill; voices fell silent. Bliksem's face appeared on the large screen, looking straight into the camera. The people in the bar fidgeted uncomfortably on their chairs.

"Citizens of Aris. My children. I speak to you now as a father, not as your ruler." Bliksem paused, licking his lips. "For years, Aris has prospered from the growing trade in Faze; you have all benefited from this bounty which the Vinayaki provide us."

Jeering broke out in the bar. One of the Oddities stood up, spitting at the screen, gesturing towards his deformed arms.

"Is this a benefit?" he shouted.

The people in the room looked at the man, nodding in agreement. The master of Aris was temporarily drowned out by loud shouting and curses. Sophia stepped forward.

"Quiet, I want to hear what this sick maniac has to say," she yelled over the crowd with an air of authority. Sophia had only recently turned twenty, but the gang members showed their respect as they fell silent.

Bliksem was now talking about meeting the supply and demand of Faze. Sophia knew what was coming. Her father was right.

Bliksem continued, "as from midnight tomorrow, all children over four years of age must be presented to the gate for work parties, education and development. For the future benefit of Aris. Of course, we will care for them. They will have a good chance in life, they will become pillars for our society, for a more prosperous Aris."

"Outrage," someone shouted out.

A woman armed to the teeth with guns and a bullet belt crossing her body stood up, screaming at the screen. "I will not give up my babies to be turned into addict slaves just to fill your bastard pockets, here or in Iris," she yelled.

Before Sophia could intervene and settle the woman down, the whole bar was up in arms. Sophia stood back, smiling. Her father was right. This would be the catalyst. This would be the beginning.

The large TV returned to the red screen for a moment, then flickered, before broadcasting live from the Baráttan pits. Sophia watched the screen. Two disfigured men were pinning down another Oddity.

The Oddities—as referred to by Major Bliksem and the System—were a by-product of the Faze program, leaving generations of people with all manner of afflictions. An evolutionary benefit, some would say, but to other people, a crippling disability. Either way, being born disfigured, or with a disability meant one of two things in Aris: slavery, or

15

being forced to fight in the Barắttan pit. Both inevitably ended in death.

The protesting Oddity on the screen was pinned down, and he attempted to scramble free. The crowd in the arena roared at his anguish. Eventually, subdued, he was tied to a post protruding from the ground. The Oddity screamed out for mercy. A third man unleashed a flamethrower onto him. The Oddity's skin bubbled and popped, skin slid from his skull, eyeballs bulged from their sockets, bursting from the intense heat. Sophia was disgusted; she turned her face away from the screen. No one else in the bar was watching the sickening, gladiatorial debacle, but tampering with the screens in any way was punishable by death, so they stayed on.

$

Sophia's hair had come loose. She removed the string holding her dreadlocks in a ponytail and shook them free. They fell to her shoulders.

"Hello, gorgeous," said a creepy voice interrupting her thoughts.

The smell of stale breath wafted too close for comfort and Sophia turned to see Steev. His teeth were so thick with plaque you could scrape the muck off and lay bricks with it. Sophia looked him up and down; his clothes were worn and dirty. The short-sleeved T-shirt he wore revealed thick hair covering his hands and spreading up his arms. Sophia cursed herself for not seeing him coming.

Steev leered at her, undressing her with his eyes. "Long time no see. You look beautiful as ever."

The aftertaste of that sentence was too much for Sophia; she had to turn her head. "There is a reason for that, find someone else to perv over will you." A look of disgust crossed her face.

If Steev was offended, he didn't show it. In fact, his smile grew broader. "Don't be so cruel honey, let me buy you a drink." The sickly smile remained on his matted hairy face.

"No, thank you." Sophia said, showing her aggravation.

Turning her back on him, she walked towards the bar. Steev's face turned sinister. Growling, he spat on the bar floor.

"Slag," Steev muttered under his breath.

$

Outside, two drones hovered fifty feet in the air; their gentle hum was the only sound in the ghetto. The lights on the drones shone like beacons. The silence was further broken by a distant roar of approaching vehicles. Their headlights flashed lighting up the slum streets. Silhouettes of addicts darted into doorways. Litter was whipped up by the wind created as they drove at high speed towards the drones. These two armoured trucks had only a narrow slit available for the driver to see onto the road in front.

A Faze addict in a coma-like state was curled up in the stairwell of a high-rise tower block. Stirring from his narcotic state by the oncoming noise, he blindly walked out of the building, straight onto the road. Before he had a chance to register what was happening, the leading truck smashed into him. His torso split in half, his legs went straight under the wheels, and his upper body embedded itself in the radiator grille. His head faced forward and wobbled with the truck's momentum; a macabre bonnet mascot.

The Klón driving the vehicle didn't even blink.

The two trucks pulled into the town square, skidding to a halt. The rear doors sprung open and a dozen armour-plated Klóns leapt out, holding machine guns.

Stepping out from the passenger seat was Major Bliksem, chewing on a smoking cigar. He walked to the front of the other vehicle, where the bonnet displayed the mangled corpse. The Major looked down at the bloodied mess and laughed loudly. Just for kicks, he began raining blows down on the dead man's head. Again and again, his strong fists whistled down, covering himself in a soup of shattered bone and blood. He battered the dead addict with such force that his head rocked back and forth until eventually Bliksem tired.

He gripped the addict's head with both hands, twisting the skull three hundred and sixty degrees. The spine cracked, skin stretched, and tore until he pulled the head clean off.

Holding the severed head in one hand, he spat his cigar butt onto the road, crushing it underfoot, spitting some loose tobacco from his mouth.

"Come on. I'm thirsty," he gestured to the stationary Klóns who obediently followed him towards the doors of The Golden Goose.

CHAPTER THREE

Two Days Ago

"For fuck's sake," the deep voice emanated from the bottom of the stairs. "Adria are you ready?"

"I've been down here over an hour. Mikhail needs us at the club, we're going to be busy tonight. Do I have to come up there and kick your backside?" Vasiliy complained, wearing down the carpet pacing back and forth in the hall of the villa.

He took the opportunity to check himself out in the mirror, wearing a flashy suit, a sovereign-laden hand fiddled with his fringe.

Vasiliy looked at his vibrating phone, "oh, bollocks." Mikhail was calling. "Adria, Mikhail is on the phone now, I am going to get a fucking mouthful. Last time I am going to tell you, get your arse down here, right now!" Vasiliy hesitantly answered his phone, "sorry, that fucking whore is taking forever."

There was a brief silence on the other end of the phone.

"Don't be late. The Cracker will be taking her off our hands tonight. Tell her I have some new Cane just come in. The best we have had in a long time. That should make her move."

"Okay," Vasiliy replied.

Adria began making her way down the stairs. Vasiliy ended the call, looking up at her moving down the steps. He had to admit Adria was stunning. For a moment, he had a primal urge to take the sixteen-year-old. This wasn't the first-time that sexual impulse roared in him when it came to Adria. He shook his head, attempting to block out the sordid images flickering through his mind. He decided against it rather than face the wrath of his brother.

Adria was still a virgin and she was more valuable un-touched.

Adria, looked at Vasiliy timidly as she reached the bottom of the stairs. "So how do I look?"

Adria was wearing stockings, a mini skirt, a short-sleeved black and white horizontal striped T-shirt and she had added a black beret on top of her golden hair. Her bright red lips glowed out of her powdered white face. Vasiliy, as always, replied with scorn.

"As you always do. Like a fucking dirtbag, now get your arse in the car or Mikhail is going to slap us both. I am not ending up in his bad books just because you take all bloody day making yourself look like a tart."

Adria bowed her head, walking out of the villa door. The air was rank. Lights coming from the lab sector a few hundred feet behind the wall lit the driveway. Adria looked towards the giant natural rock face which separated the poor from the privileged, wondering, not for the first time, what life was like outside of the ghetto and Aris.

"Stop fucking daydreaming, get in," shouted Vasiliy, sitting in the driver's seat of the custom sports car.

She moved towards the vehicle easing herself into the passenger seat. Vasiliy revved the engine, and with the bass from the sound system making the doors shake, they drove down the long driveway.

Adria opened her small black purse, feeling dejected and hurt by Vasiliy's comments. Her hands shaking, she took out a small makeup mirror. She poured some Cane from a small bag and using a straw, she inhaled a long line of the ultraviolet blue powder up both nostrils. Vasiliy looked at her with disgust.

"One day your fucking nose will fall off, no one will look at you then." He sniggered to himself, "not that anyone does now."

Adria was numb to the verbal abuse Vasiliy launched at her every day. She had learned to live with the constant scolding over the years. But anything was better than living in the ghetto—free Cane, free food, free drink and a roof over her head. She convinced herself that life was better with the brothers than barely surviving on the streets.

Mikhail was kind most of the time, but it was apparent to Adria, that Vasiliy had begun to lust after her. His eyes leered over her more and more; especially now she was turning into a young woman. She could feel the tension which made her feel uncomfortable; she dreaded being alone with him now.

The car approached the solid steel gate at the bottom of the long driveway. The twelve feet high walls which encircled the villa, were topped with razor wire. And at every few yards security cameras kept track of all movement.

At the entrance stood a tall Klón. Adria grimaced at the sight of him. They frightened her. Their thick leathery skin made them look ghoulish and their immense size was intimidating.

The Klón's red eyes pierced through the windscreen registering the driver. The gates automatically opened, and the car sped out onto the road. Adria lowered her gaze, avoiding eye contact with the Klón. He seemed to stare into her soul.

She had spent the earlier part of her life hiding from the Faze program and the Klón child unit, which was created to hunt out orphans and Oddities in the slums, and for her, capture would have meant the workhouses or worse now she was older. There were two Klóns who guarded the property of the two brothers. The Klóns were physical, powerful, programmed to protect their masters and formidable fighters. Their IQ was basic and their movements somewhat clumsy; humankind had not yet created anything close to their own intellect.

$

Vasiliy pushed his foot down hard on the accelerator as they passed through the run-down suburbs which littered the way to the dock. Located on the edge of the stagnant Lake Aris, was the brothers' club. Adria, looked out of the window watching the starving people who roamed the streets. She recalled living in poverty, eating from waste bins and gathering whatever she could to survive.

Her world had come a long way since then — hot baths, shelter, food. For a while she had felt safe, but now that she had begun to mature into a young woman, she started to question her life. Strange dreams of her past tormented her. They were vague and hazy and never made any sense.

Adria could hardly remember a time she didn't live with the two brothers. At first, they were kind to her, teaching her to speak correctly. They fed and clothed her. But around the age of eight, she guessed, as she was unsure of her precise age, the two brothers—especially Vasiliy—changed towards her. She became a maid, a cook, a cleaner. The villa always had to be neat and tidy and she forever tried to please the brothers, especially Mikhail. Adria also worked at the club and at the start, she cleaned the toilets and the bar. When she hit her teens, more was expected from her. Adria poured drinks for the creepy customers, helped sell Cane to the punters at the club and now she was just like the other girls who worked there. But her body was not for sale like theirs were. Mikhail kept her safe.

Sometimes, Vasiliy would return to Iris, the System's capital, for a year at a time. Adria always felt safer when he was away. But two years ago, maybe, even three now, Mikhail left Aris instead and for a whole year she was left alone with Vasiliy. He was mean to her most of the time. He would ignore her for days on end and treated her like a servant. One night at the villa, Vasiliy was entertaining and he made Adria serve his friends drinks dressed in just her underwear. They filled her with alcohol and drugs and that night was the first time Adria had taken Cane.

And she loved it.

The blue dust had enveloped her in warmth, which she had never experienced before. Now she craved the drug every day, fighting a mental battle which she was beginning to lose. When she lived rough, she witnessed the damage caused by drugs, with the addicts and the Oddities, but that still hadn't put her off. Whenever she questioned her addiction, she would snort the azure Cane and it helped eradicate the feeling of self-loathing. Adria's mind wandered in a haze.

The Cane filled her bloodstream taking control of her. Temporarily, her mind drifted from her body. Her soul crept out through the pores in her skin and she floated away into a calm space. The feeling never lasted long, though, and her soul was gradually pulled back to reality.

Her head was resting on the window, whilst outside crowds of addicts were swarming past the car. This was the only time you saw so many wretched residents of Aris move with any motivation. Twice a day, the alarms blared a high-pitched tone, signalling to the users. They crawled from their squalor and headed to the wall. The soldiers handed out bags of Faze for free. The chemical enhanced ivory was always in abundance and in return, the addicts worked in the farms and slaughterhouses.

Adria suddenly became aware of Vasiliy's hand groping her upper leg. Fear took her and she looked down. He caressed her thigh as the car moved at high speed. 'How long had his hand been there?' The Cane had completely numbed her body of feeling.

"What are you doing, Vas?" Adria looked at him shyly.

"What does it look like I am doing. Mikhail is far too soft on you. We feed you, clothe you, keep you safe. What the fuck have we had in return, eh?"

Adria froze, his hand began to crawl under the hem of her skirt.

"Mikhail, won't like this," her voice trembled.

"Well, he is not here, is he?"

Vasiliy turned to her, a burning lust in his eyes. Adria had not seen him like this before. He looked possessed. A tear trickled from her eye.

He glared at her, "don't start with the tears… Oh, for fuck's sake."

Vasiliy reached for his phone, vibrating in his inside pocket, forcing him to remove his hand from Adria's thigh. "We're five fucking minutes away bro, calm the fuck down."

Adria could hear the other brother on the end of the phone. He was not in a good mood. Vasiliy's face turned from lust to rage. He hung up, slamming the phone down on the dashboard, making Adria visibly jump in her seat.

"Great. I am getting a fucking earache because you took so long tarting yourself up. But you owe me, don't forget it, no more fucking free rides, understand?"

Adria, nodded, her face lowered, as she tried to pull her skirt down as far over her thighs as possible.

"I can't fucking hear you?" he screamed, spittle hitting her in the face.

"I'm sorry," Adria wiped more tears from her eyes, her hands now shook violently.

"Stop fucking crying; we will be there any minute. If Mikhail notices you have been crying, it will only make things worse for you, got it?"

Adria nodded again. She cleared her eyes of tears and running makeup, rapidly redoing her eyeliner, just as the sports car pulled into the club car park. The car park was surrounded by the old tower blocks which homed the Faze workers. The windows were blacked out with filth and nothing grew here apart from moss and mushrooms, which had almost taken over one of the tower blocks.

Adria opened the car door. The handle snapped off in her hand, she quickly glanced around, breathing a sigh of relief.

Vasiliy had not seen. She threw the handle under the car and pushed the door shut. Recently, she had become clumsy. This wasn't the only thing she had accidentally broken.

Vasiliy walked around the car and stood over her. "Now what's the fucking problem?" he spat as he spoke.

Adria looked up at him. "Sorry, Vas, my head felt funny."

"Maybe that's because of all that shit you keep ploughing up your beak. Maybe it's time I stopped giving you that shit. How would you like that?"

"It isn't that," she pleaded.

Panic washed through her body. Life without the drug didn't seem possible anymore. She couldn't remember the last time she was clean. A wave of self-disgust turned her stomach at the realisation of how desperately low she had become. She was a slave to Cane, just as the city's addicts were slaves for Faze.

Her lip turned up with a grimace and she whispered to herself. "I am a dirty junky."

$

Vasiliy pulled on her top, dragged her across the gravel car park, and up a small set of concrete steps to the club entrance. The club was on the edge of the lake which sprawled out at the rear. There were no windows or visible signs that this was a club. It was for private members only, who visited from affluent parts of the world to do business.

There were only two entrances to the club, a small jetty which sat below the bar inside and the front door. Some customers chose to visit the club via the lake on boats, mainly military or science personnel from the lab sector who worked for Bliksem's Faze program.

Mikhail owned a small speedboat and he travelled the short distance from the mooring at the rear of his villa to the jetty here. The only other entrance was through the two giant, solid black doors, in front of them.

Another lumbering Klón stood on guard, dressed in an elegant suit and tie. Adria raised her gaze and his red eyes gawked at them both. He automatically stood aside, letting them through. But his gaze seemed to linger on Adria as she passed by.

$

Mikhail stood at the other end of the club, polishing glasses behind the bar. Compared to most of Aris, the club was an extravagant luxury. An exquisite red rug ran throughout the ground floor. A marble dance floor was in the centre, surrounded by sofas made of elegant black velvet.

A small rodent picking on some crumbs sat on Mikhail's shoulder as he glared at them both. Adria shuddered when she saw Mikhail's pet, Oliver. Adria was sure Oliver wasn't a mouse. He was certainly a rodent, a cross between a rat and mouse in size. She wasn't sure he even had bones, often Adria had seen Oliver slide through the smallest of holes almost weasel like. He was intelligent, sneaky and carnivorous, with sharp razor-like teeth, vomit coloured eyes and long fur. Adria despised the smelly, horrible little thing. On several occasions, he had found his way into her room at the villa and Adria convinced herself he was going to attack her. She often wondered why Mikhail kept him. Seemingly, he showed the rodent more affection than his brother. She had thought better than to question him about it.

"Where the fuck have you two been? We have got a delivery coming in tonight. On top of that, the bar is not ready; the fucking doors open in twenty minutes," Mikhail yelled at them.

Oliver ran from one shoulder to the other, sniffing the air as if he was sensing bloodshed, which equalled something to eat.

Vasiliy started shouting back. "Don't yell at me, it's this tart. She took hours to get ready and now she's got one of her fucking headaches again."

Adria remained silent, standing back a pace. She had witnessed the brothers fighting before, which had almost ended up with Vasiliy dead. They were both in their thirties, handsome, but intimidating. Mikhail was the oldest by a couple of years, but they were often mistaken for twins, as they dressed smartly and were both tall, strong and muscular.

Mikhail eyed them both up. "It doesn't matter now, just get the bar set up; I am going to make some room for the delivery."

Mikhail opened a back door to the bar, a flight of wooden steps led down to the small jetty beneath them.

Adria and Vasiliy made themselves busy, replacing bottles in fridges. The sound system had already been set up and a DJ busied himself by the stage.

When Mikhail re-emerged from below, the bar was ready to go; the doors opened, and music filled the club.

"Go, sort yourself out. I have some special guests coming

tonight, I want you looking your best," Mikhail called to Adria.

Adria understood what Mikhail meant; she wandered off into the women's toilets. Standing in front of the mirror, she looked at herself in solemn silence. Slowly she stripped down to her underwear. She then poured out a bag of Cane next to the sink, raking out several lines. She pressed a finger on each nostril, snorting up every crumb. Half a dozen young women joined her in the toilet and started to apply makeup or powder their noses as Adria had just done. They giggled amongst themselves, talking of finding a rich man to look after them. They all ignored Adria jealously. Adria had the luxury and protection of the brothers, so she didn't care what they thought of her.

Putting on a brave face, she walked out of the toilet. The club was busy with men and women, all preying over her and the entourage of scantily clad women who worked the crowd. The girls' job was to flirt and dance with the customers, bring them drinks and to sell them wraps of Cane, which they kept stuffed in their bras. Adria felt cheap and worthless.

A sweaty, ugly, customer slapped her behind before grabbing hold of her and pulling her to the dance floor. He began gyrating against her, like a humping dog. "How much for a fuck?" he dribbled in her ear.

"Sorry I don't fuck, you will have to talk to one of the other girls," Adria replied, trying not to sound too disrespectful and disgusted.

The man pushed her away and she stumbled backwards almost tripping over. She was about to shout at the man, but Mikhail was on him, he pulled the man aside using his robust physique to his advantage. He whispered in the man's ear. His face dropped, and turned white.

She watched the cretin grovelling as Mikhail stood over him. The suited Klón came crashing in from the outside and sauntered up behind the grovelling man. He lifted him off his feet as if he weighed nothing more than a small child and carried him to the front door, and out into the night. Adria noticed Oliver, scurry down Mikhail's body as he pursued the Klón outside.

Adria smiled at Mikhail. His face remained stern as he turned and walked back to the table, where he had been in deep conversation with a dwarf. The small man had slicked black hair tied back in a ponytail and Adria noticed he had no ear and a potted, scarred face.

"Are you going to do some fucking work tonight or what?" Vasiliy appeared behind her.

Adria just nodded and walked over to a group of men who sat on the plush sofas. Making idle talk with the perverts, going along with their flirting and suggestive advances meant she racked up their bar tabs. All the time, she felt Vasiliy's eyes on her, watching her every move.

As the night drew on, Adria started to tire of all the small talk, and was beginning to feel exhausted. She made her way to the toilet, where she joined the queue of girls snorting lines of blue dust. Just as Adria had filled her nasal barrels Vasiliy walked in.

"The delivery is below, come and give me a hand."

"Okay, I'll just put some clothes on," Adria replied, wiping away powder which had stuck to her upper lip.

Vasiliy scowled at her, "There's no fucking time for that, come on."

"But Vasiliy, it is so cold and..."

"I said now." Vasiliy glared at her, cutting off her sentence.

Adria knew better than to argue further. Dressed in just her underwear, she followed Vasiliy as he made his way through the crowd of ogling men to the door at the back of the bar.

Goose bumps covered every inch of her body as she walked out into the open air. Shivering, she thought about asking Vasiliy again if she could put some clothes on.

"The boat is here," he said over his shoulder as they both reached the bottom of the stairs and walked onto the jetty.

Adria looked up and winced at the bats which hung under the club's floorboards. Mikhail's speedboat was here, but no sign of the delivery.

She turned around.

"I thought you said the delivery was…"

All went black.

$

The fog cleared from Adria's mind, but a pain throbbed at the side of her head. She attempted to move her hand towards the source, but she realised someone was holding her wrists. A tie had been wrapped around her head, gagging her mouth, stopping her from shouting out for help. Vasiliy's face came into focus. She could feel his weight upon her as she suddenly realised her knickers had been pulled off. His hot breath warmed her neck, then the thumping pain soared again as a blinding flash of white light hit her. She felt strength in her arms and was about to push Vasiliy off. The intensity of the white illumination blinded her briefly, twisting the world around her, everything morphed into a blur.

Darkness took her.

CHAPTER FOUR

Adria started to stir, roused from unconsciousness by the cold. The secondary pain from Vasiliy's punch was beginning to dull. She opened her eyes and saw the bats hanging precariously above her. The lake made a gentle splashing sound against the timber beams emerging from the rancid water holding up the jetty. Mikhail's speedboat rocked, rubbing up against the algae riddled posts, causing a grinding sound. Adria turned her head towards the noise. The wooden planks she lay on were splintered and some of her hair had tangled itself in the rotten wood, the movement of her head caused fine golden strands to rip from their roots.

Her eyes came into focus and she could make out Vasiliy rummaging around on the boat.

Slowly everything started to come back to her; Vasiliy's face and the evil intent in his eyes as he laid on top of her. She could feel the warmth radiating from between her legs. Reaching down to her inner thighs, she fingered thick blood. Adria began to shake, as she gradually attempted to sit up. Her head felt hazy and for a moment, she felt as though she was about to faint again.

The creaking boards signalled Vasiliy was approaching her. His footsteps stopped next to her huddled body. He threw a wet flannel and a dry cloth onto her lap.

"Clean yourself up, and be quick about it, before anyone notices you're missing, if you even think of telling Mikhail, I will kill you."

He didn't wait for a reply before he turned and walked back up the stairs to the bar above.

Adria stared at her blood-covered hand. She didn't cry. She didn't speak.

A sickness welled up in her stomach and nausea made her dizzy. Coughing vomit into her mouth, she crawled towards the lake edge, and leaning over the jetty she retched into the polluted, murky water. Looking at her reflection in the lake, she saw a pale ghostly face which she didn't recognise as her own.

"I don't know who I am," she sobbed.

$

Eventually, Adria found the strength to clean herself up. The numbness she was feeling was replaced with a crippling pain between her legs which made her knees tremble as she staggered back up the stairs to the bar. The bar was shoulder to shoulder with people. Rich men and women mingled amongst working girls.

Adria reached into her bra, anxiously she searched praying her stash of Cane was not lost. She felt the edge of the bag under the cup of her breast and her brief wave of panic eased. She looked around the room. Mikhail was still speaking to the dwarf with one ear. The volume of noise was overwhelming and the heat from so many bodies made her sweat. She almost vomited again gulping for air. She could feel her face turning red, and her heartbeat reverberated in her chest, making blood rush to her brain. For a moment she thought it might explode. She grabbed a hooded coat which hung from a rail next to the bar and raced towards the front doors, flinging them open. She knocked into the Klón doorman as she passed him. Running towards Vasiliy's car, she unloaded what little contents her stomach held onto the ground of the car park.

Wiping the sick from her chin, she checked the car door was unlocked and gently sat in the driver's seat. With shaking hands, she quickly poured some of the blue dust out onto her mirror, making lines with a card. She snorted more than she usually would. Within minutes the pain was gone; the sickness, the self-loathing, the fear had left her mind entirely. There was nothing left. Her eyes rolled back into her head, and her body sunk down into the seat. Her soul seemed to float from her skin and bone carriage.

The car door suddenly opened, stirring Adria from her drugged coma. A young voice spoke to her, but she was in a cloud so dense the words made no sense. She waved the sound of the voice away, but the voice persisted.

"Hello, are you okay?"

Adria turned her head to the side, her eyes rolled back into place, like hitting the jackpot on a fruit machine. Standing next to the car was a baby-faced policeman who looked too young to be in the jet-black uniform he was wearing. Two Klóns stood behind him, their huge bulks creating a muscular wall blocking any chance of her running away. The young officer's eyes looked down to Adria's lap. She followed his gaze, in plain view were twelve wraps of Cane which she had removed from her bra.

"Have you got a licence for that?" asked Babyface.

Adria, tried to speak, mumbling, "No, I work for Mikhail and Vasiliy, though."

"Oh? That's what they all say, honey; do you have any papers with you? Or a permit to be out at this time of night?"

Adria became aware she was in trouble. She had never owned papers or a permit; she had never left the villa without the brothers in all the time she had lived with them.

"I work for the brothers," she protested again.

Suddenly, she heard Vasiliy's voice coming out of the club. The officer, knowing the reputation of the brothers had backed up a few steps.

"This lass is saying she works for you," Babyface said to Vasiliy as he approached the car.

Adria couldn't look up at him. Her body quivered when Vasiliy spoke.

"Nope, I've never seen this bitch before in my life. Get her out of my fucking car, she's staining my seats."

The officer motioned with his head towards Adria. The two Klóns grabbed her, yanking her out of the car. Tears flowed down her cheeks as she screamed out.

"Vasiliy, why are you doing this to me?"

Yelling in his face, she was dragged away, kicking and howling.

"Here," Vasiliy handed Babyface a hand full of cash, "you can keep that Cane, not a word to my brother, okay?"

Babyface looked at the money, a broad grin on his face. "Yeah, sure Vas, not a word from me."

"Good," replied Vasiliy.

He winked at Adria as she lashed out helplessly. As she was forced into the back of an armoured car she desperately shouted for Mikhail. The door slammed shut. Vasiliy walked back towards the bar, as the vehicle drove out of the car park, heading in the direction of Aris's prison.

$

Adria sat hunched on the floor in the back of the armoured car. A screen separated her from the three figures sitting in the front of the vehicle. She stared towards the floor, head wedged between her knees, rocking with the motion as the tyres bumped over the potholes. Every turn, every bump made her wince in pain. A lump had begun to appear on the side of her head from the blow Vasiliy had dished out.

The dull thud echoed in her brain. She shook her head in disbelief, the last few hours of her life were a living nightmare. She just wanted to curl up and die.

The car jumped on the uneven surface again, and Adria felt warm discharge, thick blood, leaking out of her onto the cold metal floor of the vehicle.

There were no windows for Adria to look out, but she was aware they had been travelling for around twenty minutes. She knew they would be nearing the main gate to the lab sector near the prison.

Silent tears rolled down her pale cheeks. As fear crept over her, an overwhelming feeling of despair began to sink in.

$

"So, what do we have here?" growled a voice.

Adria looked up. The car had come to a halt, the doors at the rear of the vehicle were open. A tall thick-set man with a large black beard stood with Babyface looking at her.

"Fuck me, has she shit herself?" the senior prison officer looked at Babyface.

"Looks like blood? We haven't touched her," exclaimed the young policeman, holding out his hands innocently.

The large man called to Adria, "come here my pretty, I won't bite you."

She had curled up in the corner like a frightened game bird, trapped by the predator. A manic stare was all she could return.

"Don't make me come in there and drag you out, sweetheart."

Eyeing up the big man, Adria submitted, painfully she crawled towards them with a groan. She stepped out of the vehicle. The prison courtyard was surrounded by thick concrete walls, which climbed so high they merged with the ceiling of the cavern. Hundreds of barred windows dotted the outside walls and there was an archway sealed with a solid iron gate guarded by Klóns. Adria assumed this was the way they had just come in.

"No good looking that way love, you will be staying with us for a while," the senior officer whispered in her ear.

His harsh male voice—the closeness of a man after what Vasiliy had done to her— only made her feel sick. Her mind told her to flee, but there was no chance of escape. The two officers talked to each other. Adria's eyes wandered around the courtyard. In the eastern corner a makeshift frame had been erected and six figures hung upside down, suspended from a rope around their ankles. Adria could not tell if they were male or female, their bodies burnt beyond recognition. Smoke still smouldered from the pit which had been dug out below them. The stench of burnt flesh still hung in the air.

"Don't worry girl; we only burn the cripples. I think the governor will have better things planned for you. Hey, you might even enjoy your stay here." The senior officer laughed, slapping Babyface on the back.

Adria's face was a void and again her attention was drawn to the iron gates. The sound of the giant gates swinging inward made an eerie screech, and the ground shook, making the Klón guards stand back. Thudding into the courtyard, was a sorry looking Vinayaki bull. His eyes were covered with leather blinkers and his tusks had been sawn off, leaving festering stumps. His nodding head looked down at the floor as he moved. Huge reins attached with two thick leather straps were wrapped around his middle and hooked onto wooden poles, dragging a heavy load behind him. The crack of the whip on his back made the Vinayaki move faster.

The man sat at the helm of the wagon was the dwarf with one ear whom Adria had seen talking with Mikhail earlier that evening. A faint hope crossed her mind. If the dwarf saw her, he might let Mikhail know where she was. The small man continued to lash the beast's back, hurling curses and abuse at the old bull.

"Ah, at last, Cracker. Where have you been you little bastard?" the senior officer shouted towards the dwarf.

The beast proceeded slowly dragging the heavy trailer, guided by The Cracker who sat up front. Adria held her breath on seeing the massive metal cage on the trailer. Inside were dozens of young women. Around their legs small children gripped the bars staring out blankly. She recognised some of the women from the brothers' club. The Cracker leapt from his seat with surprising agility as the beast came to a halt.

"Boss-man, still here, you old fucker. How long have you been looking after this scum? Twenty years?"

The two men shook hands.

Adria gazed between the cage and the dwarf. She was about to speak, when one of the girls she knew from the club shook her head with a finger to her lips, urging Adria to remain silent. Stopping herself from speaking, Adria rested her chin on her chest and pulled the hood of the large jacket over her head.

Boss-man signalled at two guards who were standing by a large door; they both disappeared inside.

"Come, this way," the Boss-man motioned for The Cracker to follow him.

The two guards returned with a string of half-naked women, their feet chained to each other with manacles, and their hands tied with thick rope. The Cracker walked up and down the line of women paraded in front of him, inspecting their bodies, occasionally shaking his head, tutting.

"You could have at least washed them before I arrived," he stared at the Boss-man, "two thousand, for the lot."

"Two thousand?" the Boss-man laughed, "I don't think the governor will accept that." Shaking his head, he added, "Six thousand."

The Cracker grinned and played with the scarred little hole where his ear once was.

"Three. That's my final offer, because those two stupid brothers Vasiliy and Mikhail lost me a virgin. I would have got a fine price for her." Adria was within hearing distance, Babyface stood beside her, shifting nervously. She looked to the woman on the wagon, who nodded at Adria, confirming she was the virgin for sale. Adria hid her face in the coat.

'What was happening?' It couldn't be right, Mikhail and Vasiliy had been like older brothers to her for most of her life. She didn't understand. 'Had they brought her up, only to sell her like a whore, this whole time?' Her entire life was a lie, a fucking lie. She felt as though someone had hit her hard in the stomach; a wave of sadness, anger and disbelief made tears boil in her eyes, her head started to spin, and she slumped to her knees.

Broken.

CHAPTER FIVE

A man walked out of the door at the rear of a tall building. A lit cigarette hung from his bottom lip. Struggling, he carried heavy bags of waste and added them to a decaying mound of litter in the road, crawling with vermin and maggots. He coughed as the sudden displacement of garbage threw up a sinful stench. Two rotten feet stuck out from the pile of filth. Sharp bones protruded from the flesh, where toes once belonged. The meat had been gnawed off by rats.

Another forgotten addict.

Only a small flickering light lit up the back street. Two eyes twinkled from a low position in a dark doorway directly opposite. Keenly, the eyes watched the man, waiting for the right time to strike.

Unaware he was being observed, the man took a long drag on his cigarette and blew out a cloud of greyish smoke, that played in the dim light. He flicked the roll-up into the rubbish; the hot ash died in the sludge with a hiss. He turned and walked back into the building, slamming the door shut behind him.

The eyes waited for a moment, darting from side to side, checking for any signs of life. Slowly they edged out from the darkness, into the hazy light, revealing their child's body. A young girl with golden locks and blue eyes crawled on her belly towards the fresh rubbish bags. She was holding a broken glass bottle in one hand. Her elbows and knees were already scraped and bruised, but she was still able to propel her small frame across the gravel track with speed.

Finally, she reached the festering heap. She tore at the bags with the makeshift glass cutlery, stabbing a hole into the bag with the jagged bottle. The first bag she opened provided nothing of value or anything edible. But in the second sack, she found several raw chicken carcasses. She immediately tore into one with her teeth, crunched the delicate poultry bones, grinding them with her dainty jaw with ravenous hunger.

A giant rat tried to muscle in on her supper, but she thrusted the jagged bottle down fast, impaling the rat to the floor. Its intestines ruptured from the rear end. The child turned the rat over, slicing open the stomach, removing the remaining guts. She made quick work of skinning and beheading the rodent. She glanced around for wild dogs, other humans or Oddities, who could also be on the scavenge nearby. She rapidly bit into the meatiest part of the rat; blood began to run down her chin. The back door suddenly opened. The man who had put the rubbish out only minutes ago grabbed her by the hair.

"Let go," she screamed.

"Shut up. I know someone who will pay a pretty penny for a golden-haired girl like you," he laughed, as he tried to pull her into the doorway by her hair. But something held him back. He turned, confused, as if the small child weighed a ton.

He pulled on her hair again, but she was set to the floor like a *concrete post.*

"Uh, what the f-"

Suddenly the child pushed the man with both hands with such force, he fell back through the door, crashing to the ground. Dazed and confused, he looked up at her. The girl stood in front of him, sobbing.

"Sorry, sorry," she said and ran off into the dark.

Faster and faster, her bare feet sped over the cold, gravel road. The girl ignored the sharp stones cutting into the soles of her feet. She ran until her legs began to tire and she gasped for breath.

₿

Adria gasped for air, coughing cold water from her lungs. The water from the hose was freezing. She had been stripped naked, forced into the corner of a rank shower room by a jet of water from a hose held by a prison guard. The room was windowless, and dirty white tiles covered every wall. She watched as the dried blood flowed from her legs in the freezing water, making small whirlpools of grime, which flowed towards a large plughole in the floor.

"Stand up," shouted the guard. "I cannot clean your filth off with you curled up like a baby. Get up." Adria pushed her back up against the wall; her arms crossed over her breasts, her skin pale, covered in goosebumps. The hose was turned off, and the guard leered over her body for a moment, before he tossed her a long thin white blouse. "Here. Look after that, you won't get another one." Adria just caught herself from falling in the mank water around her feet, clutching the garment. She accidentally dropped her arms, revealing her ample breasts and causing the guard to smile broadly. "You're going to fit in here, just fine," he sneered.

Adria pulled the blouse over her head, the plain top clung to her wet body, barely hanging below her knees. Shivering, she was led through a network of dull grey corridors with polished mirrored floors and up a flight of concrete stairs.

"Where are you taking me?" she struggled to speak through chattering teeth.

"We are off to see the governor; he likes to see all the new inmates, likes to establish the rules before you join the other scum on the wing."

$

The officer pushed Adria into an office lined with wooden panels and made her stand in front of a large desk. Weird abstract paintings, mainly erotic, hung from the walls. One wall, however, was dedicated solely to surveillance cameras which monitored the prison. One of the screens was broadcasting the shower room which she had only been in moments before. A large bottle of spirit sat on the desk. Smelling of pipe tobacco, a blue haze laid across the room. Through the large window behind the desk Adria could make out The Cracker's wagon being pulled out of the gate by the giant beast in the courtyard below. The cage was now loaded with the inmates who were put on show earlier.

The sound of a toilet flushing came from a door at the far end of the office and she watched as the door handle turned, and the door opened. Out came a short, bald, wobbly man with a pinkish-red face. He was at least a foot shorter than Adria. She avoided eye contact with him as he came up close to her. The transparent wet blouse she wore was stuck to her, showing her curves.

Adria had heard rumours about the prison governor, tales of his perversions and his cruelty had spread throughout Aris. He was a depraved little pig of a man; hence he had been given the nickname The Hog.

The Hog now drooled over Adria. His long tongue slid in and out of a cave of sharp teeth, licking his dry, cracked lips, saliva stretched from the top row to the bottom row of teeth. His piggy nose snorted and sniffed at her as he walked about inspecting her body, grunting excitedly. Adria became nervous and attempted to hide her figure, wrapping her arms about her chest. Hairs stood up on the back of her neck as The Hog's hot breath warmed her back.

He asked for her name.

"Adria. My name is Adria. The drugs were not mine, please, I cannot stay here, I can…"

"Now calm down, dear." The Hog moved in front of her; a puddle was forming at her feet from her wet body.

Adria looked down at the short prison governor, trying to hide her disgust. His skin was shiny, slippery and wet-looking. The Hog wiped sweat from his balding head and once again he snorted at her. He revealed his sharp hog-like teeth and saliva dripped off his chin as he sniffed her again. He reached out a stubby trotter-like hand and stroked her breasts, moving down to her navel.

Adria flinched, sick bubbling in her stomach.

"You must be hungry?"

Adria didn't answer.

"You are very young; I like to meet all the new inmates. I am keen to help those who help me. If you stick to the rules and cause no trouble, I am sure we will get on just fine," he looked up at her with shallow eyes. "We can talk some more when you have settled in. Take her away, guard."

Waving his hand to dismiss them, he waddled back to his desk.

Adria had been so taken aback by the foul little man she didn't hesitate in leaving with the guard. Part of her wanted to scream out at him, hit out with the anger which was welling up inside her. But she was exhausted, and her body was beginning to crave her next hit of Cane. The blue powder she had become dependent on for years called to her. Inside, her mind started to panic; a hot flush travelled through her body. The urge to scratch at her skinny white arms was overwhelming. Cold sweat broke out from every pore. A solitary droplet travelled down the side of her face, weaving into her ear.

The prison guard had linked his arm through hers and frog-marched her back down the cold stairs, through the dull corridors of the prison. The whole place seemed devoid of people. As they walked, an unnerving silence met them at every turn. Only the sound of the guard's rubber-soled shoes made the odd squeak on the polished floors.

"Why is it so quiet?" Adria looked at the guard, her body beginning to visibly quiver due to withdrawal and from cold.

The guard kept looking ahead and replied frostily. "Won't be for much longer. The Vinayaki migration has begun, most of the filth is either at the abattoir or working in the sheds."

Adria didn't reply.

They reached the first of several locked gates. The guard

unlocked the first gate, pushed her through and locked it behind her, before opening the next gate and repeating the procedure. After several barriers, they came to a halt at an enormous, barred gate. Beyond this Adria could see four levels of cells, iron stairs leading up to each one on either side of the prison wing. All the cell doors were open, and Adria guessed there were at least four hundred of them. This wing of the prison was filthy, dank and damp, and a foul smell loitered with the intent to offend the nostrils. Rats scurried across the ground floor, leaving their rodent paw prints in the muck.

"Welcome to your new home," the guard smiled at her as he unlocked this final gate, pushing her through. "We call this wing The Four Floors of Whores. You are on the third level, cell 320."

He locked the gate behind her. Adria turned and looked at the guard through the metal bars hopelessly.

"How long will I have to stay here?" her face was solemn and clammy.

"That is up to the Governor. If you're nice to him and kind to us guards, who knows? Maybe just a few months."

Her head fell to her chest, and when she looked up again the guard had gone. She turned and looked up at the ceiling of natural rock. The two walls on each side with their iron doors seemed to be closing in on her, towering over her, engulfing her thoughts, crushing the very life out of her. Adria's head spun and she stumbled as the cell doors whirled about in a kaleidoscopic haze. She fell to one knee, howling in anguish, startling the rats which darted into their foul hiding places.

CHAPTER SIX

Adria finally summoned the energy to stand upright. She looked at the prison landings and saw the doors were all numbered. She made her way towards the iron stairs that would take her up to the third floor. Already her bare feet were filthy, and every step she took on the dirty ground heralded a new foul odour.

The wing was eerily silent and Adria hadn't felt so alone and confused in a long time. She placed a grime ridden foot on the iron grid stairs and holding on to the bannister with a shaking hand, she made her way upward. The metal steps were cold and uncomfortable to tread on. Adria's whole body felt numb. By the time she reached the third landing, she was almost crawling. Fatigue was winning and all she wanted to do was sleep. Looking down the landing, she could make out the numbers on the door which was to be her cell. Her foot slipped on something dark and sticky as she moved forward. Blood? She wasn't sure and she didn't care.

The cell door had been left ajar and as Adria put both hands on the cold steel she almost fell to the floor as she stumbled in, catching herself on the corner of a table. She leant over the back of a chair waiting for her head to stop spinning.

The cell was lit by a dim bulb hanging from the centre of the ceiling, cocooned in a spider's web. Everything smelled damp and musty. The floor was cold concrete. This was far from the luxuries she had been used to whilst living at the brothers' villa.

Catching a waft of food her stomach rumbled. In front of her on the table was a large bowl of pale oats. Adria lifted the dish to her mouth, attempting to force the gluey substance down, but her mouth was too dry. Lumps of oats stuck to her teeth like papier-mâché, forcing her to spit the gruel back into the bowl. She threw it back onto the table.

The cell was surprisingly spacious, with three crude beds, an old metal-legged table and three chairs as the only furniture. There was a hole in the wall with five bars embedded into the concrete. The window was so high up, Adria could not even see what was out there. The floodlights which lit up the outer walls of the prison offered a small amount of extra light to the cell.

She noted one of the beds had far more covers than the other two and was relatively clean in comparison. Moving towards the bed, she noticed her blood-stained footprints, which she had walked into the room. Adria was too exhausted to clean her feet or footprints, and she fell into the bed. She was in a waking nightmare, sleep would be her only escape. For now.

$

The ladies' wing of the prison came alive with the approaching chatter of female voices. The noise echoed up the landings and the sound became almost deafening, although even this couldn't rouse Adria from her deep slumber. She had buried herself into the blankets covering her head with a pillow.

A crowd of filth-covered female inmates pressed up against the gate, eager to shower or return to their cells. Two heavily armed prison wardens shouted at the mob to step back. One of them removed a bunch of keys, unlocking the gate.

The crowd remained behind the bars, an eerie silence descended amongst them. The inmates parted, backing up to the corridor wall, forming a human tunnel. Three huge figures came thudding down the walkway. The prisoners dropped their heads, avoiding eye contact with the passing mounds who snarled as they moved. Their shackles rattled as they shuffled along. Even the two guards made way for the beasts, looking nervous and on edge.

A mountain of a woman, with so much facial hair she looked barely human, never mind female, lurched over, growling at one of the anxious guards. Her hot breath warmed his face.

"Are you going to take these off, or not?" she motioned with her head to her ankles.

The guard knelt, trying to keep as much distance as possible. His colleague kept a gun on her. His hands trembled as he unlocked the shackles on the three hideous women. He tried not to gag from the festering fragrance which they emitted. Looking up at them, they grinned down on him, showing their brown, jagged, tobacco-stained teeth, which were almost hidden by the hair on their upper lips.

"Thank you, sweetheart," the biggest woman growled while blowing him a kiss. Steam seemed to emerge from her foul

51

mouth as she spoke.

The guard backed away and the inmates laughed at the two terrified looking men. The three women walked onto the wing and the other inmates followed. Meanwhile, the officer who had undone their shackles tried to hide the yellow stain now warming his inner thigh.

The three hairy females walked the landing with a swagger as the other prisoners scattered towards their cells. None of them dared overtake Lucia or her two sisters, Josefina and Amalia. The three sisters made their way up the iron stairs, which creaked under their weight. Lucia's huge matted, furry feet lumbered up the levels, her toenails were so long and curved they were more like claws. When they reached their landing level, Josefina pointed out the blood-stained footprints that worked their way towards their cell door. Lucia sniffed the air, catching the scent of Adria.

"Smells like we have a new friend to play with," Lucia leered at her sisters with a broad, twisted grin. Their eyes lit up excitedly and quickly they moved towards the cell door. The sisters licked their lips as they strode in, their sly dark eyes searching the room. Amalia instantly noticed the bowl of food she had saved from breakfast. The dish had been moved.

"Some bitch has been eating my breakfast," moaning, she looked to her older sister. Lucia was gawking at the bloodied footprints which trailed off towards her bed.

"The same bitch is in my bed," whispered Lucia.

The three sisters crept towards the sleeping mound of blankets. Six hairy hands with dirt-encrusted sharp nails reached out towards the bedsheets, pawing at the lump. Adria stirred, wishing she hadn't as she opened her eyes. The day's events came flooding back to her. She ached all over and her body was wet from cold sweats. Her mind immediately started to think about the fine blue powder her body craved for with uncontrollable hunger.

A sound played in her ears. She shook her head to clear the cobwebs, but the sound grew louder. She realised the noise was panting, and it was coming from close by. She froze, her body rigid. She could feel hands stroking her back and it raised the fine hair all over her body. Suddenly the blankets were thrown off her. Adria spun around and tried to cover herself up, but she froze, horrified by what she saw. The three foulest looking women she had ever seen were in front of her. Sheer terror displayed itself on her face.

Lucia roared. "And here is the bitch. What are you doing sleeping in my bed?"

Adria's face turned a colder pale, she became immobile with fear.

"Well, well, well, what do we have here then girls? A little present from The Hog, eh? We must have been good girls this year," Lucia purred.

"Can I go first, please," an excited Josefina shook, jumping with excitement, her plump figure moved like waves under her shirt.

Amalia moaned. "Hang on, I went thirds the last time we had a little pet to play with."

"I will have her first," snarled Lucia, glaring a warning at her younger siblings. "This one is so fresh and pretty," she smiled at Adria.

Adria prayed they were just baiting her, trying to get a rise out of the new girl, knowing she had to try and remain strong. The prison was not a place to show weakness. Again, she attempted to pull the cover back over her, as if somehow the sheet would protect her. She tried to stand up, but Lucia slapped her hard around the head, causing her to fall back onto the mattress. This was followed by another slap, on the same spot where Vasiliy hit her earlier. Once again, her world turned black.

$

Adria opened her eyes and saw the small, barred window spinning around her head before settling back into place. She attempted to touch her head to quell the pain coming from her skull, but her arms wouldn't move. A sudden feeling of dread gripped her. She became aware her hands had been bound to the bed. Her eyes refocused, and she saw the three sisters glaring at her. Her neck felt tight.

"What are you doing to me? What is around my neck?" she cried.

The sisters laughed at her.

Lucia stared at her. "You have a pretty little collar on, for your new lead. If you're a good girl we might take you for a walkie later." They all laughed at her. "And as you are laid there, like a good dog, you can have a little treat."

Lucia was visibly dribbling as she climbed up onto Adria's belly.

Adria could feel the untamed wilderness of Lucia's under-carriage upon her flesh, the urge to be sick straight in Lucia's face was overwhelming, but before Adria could even begin to protest, a giant, brown, hairy nipple was forced into her mouth.

"That's a good doggy," Lucia began to groan excitedly.

Adria felt a rage building up in her, a wave of burning anger which she hadn't felt since she was a child. Her mind was blinded by white noise, a powerful strength arose from within her making her heart race. Her eyes opened full—a madness in them. She bit down hard on Lucia's brown nerve endings. Lucia howled so loudly that the whole prison seemed to come to a halt. The white noise took the last of Adria's energy and she became detached from reality. Consciousness was lost and her eyes disappeared back into her head, her body went limp like a dead fish.

And the three sisters, they had their fun.

CHAPTER SEVEN

It was morning, not that anyone would know deep underground in the metropolis of Aris. Only artificial light lit these parts of the ghettos with a few old lamp posts flickering in the addict-ridden streets. There was an endless whirring sound of the large air conditioning units which hung with the bats from the cavern roof, supplying the residents with warm oxygen. Drone satellites which offered a signal to telecommunications equipment moved in silent circles above the city.

Vasiliy nursed his broken nose with a blood-soaked tissue. "You didn't have to break my fucking nose, did you?" he moaned at Mikhail.

Mikhail was currently pacing the dance floor. Oliver, his pet rodent scratched around Vasiliy's feet, licking up the occasional drop of blood which dripped from his nose. The night before, Mikhail could not find Adria. Vasiliy played dumb as to her whereabouts. Being the brighter of the two brothers, Mikhail went through the CCTV and was livid with what he saw.

"Think yourself lucky you still have a cock. What were you thinking? How many years have we kept her safe? And intact! Not only have we lost a lot of money, but you have also made us look like a right pair of pricks. The Cracker had her sold on to a very wealthy client." Mikhail's veins pulsated in his neck, yelling at his brother.

Vasiliy became agitated and rose to his feet. "You've gone soft. That blonde bitch has taken advantage of you for far too long," Vasiliy poked a finger at his brother.

Mikhail glared at him. "You better sit the fuck down, right now."

Stepping forward, the two men locked foreheads.

"I said, sit down," Mikhail growled.

Vasiliy backed off, keeping his eyes on his brother as he sat.

"So, let me get this straight," continued Mikhail. "After you ruined her, you let one of our guys, who's on our fucking payroll, drive off with her? Did I hear you, right?"

"Okay, Mikhail, I fucked up, I said I was sorry, what else can I do?"

"You can start by getting that baby-faced tosser down here pronto. If Adria is still alive—and for your sake, she had better be—you will personally bring her back to me. Now make some calls, do whatever you need to do, get out there and fucking find her. And tell that wanker not to keep me waiting."

He looked up through watering eyes. "What is so fucking special about this girl? You're not telling me everything, what's the secret?" Vasiliy looked at his brother curiously. Mikhail was hiding something. He knew his brother better than anyone.

Mikhail bored his eyes into his brother. "You do not need

to know, now find her or God help me, I will cut you up and feed you to Oliver."

Rising to his feet Vasiliy startled Oliver who scampered across the floor. The rodent climbed up Mikhail's trouser leg and all the way up to his shoulder. He sat there upright, alert and watching.

Vasiliy grumbled under his breath, making his way to the front door of the club. The Klòn doorman was standing guard outside. He had anticipated Vasiliy's exit and opened the door for him.

Mikhail's eyes burnt into his brother's back. He reached into his suit jacket pocket, withdrawing a handful of cheese crumbs. He sprinkled them on his shoulder for Oliver who happily nibbled at the morsels. Mikhail then opened his suit jacket, removing a large, long-barrelled silver handgun from a leather shoulder holster. Flicking open the chamber. he spun it around, counting the bullets. He placed the gun onto a small drinks table and sat down, pouring himself a small glass of strong, dark brown spirit. He stared at the main door, waiting for Babyface.

$

Five hours had passed, and Mikhail's patience was wearing thin. The bar was barely lit and would not be opening tonight. The Klòn was ever-present outside the front door. He hadn't moved a muscle since Vasiliy left earlier. Mikhail had made some calls, organising a large shipment of Cane from the lab sector. The deal would be made tomorrow.

Vasiliy had done as he was asked and had spoken to Babyface. The young officer had just pulled up in the car park in front of the club in an armoured vehicle. Adria was still alive as far as Mikhail knew and Vasiliy was on route to the prison to negotiate her release with The Hog.

Babyface exited the vehicle and walked up to the Klòn, who was gormlessly watching him approach. He opened the door for him without a word. Babyface squinted as he entered the club, the hazy light restricting his vision. Cold sweat ran down his spine and his gut twisted nervously. He cautiously edged into the haze. He could make out the bulky frame of Mikhail sitting in front of him.

Mikhail stood up, blocking the limited light and his shadow fell over Babyface. Before he could react, Mikhail's muscular right arm wrapped around his neck. He did not try to resist. There was no point as Mikhail was twice his size.

Babyface choked.

"Vasiliy made me take her away, he paid me," he said, struggling to get the words out from the tight grip which squeezed his Adam's apple.

Babyface felt the cold barrel of the handgun on his temple.

"I give the orders, not Vasiliy, you know that. You have cost me a lot of money." Mikhail's dark face was stern, his eyes wild. "What were you doing picking up my girls anyway? Trying to win favour with that fat Hog? I don't like being played, you little bitch."

Mikhail pushed the barrel deeper into the fresh-faced officer's head. Babyface squirmed, trying to wiggle out of the headlock but Mikhail simply added more pressure. The officer whimpered. His face began to turn from red to purple. His tongue started to sag, hanging from the side of his mouth.

Mikhail whispered in his ear, "Oliver is hungry."

Babyface panicked, a low dry screech left his lips and he attempted to break free. Oliver's nose appeared from Mikhail's top pocket and he scuttled out. Dropping down, the rodent landed in Babyface's hair. The furry critter wiggled over his head. Babyface could feel Oliver pawing at his scalp. He went cross-eyed as the rodent crawled down his face and then sank his sharp needle-like teeth into his tongue. Oliver began tearing and ripping at the delicate muscle, pulling the flesh apart, like stretching chewing gum.

Mikhail loosened his grip temporarily and Babyface mistakenly gasped for air. The rodent took advantage of the gaping mouth. Shrinking it's body, Oliver scurried inside. Mikhail reinforced his grip. Blood began to leak from Babyface's eyes, nose and ears before his body went limp. Mikhail pushed away dropping the dead man.

Babyface's back hit the bar and slumped to floor, his pale face twisted at a grotesque angle. Mikhail observed the corpse as the right eye began bulging out of the socket. Oliver had burrowed his way through the officer's head and now exited from his eye socket, forcing bits of brain to squeeze out. The rat chewed through the optic nerve connected to the eyeball leaving the orb to roll down the dead man's face, landing on his chest. The eye stared up at Mikhail briefly. Oliver knocked the eyeball off the dead man with his nose and hurried into a dark corner with his swag.

Mikhail looked blankly down on the corpse.

$

The Hog sat at his desk, watching the screens mounted on the office wall through squinty eyes. He zoomed in on one screen specifically. Three women were getting familiar with each other in the showers.

His trousers were about his ankles, sweat seeped from his hairless head, and his trotter-like hands worked hard between his legs, engrossed in the aquatic ménage-a-trois.

There was a knock at the door. The Hog jumped in his seat, cursing the interruption. Quickly, he pulled his trousers back up and wiped his sticky hands on his shirt.

"Come in," he snapped.

The door opened and a young prison officer walked in confidently, neatly dressed, his dark hair groomed and slick, and his face was shaven clean.

"Ah, Luca, good to see you," snuffled The Hog. "What can I do for you?"

The young officer glanced at the screens to his right, attempting to hide his disgust. "Morning governor, there is someone at the gate asking to see you. He said he has already spoken to you regarding a new inmate? Vasiliy, I think he said his name was?"

"Oh, yes Vasiliy, have you not heard of him and his brother Mikhail?" The Hog raised an eyebrow.

"Yes, I've heard of them, drug dealing scum," replied Luca, as if something had jogged a cog in his memory, setting thoughts rolling.

"Now, Luca, one must not judge. We all do what we must do to survive. Apparently, the new girl who came in yesterday was part of their merchandise. A simple mistake. I've had dealings with the brothers before. I would like to keep doing business with them so send him up and we can sort this horrid mess out." The Hog stood up, waddled around the desk, putting his fat-fingered hand on Luca's back.

"A new inmate? I wasn't informed we had a new inmate," Luca spoke sternly.

"Sorry about this Luca, she came in late last night, nothing for you to worry about, I am sure she will be leaving us today." The Hog looked thoughtful for a minute. "Pity though, I really would have liked to have seen her progress amongst us here, such a young pretty flower. Come, look." The Hog gently put some pressure on Luca's back, moving him towards the surveillance screens.

"There she is," pointing towards the monitor which was broadcasting from a hidden camera in Adria's cell.

She was unconscious, naked, and tied to the bed, her golden hair hung to one side. Luca tried to hide his thoughts.

"I had better get her cleaned up then before Vasiliy sees her like this, we don't want to upset anyone," Luca said.

"That's a great idea," The Hog smiled, looking up at the handsome officer with sly eyes. 'Off you go then, let the gate know to send Vasiliy up, there's a good man.'

$

Adria stirred. Her body felt sore. The sheets under her were cold with sweat and her stomach groaned with cramps as though a fist gripped her intestines. This was just another side effect from Cane withdrawal. Her nose was beginning to ache. For the first time in years her nostrils were empty of the blue dust.

The sudden reborn sensation of being able to breathe through them again made her right eye water constantly. Her body was pimpled from the cold and her wrists were still bound to the bed frame. Thoughts ran through her mind making her dizzy and nauseous.

Vasiliy's eyes passing over her. The three sisters and their rotting grins and filthy hands. Anger began to boil in her toes, a heat began to rise through her legs. This time she didn't panic; Adria controlled the rage. Her heart started to bounce in her chest. The white light blinded her, but this time, she kept her eyes focused on the bright vision. The room turned black and white. She clenched her fists so tight her pale skin turned bright red, her blue eyes changed into dark holes. With brutal force, the bonds which held her snapped. She sat up, unbuckled the dog collar which was strangling her neck. She looked down at the burns where the rope wore away at her wrists. For the first time, the white light hadn't made her pass out. She didn't understand where this strength, this power came from. Her body and mind were so fragile, but somehow, she had managed to break her bonds.

$

The cell door flung open. Adria braced herself. A tall man with a light brown complexion walked in. She reached for a sheet on the floor, attempting to cover herself. The man turned away for a moment while she hid her modesty.

"Don't be scared," the officer said. "My name's Luca, I'm going to help you escape."

63

Adria gingerly stood up and her knees almost gave way. She had to hold out a hand against the cold cell wall to regain her balance. Luca looked at her, he knew instantly seeing her in the flesh... she was the one they had all been looking for.

"Your name? What's your name?" he asked with an urgent look in his eyes.

Adria looked at him suspiciously. "My name is Adria."

Luca's face lit up.

She was puzzled. "Who are you? Why would you help me?"

Her lips were cracked, dry blood had set hard in the corner of her mouth causing pain when she talked.

"We don't have much time. It is not down to me to tell you but we have been trying to find you your whole life."

Adria looked confused, "who's we?"

"There's no time now," Luca hurried his words. "You must trust me, I will get you out of here to somewhere safe. If you stay here ... well, Vasiliy is here for you."

Just hearing Vasiliy's name sent a wave of revulsion and vulnerability over her, and for a moment she wanted nothing more than to hide under the bedsheets. Luca could see the fear in her eyes, which made her hesitate, and he held out his hand.

"Trust me," he said.

$

Panting, the young girl laid as still as possible while holding tight to the scraps of food she had just taken from outside the club. Keeping still, fearful that her breathing was too loud and would give her away, she attempted to bury her mouth in her ragged coat. The stench from the garbage was making her gag.

"Come out," a deep voice spoke. The young girl shook. She was frightened and she remained hidden amongst the rotting garbage. "I won't hurt you. Are you hungry?"

The blonde child's ears perked up.

"Vasiliy, what are you doing over there?" came another man's voice.

"I think I have caught our little rat, brother."

"Oh, really?"

The sound of the other man's footsteps came closer. The girl began to shift her body, readying herself to flee. Suddenly the cardboard and rubbish she hid under were pulled off her. Standing over her was Mikhail and Vasiliy. Mikhail held his hand out to the frightened child.

"It is ok, we won't harm you, trust me."

☙

Adria, shook her head, clearing the memory away.

"Come with me. Please, trust me," repeated Luca.

Adria was frightened but she looked at Luca's hand and then into his eyes. There was an urgency in them, but also something kind. Having nothing else to lose, she placed her hand in his.

CHAPTER EIGHT

Alan's glass eye was coming loose, rolling around in the socket. Raising a hand off the steering wheel, he slapped himself in the face with a groan, forcing the eye to stay still. He pulled the vehicle over, up onto the curb. The old rusty van's brakes screeched before coming to a standstill. The streets were quiet. Faze addicts were busy working for their next bag of drugs in the lab sector.

A stray dog walked in front of Alan's van, sniffing the ground, rib bones visible through his fur. Alan stepped out of the vehicle, moaning. His right leg was causing him pain. It was an old wound which would not go away.

The dog crawled towards Alan submissively on his belly. He looked down at the mutt, with pity in his one good eye. He rummaged in his pocket and the dog wagged his tail, excited by the rustling sound. He produced some potato crisps, and bending down he ruffled the mongrel's fur, holding out the snacks in his palm.

"You poor thing. I wish I had more to give you," he patted the dog, and then turned to look about him.

Alan was on the northeast side of the ghetto. There was the odd streetlamp here giving some light to the high tower blocks which arose around him. A horrid smell was in the air, and the sound of more dogs in the distance could be heard barking and yapping. Alan gazed up at the flats, sighing heavily.

"Here we go then old man, my cardio for the day," he said out loud. He walked gingerly, as his lousy leg was making him limp slightly, and he made his way up to the main door of the tower block. The doors creaked from a lack of use as he forced them open. Inside, it felt colder, and a musty, damp smell followed him up the stairs. He had removed a torch from his quarter-length coat pocket, lighting up the flight of stairs as he ascended. He shone the torch up the stairwell. His face reddened as he breathed heavily. Remembering how many floors he had to climb, he took another deep breath and continued. A drop of fluid fell from above, landing on his forehead. Alan wiped away what he hoped was just water, but he didn't check. He thought that would be best.

By the time he reached the tenth floor, he was panting. Alan was not known for his athleticism. He filled his lungs again, resting against the landing wall, and shone the torch down the passageways which disappeared into darkness on either side of him. He shivered. The place gave him the creeps.

He began to climb again when he heard feet coming up the stairs behind him at a rapid speed. He reached behind his neck, pulling out a sawn-off shotgun which was strapped to his back. He hopped up the remaining flight of stairs with a grimace until he was in a small landing in the stairwell.

Alan positioned himself in a corner, aiming the gun towards

the top of the steps. The sound of approaching feet stopped. But Alan sensed whatever was coming was still moving up the stairs.

Slowly creeping low out of the darkness, came six yellow eyes, all fixed on Alan. They panted eagerly, hungry for flesh. There were three large, fierce-looking dogs, and the one at the front showed his white fangs, snarling. It crouched ready to pounce. Alan pulled the trigger as the dog was in mid-air, leaping towards him; a big black muscular canine foaming at the mouth. The blast from the shotgun echoed throughout the empty building. Alan's ears rang out, making him temporarily deaf. The dog gave out a yelp. The shotgun's ball bearings riddled the canine, and he landed on his back in a bloody mess.

The two remaining dogs came at Alan, and blasting another round, he blinded one of them, causing the dog to whimper and turn away. He cocked the shotgun attempting to reload the barrels. His fingers trembled, and fumbling with a fresh cartridge, it slipped out of his hand.

"Shit," he moaned.

The cartridge rolled away with his torch, which he had positioned under his bad leg. He was now blind and deaf, in total darkness; the last dog standing was just about to wrap his jaws around Alan's neck.

A figure came out of the shadows, bundling the rabid dog to the floor, fangs of white, bit at each other in the dark. The torch was knocked about, rolling around them, casting their furious fight in shadows on the walls. Alan finally slid a cartridge into the barrel, and leaning over he grabbed his torch, turning the light onto the melee.

The dog he had fed by his van was his saviour. The mongrel stood, snarling at the rabid dog and his blinded fellow as they backed off down the stairs. Alan looked at the mongrel in silent disbelief. Wagging his tail, he leapt on him licking at his face.

"Get off me, bloody mutt," he said. Patting the dog's back, the dog wiggled with glee, as though he had never been shown affection before.

A bright light appeared from above, lighting up the landing. A gruff voice shouted down the stairwell. "What's all the commotion then? Is that you, Alan?"

Alan looked up from where he sat, with the dog on his lap. "Yes, it's me, Jon, how did you guess?" He grinned upwards, his glass eye twinkling in the torchlight.

"Is it finally time?" Jon looked up from his wheelchair, studying his old friend. Alan was starting to look old. Not as old as himself, but getting there, he thought.

"Lost all your hair now then Alan. You're starting to look as old as me, mate."

"Yes, to both," Alan smiled.

Jon began to cough, frail hands attempted to cover his mouth. "That's good news, I don't think I will last another week, my lungs have had it," he coughed again.

"Does it have to be this way, Jon? There's still time for you to change your mind," Alan pressed him. "There can be another way."

"Yes, it does Alan, this was my idea, my decision. If you came here just to talk me out of it, I am not listening. Now tell me the details, is it tomorrow?"

Alan looked as though his mind was elsewhere. Jon recognised that look.

"Still haven't found her?" Jon asked.

Alan shook his head, he sat down on a threadbare sofa. The

room was full of damp, cold walls which caused the wallpaper to peel away, hanging in shreds. His new-found friend had followed him in and made himself busy sniffing around the littered floor for any crumbs which might be lingering in hidden places.

"No, nothing," Alan's face was grim. "We can't wait any longer, I never thought I would give up, but the rains are coming. I've put this off for far too long. Tomorrow we leave Aris."

Jon reached out a hand, placing it on his friend's knee.

"Alan," he said, "you never gave up old friend. No one else would have continued to search for her this long."

Alan placed his hand on top of Jon's. A tear glistened in his good eye.

$

Thud. The throwing knife splintered an old, upturned pine desk which was standing against a crumbling wall. Splinters shot through the air.

Thud. Another knife punctured the wood, only a hair's width apart from the first knife. Both blades were shortly followed by two-morning stars, with razor-sharp edges which penetrated even deeper into the wood. The desk was given a momentary respite before a flurry of arrows pinned themselves around the blades.

"You are on form today, my brother," Marica looked at Hanisi with a wry smile as she walked up to the splintered desktop, pulling the arrows free. She turned, walking back towards her brother grinning.

"No need to be sarcastic," he said. Walking past her, he struck out his leg, knocking Marica backwards over the outstretched limb. Marica somersaulted in mid-air, landing cat-like on her feet.

"You need to be quicker than that, little brother," she mocked him.

Hanisi smiled a mischievous smile. "Little brother, really? Well, those extra twenty minutes in the womb must have helped my aim, my arrows hit the mark unlike yours," he teased his twin sister.

The twins were at the far northern end of Aris, not too far away from the large cavern opening which exited out into the blistering heat of the desert plain. They were on the top floor of a roofless derelict building. The setting sun's rays had crept into the cavern's entrance, offering a hint of light. This gave them a brief window to practice their weapon skills in the open. Today was hot and humid, but the air was much fresher here. The further you travelled into the ghettos, the more stagnant the atmosphere became.

The twins had been training all day, dressed in black trousers and tight-fitting black shirts, accentuating their lean muscular figures. They both kept their heads shaved to the scalp, mapped with tattoos. Hanisi had a black tiger which clawed up his back and over his head, a full roaring mouth opened at the front of his skull. Marica's tattoo had a similar design, but with a magnificent dragon. Just like their parents before them, this was a family tradition. The twins had been trained in all manner of skills by their parents; lightning-quick on their feet, they could move with great stealth and both were experts in hand to hand combat and archery. They were taught the tricks of contortion, were experts on the high wire and trapeze. Now in their late twenties, they were in their prime.

"We should head back before nightfall," Hanisi said to his sister, looking at the rays of light shrinking back out of the cave mouth onto the desert floor.

They strapped their bows to their backs and retrieved the rest of their weapons from the sad-looking desk.

Creeping down the decaying staircase of the old building with cat-like agility, neither of them made a sound. Their dark clothing hid them amongst the shadows. Ever vigilant of the Klòns and drones that were never far away.

As they made their way through the crumbling streets and alleyways of Aris, they were unaware of the shadowy figure who had been watching them all afternoon. The slight figure tiptoed behind them, keeping a safe distance, his small, withered hand held a radio to his lips. He spoke into it with a hushed voice.

"The twins are on the move, heading back towards the main square."

A sinister rasping voice answered, "We have a view on them, keep radio silence for now."

A weak hand replaced the radio into his long coat as he continued his sly pursuit.

$

The twins crept along the cracked pavement keeping close to the buildings. The streets were deserted apart from the stray dogs and cats which roamed, sniffing out anything that could be eaten. Huge rats scurried by their feet as they made their way towards the square. The daylight which came through the entrance of the cave faded behind them.

Marica tapped her brother on the shoulder. They crouched behind an old, rusted car. Marica opened the bag she was carrying and took out their night vision glasses. As they put the goggles on everything turned shades of blue and the stray animals and rodents glowed red from their body heat.

The twins darted across the road to the other side. Jumping through a gap in the wall, they paused for a moment. Hanisi looked back through the opening. The drones and Klòns would be patrolling the ghettos now hunting for children and Oddities.

They both tiptoed, avoiding the debris on the floor where nocturnal roots and weeds were winning the war against concrete and rotten floorboards. They moved from building to building, avoiding the main drag. Cameras dotted the main roads and they couldn't risk being spotted. The twins came to another wall, and they had to crawl through a tight gap, which led them back onto the pavement. They both crawled through, standing up they dusted off their knees.

"Can you hear that?" Hanisi whispered to Marica. They both strained their ears, a distant humming was coming closer, growing louder and louder.

"Drones," Marica cried out, pointing to the horizon, over the decaying rooftops of the city. "There, two of them." Marica grabbed her brother's hand. "Quick in here," she said as the drones' motors grew in volume.

They nimbly picked their way over a broken doorstep, littered with glass and bricks. The twins' feet danced lightly over an old shop sign which lay amongst the decay on the floor.

"Up those stairs." Hanisi led the way.

They both darted up a broken escalator, onto the first floor. Bats flapped in panic and rodents scurried, frightened by the rare arrival of humans. The twins slid under an old counter, laying on the floor in silence.

They listened out for the sound of the drones. Nothing, but this did not mean they were not still out there. Drones could go into stealth mode when travelling at low speed. They could also pick up soundwaves, so the twins lay rigid, still, silent.

'Not now, not today, of all the days to be trapped or caught, why today?' Hanisi thought to himself.

$

They lay motionless, not talking, for more than an hour. This was something the twins were used to. Marica remembered the dozens of times they had hidden from the Klòns as children. Their parents had brought them up in a giant hidden underground bunker on the Westside of the city, below a wasteland. The twins' parents would often leave them on their own, sometimes for days at a time as they went out scavenging and hunting for food. Their parents chose to live in hiding, rather than give themselves or their children up to the System.

Every day they trained the siblings in combat for hours on end, certain that one day the people would rise against Bliksem and his program. In the bunker, they learnt their trade. Throwing knives at a moving target—a giant wheel with coloured rings. They fought each other with blade and bow, wearing protective padded outfits, although Marica could still remember the multiple bruises inflicted by her twin brother.

Eventually, when the twins were around ten years old, they began venturing out to scavenge for food or anything of use with their parents. Many times, on their adventures, they were forced to hide in similar circumstances. They had never been caught, until one day after a successful scavenge, they were all heading back to their underground abode when a patrol of Klöns came into view. The twins' parents hid them by the lake, under an old wooden boat.

Marica remembered shaking, holding on to her brother, whose eyes seemed very distant, as if he already knew their parents' fate. He was right. They both heard gunfire shortly after. Then there was silence, for hours, it seemed like an eternity. They stayed under the old decaying fishing boat, till the temperature dropped as the night air crept in, forcing them to leave their shelter.

Later they returned to the bunker. The entrance was hidden under moss-covered rubble. The twins' parents had not returned. They never did. The twins didn't know if they were still alive or not. Marica no longer talked to Hanisi about them. He never wanted to talk about them. He became angry and agitated if she pushed him. She knew deep down that the unanswered question was eating away at him.

$

The shadowy figure sat at the bottom of the broken escalator radio in hand. A long, dark hooded coat kept the man hidden in the darkness. All was quiet, but the figure was positive the twins were right above him, and his patience was running out.

"Where were those damn Klóns," he thought to himself. He would be rewarded with a large bag of Cane for his services. His body was twitching, itching for a hit. Just thinking about the blue powder hitting his system made his mouth water, and for some reason his anus sweat. He was growing impatient. Then the outline of a Klòn appeared in the crumbling doorway of the old department store.

$ $

Another hour passed when the twins finally spoke.

"Ten more minutes, then we will have to move," Hanisi whispered.

Marica replied with a silent nod. Then they heard a voice from the floor below. Hanisi peered through a crack in the floorboards. He could make out a figure. The heat sensing glasses he wore showed a hooded man, gesturing, making signs with his hands towards someone else. Hanisi pushed his eye right into the crack in an attempt to see what, or whom the figure was gesturing to.

Suddenly, the first floor lit up.

Two drones soared in through shattered windows which overlooked the abandoned streets. The disc-like flying machines were not armed, these were surveillance drones. They sent a live stream straight back to the lab's headquarters. They hovered over and around, searching the derelict site. Their lights made eerie shadows appear then disappear as they scanned for signs of life. A red light appeared on both drones. The twins knew they would be discovered at any moment. The red light warned them the drones had put on their thermal detectors. Abruptly the familiar sound of Klòns running, as they charged up the broken escalator, reverberated through the building.

"Run," Hanisi grabbed his sister's hand and the twins broke cover.

Running towards another flight of stairs, bullets sprayed, ricocheting off the wall leaving a trail of holes behind them. Hanisi risked a glance over his shoulder and saw there were at least eight of the synthetic humanoids in pursuit.

The two drones soared over the twins. Hanisi and Marica let go of each other's hands and ran for their lives. Reaching the top of the escalator, they found themselves on another crumbling floor and they ascended a flight of concrete steps. The drones still buzzed irritatingly over their heads.

"We need to shake these off," Marica yelled over the humming. Her breath was short..

Hanisi shouted back, "Now."

They both fell to the floor, rolling onto their backs, simultaneously launching two morning stars, which they kept on hooks attached to their belts. Sparks burst as they hit both drones', causing them to erupt into flames. Their lights faded, and their buzzing ceased. One drone exploded in mid-air. The second spun out of control, flying into a wall and exploded on impact. The disintegrating wall leant inwards.

The twins jumped to their feet, and ran up the remaining steps, just as the wall caved in on the staircase. Two of the chasing Klòns were crushed under the rubble. Broken, their red eyes faded to grey. The crumbled wall blocked the path of the chasing pack, and the remaining Klóns began punching the concrete barricade out of their way with their giant fists.

Stepping out onto the fourth floor they found they had reached the top. The remainder of the building had fallen in on itself years ago. Now they stood on a skeleton of iron rafters, with exposed wires and splintered floorboards. Above their heads, the cavern roof dripped with moisture. Hanisi looked back down the stairs. The Klòns were still manically smashing their way through the broken wall in a frenzy.

"Let's go this way," Marica said as she pointed to an iron rafter, balanced precariously over the open floors below and leading to the outside wall of the building.

Hanisi filed in behind Marica on the iron girder. Putting one foot in front of the other, the twins balanced precariously. They ignored the sixty-foot drop either side of them. One wrong step and they would fall to their deaths. They had almost reached the end of the rafter when a deep booming voice of a Klòn called out.

"Stop."

They did not falter and continued until they had reached the outside wall. The only escape route was the roof of the building adjacent to the one they were standing on.

"We can make it," Hanisi said.

He positioned himself in front of his sister and leapt into the night air, before landing with acrobatic dexterity. Turning, he held out his hands for her. Marica launched herself just as gunshots rang out from the Klòns automatic machine guns. Bullets whizzed past Hanisi's head, showering the gravel on the flat roof at his feet. The shots ceased. Hanisi looked up, his sister was nowhere to be seen.

"Marica," Hanisi called out desperately.

His sister yelled back, "Help."

Hanisi followed her cry and saw her fingertips, desperately grasping the edge of the gutter. The Klòns started firing again and bullets pinged all around him as he crawled frantically towards his sister.

He grabbed her hands and shouted, "come on quickly," as he pulled her up onto the roof.

They turned and fled into the darkness. The Klòns were too large and cumbersome to jump the gap between the two buildings, forcing them to give up the chase. The hooded figure watched as two silhouettes leapt from roof to roof until they disappeared on the horizon. He sniffed a line of Cane from the back of his hand. Smirking, he disappeared into the cover of a broken building.

CHAPTER NINE

The two silhouettes disappeared over the rooftops. The screen froze and Bliksem spun around on his chair to face Stór. There was little doubt that what he had witnessed displeased him.

"We know where they are headed, sir. We can take the whole filthy lot in one go," Stór reasoned, still gawking at the frozen screen.

"I really do hope this is the case. What good are you to me if you can't even catch two circus freaks?" Bliksem snapped. They had watched the whole scene unfold from Bliksem's office, buried underneath the Baráttan pit, deep in the lab sector. The footage had been beamed back live via the drones. The office was pristine, with polished floors, and not a speck of dust in sight. His desk was immaculate, and the pens and paper which adorned the wooden top were placed in perfect symmetry. Multiple screens attached to the wall broadcasted live images from the whole city of Aris, including the giant underground farms where fruits and vegetables were harvested under ultraviolet lights; the Vinayaki slaughterhouses, the ghettos, and the drug labs where Faze and Cane were produced. Bliksem had eyes and ears everywhere.

"I have never let you down before. We will crush them all. They've set their own traps," Stór mumbled.

Bliksem glanced at the screen, then back at Stór.

"Don't be so confident. If this limping, one-eyed bastard is who I think it is, don't underestimate him. He's cunning. And where is he now? This One-Eyed Alan?" Bliksem's eyes maddened.

Stór looked nervous. "Corporal Adar was assigned to him, but we have not been updated on his location for some time."

Bliksem's eyes squinted, his face reddened, and veins pulsated on his neck. "Bring me the corporal now," he sneered.

Stór did not reply, he simply turned and left the office. Bliksem sat for a moment staring at a photo of the one-eyed man. The crowd directly above him in the Baráttan pit, jeered as the slaves warmed up for the match.

Just what he needed—some mindless violence to relax him.

$

Bliksem left his office and walked down the dull, white corridors of the lab sector. Now and then, he passed large windows on either side. They looked into the different labs where scientists worked. He stopped to watch as two men in white lab coats tested a new Klón. Checking his reflexes, they tapped his knee with a small hammer. He jerked a huge leg upright. His dull eyes hanging from their sockets.

One of the problems with human clones, was that their eyes disintegrated far more rapidly than those of a natural human. Their blood cells, also, died early and had to be replaced regularly with metallic-looking synthetic blood. This Klón was missing an arm and silver blood was being fed into him via a drip. His artificial eyes were being repaired.

Behind Bliksem, was another glass wall, looking in on the Faze production area. Here hundreds of scientists worked daily, manipulating the Vinayaki ivory by adding chemical compounds to create a drug, which turned ordinary people into desperate zombies. The highly addictive Cane was also produced here, for vast profits.

Bliksem smiled to himself, reflecting on how far he had risen in status. Thirty years ago, he lived in the capital, Iris, had attended military school and graduated with honours. He quickly rose to the rank of Major. Aris was once an ore-mining city, but when the ore began to run out, there was civil unrest. Major Bliksem was sent with an army to crush the revolt. He was successful and the reward for his actions was the city itself.

Faze was already being used to keep the population of the System under control, and there was no better city than Aris to produce the drug in vast quantities due to the annual migration of Vinayaki.

The ex-miners had been deceived into taking Faze. Bliksem had proclaimed the drug was an immunisation against the flu. The issue of Faze was mandatory for ninety per cent of the population, and humans become immediately addicted. There was no known cure, and no going back. Once taken you were addicted, and to go cold turkey would cause the body to cease functioning, death would shortly follow.

Faze alters the brain so dramatically the addict almost forgets entirely who they are. Their past life becomes a mist of confusion. The addiction is so overwhelming the user would do anything for the high. A small minority were saved from entering the Faze program and were subsequently used to run the prison or perform other manual jobs which needed a clear head to carry out.

Some of the wealthier inhabitants of Aris were able to buy their way out of the program. Faze is processed in such an abundance in Aris that vast quantities are sent to every corner of the System every year, along with large batches of Cane, the stimulant party drug, generally sold to the wealthy. Moreover, Aris had become the centre point for advances in artificial intelligence. The Klóns were just the beginning.

Bliksem's rise and that of Aris's had not been without its setbacks. Many considerable advances in artificial intelligence, weapon technology and drug manufacturing were exceeding all expectations.

The expert scientist leading this advance was Professor Alander Phillips. A genius, but unfortunately for Bliksem, a man with morals; a man without a lust for wealth, and worst of all, a man with a conscience.

When Professor Alander saw what had become of the vast population of Aris, a city full of addicts, he had begun to question his work. He then realised that humanity was to be replaced with the very monsters he was helping to create; the Klóns.

The peoples of Aris and the world were being phased out.

The professor had made a significant breakthrough in his field of study, and Bliksem wanted to further his power.

The advances Alander had made would be hugely profitable. However, aware of Bliksem's plans and his lust for power and wealth, Alander sabotaged his own work. He destroyed all his research before killing himself and his assistant, Jon Saunders. Twenty years of research was lost, a colossal blow to Bliksem.

But, twelve years later with a new head of science, they were back on track. Production of new military hardware was now at the forefront of Aris's rise. But just two weeks ago a photo had turned up on Bliksem's desk. A drone had taken a picture of a trader, who owned The Golden Goose in the old square, which still opened its doors to the small non-addicted population.

Bliksem had studied the picture repeatedly for hours. The man in the photo was driving him mad. 'Could it be him? Did Professor Alander Phillips live?' His appearance had changed, but something made Bliksem believe Alander lived. He had to know for sure. There were too many similarities. The photo played on his mind, nagging him, making him irritable and restless.

$

Alan finally reached the bottom step, limping onto the ground level of the tower block. His new adopted dog waited patiently for him at the doorway. Alan looked back up the stairs, a great sadness in his heart, knowing he would never see his old friend again. Eyeing the dog up, he grumbled under his breath while wiping beads of sweat from his balding head.

"Guess I am stuck with you now then, dog? I suppose I'd

better give you a name. That's if you're going to stick around?"

The dog tilted his head to one side as if he was trying to understand the words which came out of his new owner's mouth. Alan whistled. The mongrel walked over, sitting down in front of him. Alan removed a large blue handkerchief from a pocket. He tied the blue fabric around the dog's neck.

"Blue suits you. And there we have it! Blue, that's what we will call you."

Alan ruffled Blue's head, then made his way back out onto the empty streets, followed by his new companion. He made his way to the rear of the old van. The handles on the back doors were so rusted they were barely hanging on. With a groan, he had to use all his strength to crank them apart with a high-pitched screech.

The van was empty, apart from a large can of petrol and a canvas rucksack. He looked around, making sure he was not being observed. Sure the sky was clear of drones. He lifted the bag, and disappeared back into the tower block. In the corner of the lobby, Alan hid the bulging bag under some rubble. Hastily he limped back to the van and removed the petrol can and placed the fuel on the passenger seat in the cab. He whistled for Blue, who jumped in.

Driving only a short distance away, Alan parked the van up in a dingy alleyway. He left the cab with Blue in tow. Then he methodologically went about, dousing the vehicle with petrol. Once he was satisfied, he stepped away and removed a box of matches from his pocket then struck the sulphur, flicking the match towards the van. It exploded into flames. Alan turned and hobbled as fast as he could down the street, headed in the direction of The Golden Goose.

CHAPTER TEN

Bliksem moved up the stone steps into the arena. The stench of death hung in the air. The noise was ear-splitting. The humidity was high and he started to sweat. The harsh floodlights made the faces of the baying crowd grotesque as they screamed, shouted and clapped excitedly. The Major paused before taking his seat, looking around the small arena at the traders from around the world. They visited Aris to deal in slaves, Cane, and Klóns; waving their money in the air, yelling eagerly at the bookies to take their cash.

On the other side of the arena directly opposite Bliksem sat The Cracker, the dwarf slave trader who came from Iris every year to purchase slaves. The two men acknowledged each other with a nod. Bliksem took his seat.

The inside of the arena was surrounded by Klóns, protecting the crowd from the contestants as well as preventing players from escaping. Bliksem enjoyed the pit and the ridiculous violence on offer. The victims of the game were no use to the world as far as he was concerned. They were nothing but cripples poisoned in the womb by Faze. This way at least they could die providing some entertainment for the privileged few.

The arena was small compared to the stadium in the capital; barely a thousand spectators could sit in the circled enclosure. They were so close that often members of the audience would be sprayed in blood from the gladiatorial contest in front of them. The floor was cast iron and the fighting surface was an assault course of deadly hazards. The game itself was brutally violent. Two teams of ten played against each other to score the most goals. The winning team was the first to reach five goals. As far as Bliksem was aware, in all the history of the Baráttan pits, the score had never exceeded four.

Starting either end of the pitch, contestants waited for a metal ball to be dropped by a drone into the centre of the pitch. Both teams rushed towards this ball, and whoever reached it first, had to fight their way through the opposition. They had to throw the globe into an open-mouthed skull of a Vinayaki at the opposing end, scoring a goal. But the real challenge of the game was to stay alive. Both teams were armed with lethal weapons, ranging from baseball bats to blades and tridents.

To make the game even more entertaining for the blood-thirsty crowd, the pitch had six deep pits: three on each side. Two contained enormous iron spikes, two with burning fires stoked by slaves from below, and the remaining two pits typically included a wild animal or beast. Lions were most popular.

On this occasion though, Bliksem saw on the live stream that there was a Snow Bear in one, and at the other end of the pitch, three White Ridgeback Wolves stalked the bottom of the pit, snarling and snapping their jaws at the commotion of the crowd above.

The pitch was also littered with weapons such as flamethrowers or shotguns which could be used if one of the contenders was disarmed. The teams were made up of Oddities, mutated and deformed Faze rejects, criminals, and anyone who stood up to the System.

A large roar erupted. The elitist crowd arose from the seats as the two teams emerged from a tunnel, taking up their positions at each end of the arena. Bliksem was pleased to see his Oddity champion. Olaf strutted onto the pitch and Bliksem hoped he would survive, as he had arranged with The Cracker a hefty fee if he performed well today. A hundred games without defeat; he was a mean one. From the day he was born, Olaf's arms were thick with hair and his hands black as soot, leathered and strong. The rumour was that Olaf had split his mother in half when she gave birth to him.

All the contestants wore a simple loin-cloth to cover their dignity. Olaf's back was thick with silver hair, but the rest of his dark, scarred skin was more human-like. He was six and a half feet tall with an iron jaw bone and a scowl which would make the bravest of men turn and run. He revelled in the crowd's song and lifted his weapons of choice at them in salute. A giant double-edged axe, which was still stained with blood from the last match in one hand, and a spear with two points in the other. Olaf waved them in the air, exciting the spectators. He glanced at his teammates—who formed a line to his right—then took in the opposition. He roared down the pitch at them. Turning his eyes back to his team again, he noted they looked petrified.

Growling, he yelled at them, "you all look like scared

animals." Pointing his spear down the pitch towards the other team. "If they can see the fear in your eyes, you have already lost. Grow some bollocks. This could be the last day of your life. Find some courage. Die with some dignity." Olaf spat on the floor.

His team members answered his war cry and following his lead, they waved their weapons in the air. The crowd responded with a resounding cheer. Olaf's team was regularly being replaced, as there were only three or four survivors left by the end of each match. The only member in his team who had fought with Olaf in the last year was Inyoni, a dark slick lady with jet black, short, spiky hair. Her back was rigid like a lizard, and small scales protruded from her spine. She was also his lover, 'The Wild Woman'.

The remaining eight members of his team caused him concern. One guy had only one leg, with a wooden stump replacing the missing limb. There was also a midget standing only three-feet-tall, with a head way too big for his body.

"They're all dead men," Olaf cursed under his breath.

The crowd suddenly fell silent.

Olaf looked up at the audience towards the area where the official overseer of the game stood, and spotted Bliksem in the crowd sitting close by. His stomach turned with rage. He glared at him for a second, but the game was about to begin.

Olaf turned, straining his eyes. He took in the opposition who would start their fight to the death any moment now and struggled to make out the figures amongst the smoke and flames which crept out of the two fire pits. The game would inevitably end with both teams bloodied or dead. Olaf had learned to accept this many years ago.

The overseer nodded his head signalling the start of the

game. The crowd roared again, chanting Olaf's name. A drone hummed through the thick air and approached the centre of the pitch. Hovering for a moment, it dropped the fist-sized metal sphere to the ground. It landed with a loud clunk.

Olaf and his Wild Woman were first off the mark. They sprinted immediately towards the metal orb. The man with the peg leg toppled straight over, cursing himself. The crowd laughed at his misfortune. The midget also began running but was quickly left behind. The remaining team players scattered, unsure of what to do. Olaf ran past the fire pit, then leapt over the howling white wolves which snapped at his heels. Inyoni was by his side. Their eyes stared dead ahead, and Olaf could see at least five members of the opposing team also charging towards the ball.

Inyoni carried two swords on her back and a trident in her hand, but within arm's reach of the ball, a spear whistled past her right ear. She raised her trident, showing ripped biceps which glistened in the floodlights, launched the projectile with ferocious speed. Flying true, the prongs punctured the neck of a man, his jugular erupting crimson. He fell on his back, blood jetted upwards. The crowd resounded with approval.

An arrow whizzed past Olaf, causing him to be taken by surprise when a figure leapt out from a cloud of smoke, striking him with a club. It connected sharply with his upper arm, knocking him off balance. Olaf stumbled to the floor, just managing to raise his axe in time to block another blow.

He looked at the attacker whose face turned from violent rage into pale terror. Shrieking in pain, the man fell towards Olaf. The midget had snuck up behind him, slicing the man's Achilles heels. Blood pumped out, puddling on the floor. Olaf quickly thrust his spear upward, ramming the point into the attacker's ribcage, sinking the tip in deep. The man gargled blood and Olaf twisted the spear causing the man to scream in agony. He yanked the weapon free, spilling the man's innards.

Olaf jumped back onto his feet, smiling at the midget, acknowledging he may have just saved his life. The midget grinned, pleased with himself. The grin froze on his face as a huge axe cleaved through his skull. The sharp blade travelled right down through his face. His tongue unravelled, leaving his body. The blade continued moving through the small man, splitting him in two. The midget fell in two halves. Olaf threw his spear straight into the eye of the midget's murderer, the metal tip popping the eyeball, continuing the trajectory through the man's skull. The back of his head cracked as the spear exited with the deflated eyeball on the end. The man slumped to his knees. Olaf then swung his axe, decapitating him.

A loud buzzer sounded. The crowd cheered and clapped excitedly. Inyoni had been first to the metal ball. She had made her way deep into the opposition's half, reaching the gaping skull which was nailed to the wall. She flung the sphere into the mouth, scoring the first goal. She strode back past the blood-splattered Olaf.

"You're getting too slow, old man," she teased him.

Olaf growled back with a broad grin, "just giving you a head start darling."

Returning to their starting line, Olaf was surprised to see the man with the wooden leg was still alive. They had lost half their number and he could hear the crackling of human fat in one of the fire pits. He turned his face up, disgusted.

"How many did we take down?" Olaf shouted.

"I got two," Inyoni called out over the noise in the arena.

91

The man with one leg shouted, "one, I got one," looking very pleased with himself.

Olaf nodded approvingly. The remaining two team members signalled they had not killed anyone. It was now five aside. They had also scored a goal—although this was irrelevant in the grand scheme of things. The score meant nothing, this was just a twisted spectacle for the pricks in the crowd. Olaf knew that.

The drone hovered in, dropping the metal ball a second time. Both teams charged towards the ball once more. The man with the wooden leg hobbled as fast as he could behind them. Olaf forced through the thick, humid air, and reached the ball first, only a split second before one of their opponents. Using the metal ball to his advantage, he shoved it into the man's face, crushing his nose and cheekbones, which splintered up into his brain. Blood ran from his eye sockets as he crumpled to the floor.

Olaf glanced to his left, where a man from his team had found some courage. Screaming with rage, he ran towards another man whose face was grotesquely deformed, swinging a sledgehammer wildly. Before it connected with the already misshapen head, he was thrown off-balance by the weight of the weapon and fell into a pit of iron spikes.

Four against four.

Olaf risked a glance over his shoulder, and saw the one-legged man had made it a few yards off the starting point. Olaf continued sprinting towards the ivory goal. Inyoni was to his right, battling in a sword fight. The other man on his team was embroiled in a fistfight. The man with the deformed head who had narrowly escaped being bludgeoned with a sledgehammer pursued him, but Olaf was too quick. The skull was directly in front of him. He launched the blood-stained ball into the yawning hole, just as Inyoni decapitated the man she was fighting, slicing her two swords through his neck.

The buzzer sounded again indicating the fighting was to stop. The combatant chasing Olaf came bearing down on him. Before Olaf could react, a gunshot rang out from the arena. A Klòn marksman, who stood with the overseer in the stands had put a bullet straight through the would-be attacker's temple. This was how cheats were dealt with; instant death if you broke the rules of the game.

Olaf could hear cries for help. The two combatants who were fist fighting had rolled into the bear pit, and the sounds of limbs being ripped from their torsos made Olaf grimace. The cameras in the bottom of the pits showed the savagery on two large screens at each end of the arena. The crowd clapped and yelled hysterically, thirsty for blood. They witnessed the bear's massive jaws clamp around the neck of one of the men, biting his head clean off. Some in the crowd couldn't watch and turned their faces from the horror which was unfolding.

The odds were now in their favour. Three—his Wild Woman, the peg-legged man, and himself—against one. The remaining member of the opposition facing them was a woman; a walking steroid, six-foot-tall, broad with hands so deformed they looked like two large stone cauliflowers. Her fingers looked as though they had been melted, fusing them together. A bright green Mohican ran from her brow, over her skull and down her spine to her bottom.

Olaf was amazed the peg-legged man had survived another round. "What's your name?" he shouted.

"Courtauld," he yelled back.

"Well, Courtauld, you may get to die another day."

Courtauld smiled back.

Inyoni called out, "She's mine, leave her for me."

"Be careful, she's a beast," Olaf replied, concern showing on his face. The drone once again whizzed in and the four remaining contestants ran forward. They all ignored the ball this time. Courtauld tried to keep up. So far, he hadn't reached the halfway line once which had probably been his saving grace. The Cauliflower-handed woman stormed towards them. Inyoni readied her trident, launching the deadly fork with furious speed. The woman slapped the trident away.

"Like swatting flies," she growled, boring down on Inyoni who had pulled her two swords from their sheaths tied to her back.

Olaf rounded the two women, positioning himself at the rear of the opponent. Courtauld was gaining on the group. The crowd laughed and jeered at him. He returned their amusement with a royal wave.

The monster swung a giant hand at Inyoni. She lumbered backwards, the fist just brushing her nose. She rolled to the floor, springing back up onto her feet, just in time to avoid another blow. Inyoni dashed towards her attacker, slashing at the air with her swords. One of the blades nicked the monster's exposed right breast.

The woman yelled and bulldozed towards Inyoni. Stepping backwards, Inyoni tripped over a severed arm, which lay dripping blood on the floor. She looked up in horror as the two giant hands clamped around her torso and squeezed her in a vice-like grip. Inyoni screamed in agony.

Olaf ran towards the beast, panic-stricken. The sound of popping and the cracking of ribs came from Inyoni's chest. She coughed, and blood splurged from her mouth. The monster grinned hideously at her, then flung Inyoni ten feet through the air, her broken body lay still on the floor.

Roaring with anger, Olaf lifted his axe high above his head. The woman spun around and swung a giant fist knocking him to the floor. He lost a grip on his weapon and cried out in pain. The brute's fist had hit him cleanly in the temple. His head spun and his vision clouded as he struggled to reach across the floor for his axe. The monster stood over him, looking down at him. She slowly raised her fists.

Olaf strained to look at Inyoni one last time before he met his fate. The woman suddenly froze, her fists in mid-air. She looked down at her stomach. The skin tore open, a sharp point erupting from her gut. Her head slumped to the side and she fell back onto the metal surface with a crash causing the arena floor to shake.

Olaf sat up confused, to see Courtauld hopping over the dead body. He had detached his wooden leg which he now held in his hand. The wooden leg doubled up as a telescopic spear. The crowd screamed in delight as the final buzzer sounded. The game was over. Olaf staggered to his feet and ran towards Inyoni, kneeling beside her he lifted her head.

"Please. Don't you dare die on me," he sobbed.

Inyoni opened her eyes, struggling to catch her breath, as blood dripped from her lips. "Olaf, my love," she struggled to speak. "Please, find my baby. Promise me you will find Zarrah."

He stared at her, replying with honest determination in his voice. "I will, I promise."

And Inyoni, The Wild Woman, was gone. Olaf held her lifeless body tight against him, feeling her body go limp.

And the crowd cheered.

֍

Bliksem rose from his seat upon seeing Stór. The giant Klón was making his way through the applauding crowd towards him.

"Major, Corporal Adar has lost the One-Eye."

A madness showed on Bliksem's face. His lips tightened, holding the hilt of his machete. He made his way out of the arena followed by the Klón commander.

֍

Olaf stared at the empty space next to him on his bed, his eyes heavy with tears. Courtauld sat on a chair in the corner of the dank cell, remaining silent, not wishing to disturb Olaf in his grief. They had both been brought back to the cell from the Baráttan pits after the game, although Olaf had to be torn away from Inyoni's body. Eventually, two Klòns rained heavy blows on him until he passed out.

Courtauld had opened his mouth several times, but stopped himself, not being able to find the right words.

Olaf finally spoke quietly, "I have to get out of here, somehow."

Courtauld wasn't sure if this was a question, or if Olaf was talking to himself. He decided to nod, still unsure of what to say. Everyone knew escape was impossible.

"There must be a way," Olaf said. He remembered the times he laid here with Inyoni. They had only shared each other for a short period.

Maybe if they had met under different circumstances, they might have never been lovers. But for the twelve months they had fought together, bled together, lay together, they had fallen in love. Inyoni planned to escape. Olaf had dismissed her plan before, but now, he reconsidered.

"There must be a way."

"How?" Courtauld looked at Olaf questionably.

Olaf didn't reply.

Inyoni had lived all her life hiding in the ghettos of Aris. She was caught scavenging with her daughter and was incarcerated. She was sent to the pits and her daughter was being held in prison. Eventually, she would be inducted into a work gang and the Faze program. He didn't know if Zarrah was still alive or an addict now, but Inyoni had told him that if there was any hope of finding her daughter, she had to seek out the One-Eyed Man.

Olaf had made up his mind. He looked at Courtauld, "have you heard of The Golden Goose?"

CHAPTER ELEVEN

Bliksem returned to his office after the bloodshed of the Baráttan pits. He had sent Stór to find Corporal Adar and he had also sent a message to the head engineer, telling him that his presence was required. Bliksem leaned back in his chair and watched the drone feed on the monitors. Impatiently, he tapped the ivory handle of his machete, which hung from his waist. Below his feet, the grinding noise of the military-industrial units made the floor rumble. These huge machines worked day and night constructing drones and weapons.

The Major turned in his chair to look at a large map of Aris sprawled out on the desk in front of him. There was a knock at the door. Corporal Adar walked in, visibly nervous, sweat showed in damp spots on his shirt. The young corporal approached the desk.

"Sir, reporting as ordered," sheepishly the Corporal fingered his collar. It felt tighter than usual.

Bliksem ignored him and continued to study the map.

Minutes passed without a word between the two men. Again, there was a knock at the door which then sprung open violently. A Klòn lumbered into the office hunched over. Two straps went over his shoulders, holding a casket on his back. Inside the casket was Techno, a legless human, hurling abuse at his carrier. He was bald and his face was scarred by fire, with round-rimmed goggles on. "No. Over there by the desk you moron. That's right. Now turn around." Techno now faced the Major. "Evening sir, apologies to have kept you waiting. Blame this brainless mannequin," Techno spat, and wiped his oil-stained forehead. His face was greasy, potted with acne, a large boil glowing with pus on his left cheek.

The Major glared at Techno - studying the hideous man's face he regretted doing so. "Are the new units ready to roll out?" Bliksem asked.

"Yes," Techno stammered nervously, swatting away foaming saliva which manifested in the corners of his mouth. "Six of each unit will be ready by the morning. I know you requested twice this number," Techno stammered anxiously, "but due to a shortage of the metals we need..." he trailed off as Bliksem bored his eyes into him.

Bliksem stood up and walked around the office, pacing back and forth, his boot heels squeaking on the polished floor. "Failures. Both of you, failures," he spoke sternly. Facing Adar's back, he didn't raise his voice, but there was a hint of menace. If Techno or Adar were brave enough to turn around they would see the Major's face was bright red. Bliksem fondled the machete's handle.

"Corporal, how is it possible for a limping, one-eyed man to escape you?"

"Sir..." the Corporal opened his mouth.

His eyes froze wide open, Adar's head convulsed, twitching side to side; spasming. The machete's blade had burst from his mouth. Bliksem had rammed the knife into the soft area between the skull and neck, puncturing through the skin with little effort, ripping Adar's tongue and breaking teeth which washed out of his mouth in a stream of blood. The mush pitter-pattered onto the floor. Techno began to retch.

"That is the cost of failure." Bliksem pulled the blade out cleanly.

Adar fell to the floor twitching. He was still alive, attempting to blubber words from his ruined mouth.

"Sorry I can't hear you, have you something stuck in your throat?" Bliksem sniggered. Then with full force, he stamped repeatedly on Adar's head. The blood splattered up the walls. Techno turned his face from the grotesque violence.

Adar was dead. The Major wiped the mess from his boots onto the cripple-carrying Klón's trousers, who remained still with a blank expression on his face. Casually Bliksem stepped over the mangled Corporal, returning to his chair. He looked up at his head engineer.

"Never let me down again."

"I will not, sir," Techno held out praying hands, dribbling.

"Have everything ready by morning." Bliksem flicked away a chunk of Adar's tongue and a broken tooth which had landed on the map.

"We start here," the Major said, as he stabbed a bloodied finger down on a circled building, labelled as The Golden Goose.

$

The Major had moved to the comms room and two Faze addicts had been summoned to his office to clean up what was left of Corporal Adar.

The vast room was the epicentre of the lab sector where engineers and soldiers monitored hundreds of screens around the walls. Every camera and drone in Aris beamed back live footage to this surveillance hub.

Bliksem had been sitting in a large chair for the last two hours, surrounded by monitors feeding back images from every corner of Aris. A radio receiver sat in front of him, menacingly silent. His narrow eyes watched the screens, one of them in particular he focused on intently. He had watched the comings and goings of The Golden Goose all evening.

"What are you up to?" he said to the screen.

Inside the bar, Bliksem's spy was trying to discover the whereabouts of One-Eyed Alan. The spy was the same shadowy figure who had followed the twins earlier. He had received orders from Bliksem to abort their pursuit and divert to The Golden Goose. Bliksem was determined to find out if his hunch was right; that One-Eyed Alan and professor Alander, were indeed the same man.

A Klón waded into the comms room, carrying the goggle-eyed engineer, Techno.

"Over there, you giant walking turd," Techno motioned towards Bliksem, twisting in his carriage. The Klón walked towards Bliksem heavy-footed; he stopped short, turning around so Techno could face the Major.

"Sir, a moment of your time," Techno sounded excited and judging by the phlegm which left his mouth just missing the Major's crossed legs, he was very excited indeed.

Bliksem turned his head and frowned at the foul, legless

man - irritated by the intrusion of his thoughts.

"All is ready for your inspection, Major. The Chemist is also ready to see you too," the engineer removed his goggles, revealing eyelids which were fused open. He wiped the glasses as they had steamed up.

Bliksem noticed Techno was salivating more than usual. He was in some sort of enthusiastic hyper mode. Techno's ability as an engineer far outweighed his personal hygiene. Otherwise, Bliksem would have done the kind thing years ago and put him down. The thought had crossed his mind on several occasions. Bliksem looked thoughtful, then nodded with a dry smile.

"Okay, ready the battalion for inspection, I will be along shortly."

"Sir," spluttered the engineer, wiping snot away with his sleeve, then wiping it onto the unaware Klòn's back. "Come on then," the engineer barked his command at the docile Klòn.

Techno left the room. Bliksem turned his attention back to the screens. The radio remained silent in front of him.

$

Bliksem left the comms room, pushing open two large double doors. He stepped onto a metal platform which overlooked a vast underground hangar stretching out as far as the eye could see.

He paused, looked down and surveyed the assembled army which was neatly formed in regiments. On the left flank were rank upon rank of Klòns; two thousand in number, their red eyes staring vacantly into space.

They were all dressed in padded body armour and carried machine guns, held against their right shoulders. On the right flank were the human armed forces, handpicked by Bliksem himself. More than a thousand stood to attention in regimental files. There was not a hair out of place and even the trained Bull Mastiffs which stood by their handlers did not move or make a sound. Bliksem descended a flight of steel steps. Reaching the ground level, Techno and Stór waited at the bottom. A tall woman was standing by—The Chemist.

"The troops are ready," Stór looked very pleased with himself.

"You are to be commended," replied Bliksem, who noticed Techno was bouncing about impatiently on his Klón's back. "So where are my new toys, are they ready?" he said to his legless engineer.

"Yes, yes, this way," the engineer spoke like an excited child.

Bliksem, Stór and The Chemist followed Techno through the hangar until they reached an area where the new weapons of war waited to be inspected.

"I have named these ones Moles," his goggles started to steam up again, and he gestured for Bliksem to inspect them. Six new machines with boring drills on metal tracks stood no higher than waist height. Techno continued, "They are programmed to work remotely from the comms room. They have a diamond steel-tipped drill and they can cut through iron. They also carry a payload of six projectile missiles. Over here," Techno was beside himself, "these are my Dragonflies," he said giggling hysterically.

Bliksem walked around them, genuinely impressed with their design. The new drones had synthetic wings.

"I have made them far slicker and slender, making them lighter and faster than normal drones. They can also carry two heat-seeking missiles."

"You are to be congratulated. We'll see how well they perform shortly, I am sure," Bliksem then turned his attention to The Chemist. She stood at the same height as the Major with long, straight jet-black hair with a fringe that was cut perfectly straight across her high forehead. Dark eyes matched her hair. She looked over the rim of her glasses and adjusted them with twig-like fingers. "Are you ready?" Bliksem looked at her. He found her unattractive; bean pole thin with gangly legs, long arms which almost met her knees and a mole on her chin, which sprung hair like a spider's legs attempting to escape from her face.

"Yes, the test chemicals are in place ready for your orders, but first I have a demonstration for you, sir."

He smiled at her and she gestured for all of them to follow her. They passed through some glass doors, and then along a surgically white corridor. They entered another room on the right, which was completely bare other than a two-way mirror, a door to the left, and a small speaker mounted on the wall. Bliksem, Techno and Stór waited here.

The Chemist disappeared through the door.

The three of them looked through the mirrored glass, where a naked, middle-aged man paced an empty white room. A padded door was the only way in or out. The Chemist's voice sounded from a speaker in the wall.

"It might be wise to step back a few feet."

CHAPTER TWELVE

Sophia put down her phone and looking around the empty bar she poured herself a shot of dark spirit, necking it in one gulp. She had just spoken to Luca and her mind raced with emotions. They had found her. 'Was it truly her?' To have discovered her now after all these years of searching when everyone had given up. She wasn't one hundred percent convinced, but she hated to doubt Luca's word. She had given up hope of finding her a long time ago, although her father had remained optimistic.

Sophia shook herself, she had to focus on the job at hand. Lifting the trapdoor behind the bar, she made her way down the wooden ladder into the cold cellar. She pushed kegs of homebrewed beer to one side revealing another door hidden behind them. She descended a second ladder which went deep underground into old Aris. The tunnels and catacombs of a past civilisation were hiding deep in the earth. The tunnels and catacombs of a past civilisation were hiding deep in the earth. Sophia climbed down, her athletic body moving with nimble speed and reached the bottom in little time, not a bead of sweat on her. The ladder dropped into a large open tunnel.

Dozens of Oddities and humans hurried about. They were busy loading weapons, cleaning guns, making explosives and filling backpacks with ammunition and grenades. Lights hung from exposed wires from the roof and were connected to a generator, which was groaning at the far end of the room. Maps of Aris and the lands beyond hung on the walls and floor plans of multiple buildings from inside the lab sector, including the prison, were pinned to boards.

At the far end of the room was Alan's worktable. Spread on top were test tubes, Bunsen burners and jars with different coloured liquids in them. Alan had been working down here day and night recently, to the point of obsession. She would bring him food otherwise he would forget to eat. Several times Sophia had found her father asleep hunched over the desk.

Sophia called out over the noise, "Ratty, where are you?"

A slim young man with a pointy nose stood up from behind a pile of bullets that he had been carefully dividing out. "Sophia, here," he waved.

"I have to leave now. You need to keep a watch upstairs. More people will be coming soon."

"Leave?" Ratty looked confused, "why, what's going on?"

Sophia tied up her dreadlocks which had come loose, and bending down on one knee, she tightened her boots. Looking up, she shouted back, "I can't explain, I don't have time, but my dad will be back shortly."

Ratty nodded, halted his counting, and followed Sophia back up the ladder to the bar.

Sophia checked her revolver was fully loaded and put a torch in her pocket. Looking back at Ratty as she opened the front door, she said, "tell my dad not to worry."

"But Sophia…"

Sophia cut him off before he could finish his sentence. "Not now, Ratty, I have to go."

Sophia and Ratty were close friends, but lately, he had begun to show feelings towards her and she wasn't sure she felt the same. This was the last thing she needed right now. Closing the door behind her, she headed towards the prison.

♭

Sophia made her way through the network of crumbling buildings and back alleys. Avoiding the main streets would mean an extra half an hour on foot for her to get to the prison, where she would pick up Adria. The route would be dangerous. The prison was adjacent to the main entrance leading into the lab sector and was heavily guarded by Klóns. The walls were well-fortified, with watchtowers manned with heavy machine guns overlooking the main gate.

But on the plus side, the gates would be busy with people now the Great Migration had started. Fine cuts of meat and Faze—bounties from Vinayaki herds—were being sold, before being transported to Iris. Traders would be coming from near and far, and she hoped to blend in with the comings and goings unnoticed.

♭

Luca had disconnected the live feed of the prison's cameras after calling Sophia with the news that he had found her. Adria held his hand as they fled down the prison's landings. Time was not on his side, but Luca knew the prison inside and out.

He had been taken from his parents when he was only eight years old after showing promise working in the vast underground farms, which grew fruit and vegetables under ultraviolet lights. He'd been picked out for being a hard worker, but more importantly, compliant. At age of fourteen, he began his training at the prison. Luca had gone along with the System, pretending to be loyal. But one day he planned to avenge his parents who had been forced into the Faze program. They had subsequently died from their addiction.

The prison was quiet as the inmates were all out on work parties; the timing was perfect. They made their way rapidly down the landing's metal stairs. Luca had left the corridor gates open so they could make their escape quicker. Leading Adria by the hand, he could feel the clamminess in her palm.

"Slow down, please," Adria cried breathlessly. Her head was still hazy, her body screamed out in pain.

The couple turned a corridor and standing in front of them were two double doors. Luca turned to her.

"I have to put these on you, just for a minute," he said while removing handcuffs from his belt.

Adria pulled away, frightened.

"Please, we have to pass through the kitchen, and we need to make out I am taking you to work duties," Luca pleaded with her.

Reluctantly, Adria held out her hands allowing Luca to lock the cuffs around her pale wrists.

"Walk in front of me, and keep your eyes to the floor," Luca opened the doors for Adria to walk through.

The smell was horrendous. The kitchen was stifling and inmates and addicts were busy boiling up Vinayaki broth from the left-over bones and offal to make the prisoners' gruel. The Klón guards watching over the kitchen crew stared at Adria as they passed. She kept her head down and occasionally Luca would push her in the back, forcing her to go in the right direction.

"Move it, bitch," Luca shouted at her, putting on a pretense.

Adria was scared. Could she really trust this man? Where was she being taken to? But she knew anything was better than being a bedspread for the three sisters. Luca pushed her out of a door to the rear of the kitchen, which opened into a small courtyard.

"Quickly." He hurried her across the slabbed floor. Adria wiped her eyes, watering from the heat and smell in the kitchen.

Glancing up at a window, high in the prison wall, she thought she could make out a figure of a man. He was looking down at them, and her heart rate soared. Couldn't be, could it?

They ran through another door into a long corridor, and turned right. Finally, they came up to a large refrigerator door. Luca pulled the handle. The smell in the kitchen was nothing compared to this; carts full of rotting Vinayaki were crawling with flies. Adria covered her nose. Luca pushed her in and followed, slamming the door shut behind them. It was totally black. Their heavy breathing was the only sound.

$

The Hog opened the door and in front of him stood the sturdy frame of Vasiliy.

"Afternoon, please, come in," The Hog grovelled.

Vasiliy walked in, sure of himself. His large frame dwarfed the small, fat prison governor.

"Take a seat, please," The Hog held out his stumpy hand.

"You have something that belongs to my brother and me." Vasiliy looked at the sticky pink digits with disgust, ignoring it as he sat down.

The Hog shuffled behind his desk and, feeling underneath the wooden top, he checked his shotgun was in reach if things should get out of hand. "Yes, so you said on the phone earlier, but I must say I find it rather peculiar. Why do you want her back when I believe you paid for her removal in the first place?'

Vasiliy's face turned sour. "Look, I don't want that bitch. She's been a pain in my side since the day we found her, but Mikhail has a soft spot for her and it was my mistake letting her go."

He reached inside his coat. The Hog watched him, his wet-looking hand reached for the shotgun.

Vasiliy pulled out an envelope and threw it at The Hog. "Here," he said bitterly.

The Hog almost leapt over the desk in order to snatch up the packet. With greedy, stubby fingers he opened the envelope and counted a lot of credit notes.

"Well, this will cover some of the cost," he said stroking the bristles which collected drool on his chin. "May I ask where my officer is?"

Vasiliy grimaced, he knew by now Babyface would be at the bottom of the lake. "That's been done," Vasiliy said aggravated, he knew what was coming next.

"This is a shame," The Hog pondered for a second. "Obviously, I can turn a blind eye to that, but…" The Hog tutted, "this is not going to cover it," he rolled his filthy fingertips on the envelope, throwing it back at Vasiliy.

His face turned red with anger and he rose from his seat. "Look here, you sad, fat perverted pig, do you have any idea who my brother and I are? Do you know the kind of people we know? Do you have any idea what we are capable of?" Vasiliy waved a finger at The Hog with a menacing laugh. "That is all you are getting, bring me the fucking girl now." He flung the envelope back, and it landed on the Hog's lap.

"Of course I know what you and your brother are capable of. I meant no offence." The Hog looked shaken. "A deal is a deal," he continued, "one of my officers is bringing her along right now."

Vasiliy walked around the office. Standing in front of the various screens on the wall, he could see Adria tied to the bed. Something wasn't right, she looked still. Too still.

$

Luca's flashlight lit up the rank refrigerator. Adria was visibly shaking next to him, her face was gaunt and her eyes wide. Afraid. Luca removed the cuffs from her skinny wrists.

"It's okay," he reassured her. "Now listen to me, there is an old cellar door at the back there, under those two carts. No one ever goes down there. Once you get down the ladder, I will have to leave you."

111

Adria looked confused. "Why?" she asked.

"I have to cover our tracks. There are things I need to do but I will point you in the right direction. Someone will be waiting for you on the other side of the wall."

"Who?" Adria was so muddled.

"Her name is Sophia. She will take care of you, but first, you must listen to me. When we reach the bottom, you will head south; eventually you will come to a drain cover, this opens into the gardens. On your left are the polytunnels. Inmates will be working in there so stay low. Directly in front of you will be the wall. At the base is an old sewer pipe covered by a sheet of metal. Crawl through and you will come out near the main gate. Then go directly right. There is an old watchtower. Make your way to the hut below. Sophia will be waiting for you there. Do you understand?"

Adria nodded, not sure what was going to happen to her, but it couldn't get much worse, could it?

Once they had reached the bottom of the ladder, Luca explained to her the way out one more time. She began to walk towards the drain cover slowly. Nervous, she looked back at Luca who lit the path with his torch.

"Go on, keep your head down. We will meet again," he smiled reassuringly at her. The drain cover was directly above her head, she could reach it easily. She listened, then pushed the grate up. Clambering out quickly, she lay on her belly and looked about for signs of life. The polytunnel to her right was illuminated by the blue ultraviolet lights inside. She began to crawl towards the sheet metal, which covered the sewer pipe which led to her freedom.

"Help me," she heard a girl screaming desperately from the direction of the polytunnels.

⚗

"When was the last time you noticed anyone move on these screens?" asked Vasiliy.

"Eh?" The Hog turned on his chair, puzzled by the question.

"I've been looking at her for five minutes," he pointed at Adria tied to the bed, "she hasn't stirred once."

The Hog waddled over to the screens, staring at them for a moment. He blinked. "I don't understand," wobbling back to his desk he punched some buttons on a keyboard, looking at the screen in front of him. His jaw dropped. "The live feed is down." He turned to Vasiliy, who was now staring out of the window, watching Adria and Luca run across the courtyard.

"Done a deal with someone else, have you?" Vasiliy screamed at The Hog.

"I don't know what you mean," The Hog suddenly felt threatened and reached under the desk. His trotter-like hands fumbled for the shotgun. Something cold and sharp jabbed the back of his neck and his hands froze.

"Sneaking her out the backdoor? Do you think I'm stupid?" he spat angrily.

The Hog was about to protest, but no words came out. He reached for his throat where blood was oozing from a jagged cut. Vasiliy had slid the knife across the fatty neckline, a short bloodcurdling squeal followed as a jet of crimson decorated the ceiling. Pushing the governor's head down onto the desk, he repeatedly brought the knife down on his skull. Vasiliy looked crazed, as his own face was splattered in the prison governor's blood. When his arm tired, all that remained was a congealing puddle of skull fragments and mashed brain.

Calmly, he wiped the blade clean.

He walked out of the office, looking back at the headless Hog as the body twitched one last time. Closing the door behind him, Vasiliy sped in the direction he had seen Adria making her escape.

Vasiliy ran across the courtyard, through the door he had seen Adria being led by Luca. He looked right, down the long, dull corridor. He scanned the floor, looking for a sign or a clue as to which direction they went.

"Why is my brother so obsessed with this bitch?" he said to himself.

He heard a clunk and he darted back into the courtyard, seeing a door open in the corridor. His eyes darted around and he threw himself behind a pile of garbage bags which had been piled up outside the kitchen door. Peering over the top, he watched Luca make his way back across the courtyard alone before he disappeared back into the kitchen. Satisfied he had gone, Vasiliy sprinted across the courtyard and through the door. Slowing he made his way up the corridor to the walk-in fridge from which Luca had just emerged. Opening the door, he stepped back, wafting the air with his hands. The vile odour made his nasal hair stand to attention. He left the door open as he entered. He used his phone as a torch, lighting up the hanging carcasses of the Vinayaki. 'Where had she gone?' He walked to the end of the fridge and noticed that Luca had not pushed the carts back over the trap door. Vasiliy smiled. He climbed down into the tunnel below and could make out a faint light to his right. Small footprints freshly trodden into the wet mud underfoot showed him the way.

☥

Adria could hear the commotion caused by the traders, who queued up at the gate, on the other side of the wall. She lay on a pile of rubble mixed with waste and junk. There was very little light hid amongst the trash. The sheet of metal covering the hole in the wall was only a few feet away. Her chest rose up and down rapidly and her adrenaline levels made her heart beat in her head. She had ignored the scream for help with her mind focused on her crawl towards freedom.

Again, she heard a desperate plea for help, and she turned her head. Lucia followed by her two sisters dragged a young girl across the ground by her hair into a polytunnel. Adria watched, her anger rising.

The girl's clothes were already torn and hanging, exposing her body. Adria's face changed from resolved and determined to anger and disgust. Before she even knew what she was doing her blood began to boil, she could feel her heart pumping, and her muscles tensed in her arms. The noise from outside the jail seemed to fall silent. The world seemed to stop, everything turned white apart from the polytunnel, where only a black outline remained. Before she was even aware of it herself, her fists clenched white, her pale face red with rage. Adria marched with purpose towards the scream for help.

CHAPTER THIRTEEN

Bliksem, Stór and Techno stepped back from the two-way mirror. The Faze addict grew agitated. He attempted to open the locked door, rattling the handle. Small vents in the isolated cubicle began to emit a green gas. The addict started to panic, screaming frantically he scratched and thumped the door he had come through only moments ago. His cries of anguish fell on deaf ears. Anxiously he moved towards the two-way mirror and began clawing at the glass, raining blows with his fists, the skin on his knuckles tore, smearing blood down the mirror. The addict vanished into the thick, sinister mist.

Re-emerging through the haze, his face had turned red. He tore at his own skin, pulling the flesh from his cheeks as he lurched forward until his face was pressed up against the glass. As he slid down, he left a trail of gore. The three men craned their necks closer to the glass and watched in amazement as the man began to convulse and twitch, spitting blood, screaming in pain and wriggling like an eel out of water.

There was a low humming noise as the green haze was sucked back out of the room leaving the man's body laying still and cold. The door opened and an angrily protesting woman was pushed into the room by a large Klón. The door slammed shut behind her. She turned nervously and her eyes caught sight of the bloodied mess on the floor. Screaming in horror, she ran over to his side, shaking the addict hysterically.

"What have they done to you?" she sobbed.

Suddenly the man's body began to pulsate in front of her eyes, and she stood back in dismay as she watched the body form a new dark purple skin. Bodily fluids leaked from every orifice and the addict's eyes popped from their sockets and exploded. The creamy white sclera hit the glass making Techno jump.

"Fuck me, that was gross," he laughed, clapping his scabby hands together with emphatic enthusiasm.

The pulsating limbs twisted and turned into grotesque, odd angles. Bones snapped, skin turned a dirtier purple, a road map of veins pulsated and bulged.

"Impressive," a rare, dry smile appeared on Bliksem's face.

Techno cackled with joy, bouncing excitedly inside his box on the back of the Klón. Stór's face remained gormlessly void of any excitement.

The woman backed herself into a corner, crying and shaking with fear. Unexpectedly the man began to pull himself up to the mirror, sniffing the air. The hollow eye sockets seemed to acknowledge the three figures behind the mirror.

"My god," Bliksem said, mouth ajar.

The purple beast had grown twice its original size, and the withered addict was now solid muscle. He sniffed the glass and sensed their presence. His nose twitched, and stretching

117

his neck, he spun around, facing the petrified woman. Techno noticed a yellow puddle had formed by her feet, making him laugh so hard he spat saliva over the glass. Bliksem moved a few inches away from the engineer, disgusted.

The hollow sockets were directed towards the woman. She slid into a corner, curled up on the floor, and hid her face from the hideous sight. The beast's jaw opened, teeth snapping together as he launched forward with shocking speed, surprising the onlookers. Flesh and blood splurged up the white walls. The purple monster ripped open the woman's belly, stuffing his head inside, gorging on the guts and entrails of the now lifeless woman. The hollow-eyed man bit and chomped, tearing at the body, piercing through the sinews and muscles which held the limbs in place, ripping the woman's right arm from the socket.

He stood in a pool of blood and guts, holding the severed woman's arm as his attention turned to the two-way mirror. The mutated addict gnawed at the soggy end, gawping blankly through the mirror. Blood ran down his face. Suddenly he dropped the limb, rushing towards the mirror, teeth snapping. Bliksem stared into the deep, dark, hollow sockets.

$

Alan gasped for breath. He was sat amongst the rubble of a broken doorway. His new best friend Blue rested his head on his lap.

Ruffling his fur Alan spoke, "we better get going boy." With a groan, he pushed himself up off the floor.

Looking out from the doorway, he could make out the flames of his van which he had left burning behind him. Alan had waited over an hour here, making sure he wasn't being followed. He was about to set off again when his phone vibrated.

"Hello," Marica said, sounding vexed. "We've just had a run-in with the Klóns. The operation has been compromised, what should we do?"

Alan paused a second. Speaking calmly, he said, "go to the cargo, make sure it is safe, then meet me back at the Goose by midnight."

Marica confirmed that she understood before hanging up.

Alan stood staring into the darkness. He removed his glass eye, pulled a handkerchief from his pocket and polished the glass, a pained look crossed his face.

₿

Bliksem was very pleased. The demonstration of the chemical which made the dead rise again would be most useful.

He congratulated his chemist and returned to the comms room. People were still coming and going from The Golden Goose on the screen in front of him. Stór and the engineer had joined him. Sitting in his chair, he removed the blood-stained machete from the sheath which hung from his waist, playing with its tip, tapping it gently with the end of his thumb.

"Well then, let's see if these Moles of yours work, shall we?" Bliksem stared at the engineer, who was foaming at the mouth, giddy with excitement.

"They will work," he dribbled.

Bliksem entered some digits on a keyboard and the main screen which was projecting The Golden Goose, switched to a bird's eye view of the ghettos. A drone moved towards the Faze addicts, leaving the main gate and the camera on-board focused on a cluster of around five hundred of them, all staggering in the darkness returning to their hovels.

$

The Faze addicts' day was over. Moving in a herd they bundled out from the main gate of the lab sector, shuffling their feet in their dirty rags. They dispersed into the ghetto, hugging their day's pay close to their bodies. The small bag of Faze which would soon find a way into their bloodstreams, would keep them alive—for tonight. The bell would sound early the next morning and the addicts would crawl from their squalor, near to death, their bodies screaming out for their morning hit.

Two men sat huddled in a shop front doorway with a small dog. One held a flame under a spoon to melt the hard, brown chemical, Faze. Once the addict was happy with his work, he picked up a syringe off the floor. Dipping the needle into the murky brown liquid he pulled back the plunger, sucking in the filthy medicine. The addict's arms were bruised, veins ruined with the track marks from dirty needles. He undid the fly on his trousers, releasing his cock. He gripped it, throttling the shaft tight until the veins became apparent. He jabbed a vein with the syringe, filling his blood system with Faze. Almost immediately, he passed out on the floor. His friend repeated the process but injected into a vein in his neck instead.

The two addicts were both staring, unseeing, into space after cooking up their evening dosage. The bitch curled up at the addicts' feet twitched her paws, her eyelids flickered as she dreamed of a better life. The air was damp, bringing a chill to those with no hope. The two addicts lay under a torn blanket, zoned out from the world, their clothes ripped and bloodied from a day's work hacking up Vinayaki.

The bitch stirred, looking around, her ears pricked up. A sound in the distance had woken her. The humming noise grew louder making the dog stand up, fur on end. She began a low growl, sniffing at the air. The dog walked out onto the crumbling potholed tarmac, looking westward down the street and watched as distant headlights appeared on the horizon. The canine began barking and howling, as the sound of roaring grew louder with the nearing lights.

One of the men in the doorway stirred. He threw a stone at the dog shouting, "shut the fuck up, mutt."

She yelped as the stone hit her hind leg, but unperturbed, she continued to bark with even more intensity. Other inhabitants of the ghetto began to stir, looking out from behind broken windows or peering out of the dark places in the street. Both men sat up, shaking their heads attempting to clear the cobwebs of Faze, which cocooned their brains. They rose to their feet, staggering over to where their mutt bayed and yapped.

The silhouette of two huge lorries pulling trailers headed straight towards them, getting closer and closer as more people came out onto the streets. It was a rare spectacle to see moving vehicles in this part of Aris.

A bewildered population emerged from their dwellings

to witness the commotion. The two lorries were rolling at high speed, crashing and ploughing over everything in their path. The headlights blinded the two addicts, but they jumped out of the way just in time. Their canine friend was not as fortunate. She gave out one last yelp as the wheels went over her. Crushing the poor animal into the road, leaving nothing but a dirty smudge and shattered bones behind. The lorries continued for another five hundred yards, then pulled up next to each other. The engines fell silent and the headlights dimmed.

A bewildered crowd had now gathered in the street, keeping a safe distance from the rear of the vehicles. The two addicts sat by the bloody pool, which only minutes ago was their pet, and sobbed.

Then the earth began to shake and tremble, people began to scream and scattered into their dark hiding places. The addicts' remained with the matted fur and bone bloodstain, watching in horror as the tarmac in front of them cracked and began to rise. They shook their heads to wake themselves from the nightmare unfolding before them.

A deafening, roaring noise echoed from all directions. The tarmac on the street started to lift in random sections. The addicts', looked on, open-mouthed, as the pointed end of a giant corkscrew pierced through the tarmac, boring out from the ground below.

The Mole wheeled out on rotating tracks. The spinning drill came to a stop and the spine of the Mole split open like a Venus flytrap. Two mechanical arms came out of the rear of the vehicles holding six capsules. The two men looked about, as more of these Moles emerged from beneath the earth. Some people still stood about, shocked, whilst others fled in fear.

The Moles suddenly launched the capsules. Some rolled into the groups of shocked addicts, some flew high into the air.

The two addicts stood up, watching as a missile fell back to the earth, crashing through a tiled roof. Screams of horror came from inside the building. Another capsule landed next to them. They remained frozen, terrified, as they watched curiously as the capsule opened at both ends.

A green veil of mist arose from the projectile. Coughing, they collapsed, their bodies jerking and twisting. The collar bones on one tore through his flesh. The clear white bone jutted out like small ivory tusks which snagged one of his ears, tearing it from his head. In the street and nearby homes, howls and screams of terror filled the air. They ended quickly, leaving an eerie silence hanging over the squats. A thick green haze engulfed the scene.

$

"Someone was following us, I'm sure of it. A man in a hood, so I couldn't see his face," Hanisi gave his sister a concerned look.

Marica had just spoken to Alan on the phone. The whole operation was at risk. Gravely, she looked back at her brother.

"Well, we've lost him now, whoever he was. We need to be more careful," replied Marica. "Alan wants us to check the cargo hasn't been discovered." She considered this for a moment.

"Then we better move now," Hanisi put a reassuring hand on her shoulder. "The cargo will be safe, sis."

"We're to meet Alan back at the Goose by midnight. If we're not there, he will assume the operation has failed," Marica said.

"Better get our arse in gear then," said Hanisi.

He crawled out from under the old, abandoned car where they had been hiding since they made their way down from the rooftops. Hanisi held his hand out for his sister who dragged herself out from under the wreck. A chill spread over the decaying streets of Aris as they darted through the deserted streets, zigzagging in and out of hollow buildings. They jumped and leapt out of window frames and doorways with stealth. They didn't have much time to spare. The cargo was on the other side of the city. If the cargo had been discovered, then there would be no point going back to the Goose. Hanisi's priority then would be to his sister. Her safety would come first.

This part of Aris was basically deserted. The occasional hovel housed Oddities living in hiding. The offspring of addicted parents. Half-human mutations which were shunned, hunted and persecuted by the System. The two siblings came to a stop.

They had reached an old bridge, where ancient towers lay bent and grotesquely twisted at each end, drooping like dying flowers. Huge holes littered the bridge, which spanned over an ancient dried-out riverbed. Put one foot wrong and they would fall to their deaths.

The twins looked up and down the dried-out river. It looked safe enough so they ran over the bridge, dancing over the cracks and wreckage. They reached the other side, pausing for a brief second to get their breath back before speeding off again.

Great houses and buildings which once stood on this side of the river had mostly all crumbled to the ground. They headed further east where the piles of rubble which they had to manoeuvre through became less frequent. Eventually they reached an area of flat concrete, that was once a vast car park. Beyond which was a stadium that was way past repair. Giant blocks of concrete dotted the landscape and the twins hid behind one.

"It looks quiet," Marica looked at her brother.

"I'll go first," Hanisi replied. "Wait for my whistle and keep your eyes open."

Before Hanisi could turn and run, Marica grabbed his hand. "Please be careful," she pleaded. "You're all I have."

Hanisi kissed her on the forehead.

"I'll be fine. See you inside shortly. Wait for my whistle. If you hear nothing and I am not back in twenty minutes, you must leave Aris."

Marica looked at him puzzled. She couldn't leave Aris without her friends; Sophia was like a little sister to her. But before she could argue, her brother disappeared into the gloom.

₷

Hanisi tiptoed through the skeleton of the stadium. Rumours around Aris had spread over the years that the grounds here were haunted. Not even the Klóns ventured out to this part of Aris, but for Hanisi the stadium was home. He had never seen any ghosts. This had been where he lived as a child in relative safety, which was the reason the cargo had been kept out here.

He picked his way through the old concourse where nature was gradually taking back the landscape. Mountains of moss grew in huge mounds as tall as a man, dotting the area where once a previous civilisation had watched tournaments. Strange fluorescent and ultraviolet plants littered the floor and huge mushrooms and other fungi spawned from damp rocks.

Hanisi looked upward to the cavern roof, as a drip fell on his forehead. The rains had come at last. He smiled. Above ground the monsoon rains filtered down through the layers of sand and rock, dripping steadily down on Aris.

Navigating through biting plants, Hanisi cursed at them when they stung and spiked him. Eventually he waded out from the psychedelic fauna into the centre of the arena. He waited for a moment, attempting to listen over the water now dancing a calypso on the rocks and plants. Satisfied that he was alone, he moved next to one of the giant moss mounds, pushing his weight against the soggy lump. The moss slid across the floor, revealing a hatch buried in the soil. He knelt, placing an ear against the round metal door and strained to hear anything which would cause alarm.

Hanisi removed a key from a chain which hung on a piece of string from about his neck and unlocked the hatch door. He heaved it open. His eyes struggled to adjust to the darkness. At first, he couldn't see anything and his heart rate quickened. Slowly his hand moved towards the dagger which was attached to his belt.

Suddenly a pair of eyes appeared below him. Like stars waking in the night sky, dozens of shining, tiny eyes looked up at him. The cargo; The children of Aris...

They were safe.

CHAPTER FOURTEEN

"What's your name?" asked Mikhail. He helped the small child out from her hiding place within the rubbish heap.

"Adria," she said softly.

He lifted her onto his shoulders, "Where are your parents?" he asked.

"Par...ents?" she didn't know many words. Her name, "food", and "sorry" were about all she knew.

Mikhail looked at his brother and smiled as they walked back towards the bar. Vasiliy eyed her up—she had thought with curiosity at the time—but now she realised he was jealous. He had always despised her. How his moods would change. In the presence of Mikhail, he would be sweet and charming, but whenever they were alone even from a young age, she always felt unsafe.

'He raped me because he was jealous of the way Mikhail loved me? But if Mikhail loved me, why would he want to sell me? Had she got this all wrong?'

Adria shook her head.

☥

The vision faded, and Adria walked forward. Her plain blouse and her long blonde locks splayed behind her and made her look ghostly. Her eyes had hardened, darkened. Her lips formed a tight, straight line, and her fists were clenched white as she approached the polytunnel.

The screams for help had died down to a soft whimper. Adria only felt hate and anger. The physical pain from being raped had numbed, even the craving for Cane had evaporated. The world she was in now was black and white.

She glided closer towards the polytunnel like a thin apparition, her pale skin adding to her ghoul-like appearance. Her eyes were wide open now, dark and soulless. She stared at the three large silhouettes within the plastic sheeted shed. Reaching a small gravel path, her bare feet moved silently upon it. Her light frame continued to move without effort. The hard stones underfoot had no effect on her, she was totally unaware of sound, smell and touch. All her senses and emotions were void apart from one... anger.

Just in front of the entrance to the polytunnel, another small shed sat to the right, and the wooden door was ajar. Adria's eyes were drawn towards the opening. Her thin, pale hand pulled the door open. On the walls hung an array of gardening tools: a spade, a fork, a rusted rake, and scythes. Adria tilted her head to one side as if examining the objects. She licked her dry lips, her eyelids clamped shut and a burst of strength rushed through her body. Veins pulsated in her arms and neck making her body judder and tremble.

$

The three sisters surrounded the young girl who lay muddied and bruised on the polytunnel floor. Looking up with innocent eyes she attempted to reattach her ripped blouse. "Please, don't hurt me," she sobbed.

The blue ultraviolet lights which lit up the tunnel made everything look one dimensional and made the three sisters even more grotesque as they drooled over her.

"I am going first this time," snarled Amalia.

Josefina pushed her sister. "It's my turn," she spat back.

Lucia watched her two sisters fighting with dry amusement. "You can both take her at the same time. I will watch," she stood back with a broad smile revealing her hideous, broken teeth.

The petrified young girl laying on the floor looked up frightened and bewildered at the sisters' fighting over her. Josefina and Amalia silently agreed to share the girl's flesh and turned their attention back to her, their huge shadows creeping over her. The young girl tried to crawl away, but Amalia clamped her filth-ridden hairy hand on her shoulder and spun her over onto her back.

"Please..."

Josefina slapped the girl hard around the face, almost knocking her out. Pointless to resist, the girl whimpered as the two sisters began to paw at her clothing with their hairy fingers. Lucia watched on grinning, twiddling with the matted hair which protruded from a mole on her upper lip.

"Come on, girls, be quick," she growled, "I still want to have a go."

"Hold her wrists," Amalia snapped at her sister.

Josefina was staring blankly in front of her.

"What are you gawping at?"

Amalia followed her gaze, and her mouth dropped open. Lucia had already seen the figure at the end of the tunnel and stepped over her sisters snarling. The young girl on the floor took the opportunity as Amalia and Josefina rose to their feet and ran into a corner and huddled up crying.

The three sisters stood shoulder to shoulder staring at the entrance to the polytunnel, where the pale figure of Adria stood. This wasn't the same scared little girl they had raped the day before, far from it. She was paler, with a demented look on her face which seemed to bore into their souls. Lucia noticed the shimmer of metal in Adria's hands; two scythes held in a tight grip down by her sides.

"Come to help us with a spot of gardening, sweetheart?" growled Lucia.

Adria remained silent. The three sisters looked at each other, puzzled.

"Go take them tools off her," Lucia gestured with a nod to Amalia.

"Why me?" she began to protest, but one look from Lucia made her catch her tongue.

Slowly Amalia made her way up the aisle of tomato plants and herbs which grew under the bright blue lights. Edging closer, she watched Adria nervously.

"Hey, you'll want to put them down, before you get hurt," she said pointing at the scythes.

Adria remained still, silent, statue-like. Amalia thought to herself that if she hit her hard enough, she would smash; she reminded her of a china doll.

131

"Come on, you're not upset about yesterday, are you? That was just a little fun, no harm done, was there?" Amalia was almost within arm's reach when she turned to look at her sisters and shrugged her shoulders at them.

Just then Adria leapt forward. Although Amalia was far taller and stronger, Adria had managed to pull Amalia back towards her, holding a scythe to her neck. Her eyes remained firmly on Lucia who stepped forward, then halted, thinking better of it. Amalia was speechless, she dared not move with the sharp, cold metal on her neck. She was confounded by the strength Adria possessed.

"What do you want?" Lucia bellowed down the aisle.

Adria suddenly screamed a deafening high-pitched howl. "Vengeance."

One of the scythes Adria held, came up between Amalia's legs, as the one in her other hand slit her throat. She let the body fall. Amalia's guts left a crimson smear down Adria's plain white shirt.

Lucia and Josefina both roared with anger and sped towards Adria. Josefina was the fastest and she sprung forward, almost within touching distance as Amalia's body crumbled to the floor. Josefina reached out for Adria's neck. Spinning with great agility to her left, Adria brought down both scythes as she turned. Josefina howled, as her two clawed hands flew into the air. Falling to her knees screaming, jets of blood spurted from the soggy stumps, splattering the plastic ceiling.

Lucia froze only a few feet away. She turned her back and started to run. Adria coolly began to follow. She passed the howling Josefina, who held out her bloody stumps, begging for mercy. Calmly, she slit her throat. Josefina gagged, trying to grip onto Adria's flailing shirt and fell face down in the dirt.

Lucia was in a mad panic, attempting to tear a hole in the polytunnel with her sharp nails. Adria was calmly striding towards her down the aisle, barely any white showed on her blouse now. It was completely drenched with blood and clung to her body. Lucia's eyes flicked from side to side, desperately searching for anything she could use to protect herself. From the corner of her eye, she spotted a small handle sticking out from a plant pot. Quickly, she moved and pulled the handle from the soil, revealing the sharp prongs of a hand fork. Better than nothing, Lucia puffed up her colossal frame and snarled at Adria.

"You're going to pay for my sisters, you fucking slag."

Lucia launched her hefty weight towards Adria, who attempted to sidestep out of the way. Adria caught her foot on a bucket which was laying on the floor and it threw her off balance. Lucia swung at her and the sharp fork connected with Adria's right shoulder. The pain woke Adria from her trance and she dropped the scythes. The polytunnel began to spin. Seeing her chance, Lucia swung an almighty fist into the side of Adria's head, sending her crashing over into the tomato plants.

Adria opened her eyes.

The smell of fresh tomatoes hit her nose, then the throbbing pain in her shoulder. She heard snarling and looked up just as Lucia reached down and clutched at her throat, squeezing tightly and lifting her off the floor. Her face began to turn purple. She coughed and her feet kicked out, but her body was finally giving up.

Lucia's hands squeezed tighter and tighter. Then suddenly the grip loosened before completely letting go. Adria fell to the floor, oxygen filled her lungs and she coughed blood. Lucia's body lay flat, face down. Protruding from her lower back were the two scythes. Standing next to her, was the dark young girl who Adria had saved only moments ago. Through their tears they smiled at each other.

$

Sophia crouched down in the abandoned hut at the foot of the old watchtower. She nervously watched the entrance to the old sewer tunnel through a crack in the wall. She was expecting Adria to appear at any moment.

Sophia had jumped onto the rear of a trading truck just before reaching the gate. When she had rolled off, she made her way up the small rise—mainly on all fours—and into the hut. The high walls of the prison towered above her. Cold stone slabs were stacked on top of each other twenty feet tall, and razor wire was laid menacingly along the top. Pieces of ripped fabric hung from the sharp barbs, stained with blood which trailed down the wall. They gave her goose bumps.

"Some poor bastard didn't make it out."

Sophia had been here over an hour and was beginning to worry. Once again, she checked her gun was loaded. Suddenly a face emerged from the sewer pipe. A young girl. Her heart raced with excitement for a moment, but something wasn't right. The girl she was looking at was far smaller than Luca had described. Her hair was short and dark, not long and blonde. Her skin was coffee brown. The girl suddenly ducked back down into the sewer. Sophia heard the deep voices of approaching Klóns and she turned her back on the girl.

"Fuck it," she said under her breath.

Scanning the bare hut, she saw there were no windows to escape through, nowhere to hide, and only one way in and one way out. Two huge shadows came into view by the entrance. Sophia could hear their footfalls just outside the door and her hand tightened on the revolver as the two huge Klóns came crashing in through the doorway.

$

"What is it?" Adria whispered from inside the sewer pipe. The young girl who saved Adria's life moments ago laid in front of her just outside the opening to the tunnel.

"Two Klóns. They've just gone into the hut over there," she pointed in the direction.

Adria was about to respond when she heard a scuffling behind her. The sewer pipe was tight and black. She strained, looking back over her shoulder, but she dismissed the sound. Probably just a rat, she thought. Crawling out, she laid next to the young girl. Two hundred yards to their left was the main gate into the lab sector. A queue of vehicles lined up waiting to gain access. Klón guards and human soldiers were searching the traders' vans and cars. Passes and identification were being checked all under the floodlights which washed the scene from the high walls. Adria turned her attention back to the young girl.

"The Klóns went inside that hut?" she asked the teenager.

She nodded back.

"Okay, we will wait here for a min-"

Before Adria could finish her sentence, a firm hand grabbed the back of her shirt. She turned, her heart skipping several beats. She froze terrified and wide-eyed. 'No! How?' There was no doubt. Vasiliy hit her hard over the head with an axe handle which he had found by the polytunnels.

He had watched the two girls crawl through the tunnel before he made his move. His car was only parked a few yards away on the other side of the road. Vasiliy threw the handle aside, slinging Adria over his shoulder.

The young girl lay still, petrified.

He looked down at her for a moment putting a finger to his lips. "Shhh," Vasiliy walked away.

Adria's body flopped about on his shoulder.

CHAPTER FIFTEEN

Olaf watched Courtauld. He was hopping across the cell floor as his wooden leg was taken from him after the battle in the Baráttan pit. Courtauld removed his trousers and sat on a bucket in the corner of the room.

"Sorry," he said.

"A man's got to do what a man's got to do," Olaf replied. "One of the pleasures of prison life; listening to another man crap. Wow, what have you been eating?"

Courtauld's face reddened. The cell had no windows and only a dim light lit the room. The walls were coated in a thick layer of mould and the floor was cold, hard and damp. The blankets which made a makeshift bed on the floor were of little comfort. Other than the bucket—which Courtauld now occupied—there was nothing else in the room.

The sound of keys jangling and being placed in the lock of the cast-iron cell door made Olaf jump to his feet. The door swung open and a Klón stood back in the doorway, allowing the dwarf to step into the cell.

The Cracker's nose turned up at the smell in the room. He threw Courtauld, who was in the middle of pulling his trousers back up, a dirty look. Olaf knew of The Cracker; an Oddity, a slave-trader from Iris. He looked down on the small man with hatred in his eyes.

He looked Olaf up and down, studying him. Moving around him, he inspected his new prize. His small hands played with the hole where an ear should have been.

"You're even more impressive close up," he said, with a hiss in his voice. "You will go down well in the pits of Iris."

Olaf raised an eyebrow. "Iris?"

"Yes, I've bought you... and your funny little friend over there. Actually, he came for free." The Cracker sneered at Courtauld, "but I will find a use for you."

Courtauld looked hurt by the comment.

"And if I say no?" Olaf puffed up his massive frame.

The Cracker watched the Oddity's biceps pulsate through the thick hair which grew up his arms and down his back.

"You don't have a choice, do you?" replied The Cracker. He pulled on his slick, black hair, tightening his ponytail.

Olaf looked towards the open door. Another Klón had joined the first one. The urge to make a run for it faded. Now was not the time, but maybe this could be the chance. The chance he needed to escape.

The Cracker had him tied up, reeled in thick rope from shoulder to waist, his arms strapped tight by his side. He was pulled along by two of The Cracker's massive bodyguards. Both of which would be a match for Olaf. They mocked him as they dragged him out from his cell.

He was led out of prison and into the courtyard. Behind

him, he heard The Cracker's whip. Courtauld was forced to hop, still without his wooden leg. The Cracker laughed at him, snapping the whip around Courtauld's jumping foot. He had fallen over several times and had felt the harsh sting of the lash on his back. Warm blood leaked from deep gashes which crossed his bare back.

Olaf was burning with rage. He hated bullies. He particularly hated The Cracker, who dealt in the living flesh of his kind, but he remained silent. Patiently waiting for the right time to act.

The Vinayaki which pulled the large cage of slaves lay in the courtyard sleeping. The shackles and reins from the trailer were still attached to his scarred, whiplashed hide. He eyed the giant beast with pity. Flies hovered around his festering stumps where once the great tusks would have adorned his enormous head. The Vinayaki were docile, placid beasts. Olaf was saddened to see the animal in such a state.

As they approached the rear of the trailer, he looked around at the high walls and barred windows surrounding the courtyard. Water fell from the cavern roof, informing him that the monsoons had arrived. His eyes passed through the cage which was filled with desperate women and children sobbing. Some had clearly been handled roughly.

One of the thugs pulling Olaf lifted a hefty set of keys off his belt and climbed up onto the trailer. Behind him, Olaf heard Courtauld fall again, this time he groaned in pain. He looked at his new friend. His back was ruined, skin hung revealing raw flesh. He looked up at Olaf, a mouthful of blood had painted his teeth red—the result of biting his lip when he fell.

"Sorry, am I holding you up, big guy? Didn't realise you

were in a hurry," he laughed bravely.

The Cracker was standing over him, sneering. He lashed the whip with crazed pleasure apparent on his face.

Olaf growled at him. "One day Cracker, someone is going to fucking do-,"

Olaf's voice was silenced as the prison sirens rang out, piercing the yard with a deafening sound.

$
♯
$

Luca ran through the hot stinking kitchen. He had to make sure everything was in place. The time had come.

Years of planning, sneaking about and deceiving the System was over. He had to reconnect the CCTV feed before anyone noticed he had tampered with it.

Walking out of the steamy kitchen, he turned right and made his way along the corridor. Green and yellow mould crept up the walls. The lower level of the prison was always damp and cold, the air rancid. Ascending a set of stairs, sirens suddenly rang out, hurting his ears. Panic gripped him. 'Had Adria been discovered missing? Not now, please,' he begged an invisible deity.

The prison was in chaos, inmates fled back to their cells, and Klón and human guards ran about doing their duties, locking doors and gates. Luca had made his way back to the top level of the prison. He turned a corner into a corridor which led up to The Hog's office. Just to the right of the door was the electric terminal room, which housed the CCTV feed.

Luca was about to step into the room when suddenly The

Hog's office door swung open. He spun on his feet as if to make out he was approaching the office. Standing in the doorway was the Boss-man, Luca's superior officer.

"Sir," Luca snapped to attention.

"The governor is dead," the Boss-man gave him a bewildered look.

"What? How?" Luca tried to look concerned. He wasn't. He was pleased.

"That drug dealing scum, Vasiliy, was seen leaving the office not long ago. Search the jail and find him," he ordered.

Luca saluted him. Turning around, he went back the way he had come. The Boss-man's eyes lingered on Luca's back as he walked away. Fear gripped him at the realisation that Vasiliy may have been on his and Adria's scent. He darted into an empty office and scrambled for his phone in his pocket. He dialled Sophia's number. The phone rang and rang.

He then called One-Eyed Alan.

After speaking with Alan, he had to think for a moment.

Time was against him and it was too late to run back to where he had left Adria. He could not risk failing in his mission. Sophia would have found her. He convinced himself they would both be safe.

He had to make his way back down to the ground level. The constant ringing of the sirens punished his eardrums. He glanced out of the window and saw a commotion in the courtyard. Inmates and guards swarmed about like ants. A Vinayaki bull was thrashing about, spooked by the alarms. Two brutish-looking men tussled with a gorilla-like Oddity, trying to force him up some makeshift steps and into the caged trailer. Meanwhile, a dwarf was cracking his whip at the Vinayaki bull.

But there was something odd and comical about the whole scene. A one-legged man was hopping about, trying to balance himself amidst the madness.

$

Sophia watched the two Klóns burst into the derelict hut. Standing her ground, her hand tightened on the grip of her revolver. The two Klóns halted in their tracks, staring blankly at her. Sophia tilted her head smiling at them. They both looked at her confused, one of them about to speak. When the siren blared out, they both turned and ran out of the hut. She turned her attention back to the hole in the wall, just in time to see the young girl lift herself off the floor and begin running away from the prison.

"Bugger it," she said out loud and gave chase to the dark girl.

"Will you stop?" Sophia cried out at the girl.

She turned around, sobbing. "What do you want?"

Sophia could hardly hear her gentle voice over the sirens. Monsoon rainwater was now lashing down, from the high cavern ceiling. The pair of them were wet through. The young girl was only wearing her prison-issued blouse, and she was shivering with cold.

She repeated herself, "What do you want?"

Sophia approached her slowly, not wanting to scare her. "I am looking for a friend, she was meant to meet me over there," Sophia pointed to the hut, which was now several hundred metres away. "She is a little younger than me, with blonde hair. Her name is Adria?"

"A man took her, a big man. He hurt her and carried her down there."

The teenager pointed to a dark alleyway, which was concealed between two old decrepit buildings. Sophia panicked, running towards the alley, unholstering her gun as she ran. She turned into the small road when she was blinded by a set of headlights that came roaring out from the darkness. Wheels spinning, Vasiliy's sports car came tearing out of the alleyway, almost knocking Sophia over. She just managed to roll out of the path of the vehicle in time.

The car disappeared into the distant gloom.

Sophia hit the road with a fist. "No," she screamed. 'No.'

$
♌
$

The three men stood over Adria. They argued with raised voices, making her cry. A gentle hand had taken hers. Adria looked at the figure next to her. She was a young girl, around five or six years old. Her features were hazy. The girl spoke to her.

"Come on, let's go over here," she began to lead Adria away, when two large hands suddenly grabbed her, lifting Adria into the air. They held her tightly, making her cry even more.

He shouted at the other men. The girl who was holding her hand had run off and hid behind one of the men's legs "What have you done Alander? All our hard work; ten years of my life wasted, and you are not going to take it from me."

The man trembled with rage.

Adria cried out. The man with the young girl at his ankles stepped forward. Suddenly there was an almighty explosion and she was thrown from the man's arms, sliding across the white floor. There was fire everywhere and the heat warmed her small face.

Screaming—she could hear screaming. Someone howled in agony. Looking up she could make out the man who had just dropped her through the smoke.

An iron beam had fallen from the ceiling crushing his legs. The fire was approaching him, his face melting. Out of the smoke, a Klón came crashing into the burning room, grabbing the man's hands and dragged him out from under the beam. He let out an agonising howl as his legs became detached from his torso, leaving a trail of blood. The Klón carried the top half of the man away.

Adria was surrounded by fire. She covered her eyes.

$

Bright light hit her eyelids. Opening them slowly, Adria saw Vasiliy standing over her.

"Come here, bitch." He had bound her wrists and ankles. Lifting her out from the boot, he tossed her over his shoulder again and marched into the villa.

$

Sophia watched the car vanish from view and her heart sank. Holding back tears she looked up. The young girl stood over her with a sad look on her face. Sophia lifted herself off the floor, dusting herself down. She returned her revolver to her holster.

"Do you have anywhere to go? Family?" she asked gently.

"No," the young girl shook her head.

She was undeniably pretty under the grime that covered her coffee-coloured skin.

"How old are you?" Sophia asked, her eyes strayed in the direction Vasiliy had driven off with Adria.

Shyly the young girl said, "thirteen."

"You had better come with me then."

The sirens were still echoing from the prison, irritating Sophia. She held out her hand and the teenager took it.

"Do as I say, the streets are not safe."

"Where are we going?"

"To find Adria," Sophia's face was determined. "Anyway, what's your name?"

"Zarrah," the girl said, "It's Zarrah."

CHAPTER SIXTEEN

Marica had concealed herself behind a crumbling concrete pillar. Stray cats were roaming the old arena and were busy wreaking genocide on the rats and mice. The air was wet with moisture, dampening Marica's soot-black clothes. The wasteland was silent apart from the occasional flutter of bats' wings from above. Illuminance from psychedelic fauna offered a little light in the darkness, and bizarre-looking mushrooms emerged from the ground, blowing out their spores in small clouds of dust before shrinking back into the earth. She was still waiting for Hanisi's signal, indicating the cargo was safe and for her to join him.

She lay on her back staring up at the cavern ceiling, beginning to feel anxious. A drop of water fell onto her face. The rains had come. Marica and her brother had planned to flee Aris several times in the past, but the agonising possibility, the slim hope, that their parents were still alive somewhere in the city forced them to stay. On top of that, it was impossible to leave Aris most of the year, only when the rains came. Outside was far too hot during the day and the nearest habitable city was two hundred miles away. The rough terrain made the journey slow and perilous. People attempting to flee the city in the past had been cooked alive by the hot sun. This time, they had no choice but to leave. Tomorrow the uprising would begin.

Marica had every faith in Alan, his plans had been years in the making. But she couldn't help feeling worried. It was a battle the gangs of Aris could not win. The bottom line: victory over Bliksem was not the priority. The whole thing was a diversion to get the children, old folk, and the Oddities out of the city. The forthcoming battle would inevitably cause loss of life. The loss of her friends.

She was stirred from her thoughts by the sound of a distant engine getting closer. She rose to her knees, peaking over the rubble. Through her infrared glasses she could make out the shape of a small van snaking towards her. Creeping along at a low speed, the headlights were dimmed. The van stopped not far from her and she remained as still as the pillar she hid behind. Two men leapt from the cab. Finding a comfortable position, they began to piss onto a wall. Marica cursed them, they were either traders or a rogue gang of chancers. Their presence here could give them away.

The rear doors of the van violently opened and an obese woman bundled out. Her yellow eyes were like pinpricks submerged in her lard filled cheeks. In one hand she held a small handgun, in the other was a half-eaten chicken drumstick. Taking a massive bite from the poultry bone, she spat out the debris as she shouted at the two men.

"What are you two wankers doing now?"

"We're having a piss, Mum," one of the men said, shouting over his shoulder.

"Could you not hold it in, idiots? We need to get out of the city, we don't have time to hang about."

Marica watched the three individuals with tight lips, concerned by the noise they were making. She cringed, as she heard Hanisi whistling, signalling for her. The three figures by the van stopped bickering and the two men removed revolvers from their hips.

"Mum, what was that?" asked one of the men, his voice had a strange almost purring quality.

"Will you be quiet," she glared at her son, ears open.

Again, Hanisi whistled, louder this time. One of the men pointed towards the arena and the three of them began walking towards the sound. Directly towards Marica.

$

Hanisi was beginning to worry, Marica had not replied to his signal. He removed his bow from his shoulder. Looking down into the bunker, he whispered to the dozens of small eyes which looked up at him hopefully.

"Keep quiet, I'll be back," he closed the lid, pushing the large mound back over the hatch, then disappeared into the foliage and the sharp, stinging thorns.

Hanisi crawled along the concrete floor and climbed up the outer wall of the arena. From here, he had a view all around. Still wearing the infrared glasses, he picked out his sister. She was on her knees, a man and a huge woman standing over her.

The man held a gun to the back of Marica's head as the two strangers argued with each other.

"Oh Mum, please can we keep her, she's beautiful," said her son.

It was hard to believe he had been born of the woman. He was tall and skinny with long, greasy, straggly hair.

"No, we cannot. Stop thinking with your pecker for once, we must get this shipment out of the city. We don't have time for you to start playing fucking lover boy." The fat woman looked down on Marica. "The question is, what is a lovely looking lady like you, doing out here all on your own? Seems very strange if you ask me," she rubbed one of her many chins. "What are you doing out here?"

Marica remained silent. She noticed the woman's face had an odd feline look about it. Her nose was dark compared to her massive rosy cheeks, long whiskery hairs sprung from her upper lip, and sneaky jaundice coloured eyes looked at her curiously. "Let's keep her, please Mum," the son repeated.

Marica was silently praying her brother would come to her aid.

☥

Hanisi rose to his knees, an arrow loaded in his bow. He wouldn't usually doubt that he could take them both down, but this was his sister's life on the line. A bead of sweat rolled down his face meeting his lips. The tall man holding the gun was in his sights. He would bring him down first, then the woman. But before he could steady his aim, the cold barrel of a gun pushed into his temple.

"I would drop that if I was you," said a whiny voice.

The large woman's other son had gone to investigate the whistle, and catching sight of Hanisi climbing the wall, he had followed him. Hanisi dropped his bow, a look of anguish on his face.

"Mum, I've got another one here," he cried out with a shrill. "He looks just like her," he waved his gun towards Marica.

"Bring him down here then. Stop farting about," she yelled back.

"Oh, goody." The man got very excited. "Come on, up you get."

He tapped the gun against Hanisi's head. Rising to his feet, he was pushed towards a flight of stairs which led back down to the ground floor.

$

Marica had given herself up, she didn't want to risk the strangers letting off a gunshot and bringing attention to the area. Hanisi was pushed to the floor next to her. Looking at each other, they both shrugged their shoulders. The two lanky men went about wrapping the twins up in parcel tape from waist to shoulder, their arms trapped inside unable to move. The large woman covered them with a pistol, eyeing them suspiciously.

The twins remained silent as the woman stared at them, examining them. Her two sickly thin sons—their long matted hair hung over their faces—kept whispering something into their mum's ears.

"Okay, in a minute," she scorned them both and they bowed their heads submissively. Looking back at the twins, she spoke, "If you won't talk to us, I know someone you might talk to. I bet Bliksem would like to hear about this, two strangers out here in the wastelands. What are you hiding out here? Guns? Drugs?"

Marica tried not to show any emotion on her face, but every time she heard the name Bliksem her blood boiled. She looked around her not wanting to give anything away. This was when she noticed the stray cats she was watching a few moments ago hunting down rodents. They had begun circling them, purring and crying. The large woman backed away from the twins, sitting down on a large boulder opposite them. She began to undo the buttons on her long coat which hung down to her chubby knees. Her two sons seemed to go into a frenzy, rubbing their bodies against walls and posts. Hanisi looked at his sister, his face said it all. This was weird. The woman opened her large coat and let it fall to the floor. The twins' eyes widened, horrified at what they saw. She revealed six sagging breasts, with thick dark nipples, ginger hair covering her wobbling belly. Her two sons swiftly moved in and began feeding on their mother's teats, purring excitedly.

$

A grinding sound came from under the mound of moss concealing the hidden hatch to the bunker. The moss began to move slowly as if being pushed by something invisible.

The hatch began to rise, the pile of foliage and rubble fell over. Gradually, it fully opened. Dozens of small fingertips appeared over the edge of the entrance, followed by little peering eyes. Suddenly four small figures leapt out from the bunker and were lost in the darkness. One of the figures clasped his hands around his mouth, sounding a bird call.

As the four shadows entered the overgrowth, more children crawled out, leaving the bunker.

℔

"Ouch, idiot, stop biting," shouted the big woman, she clipped one of her sons around the back of his head until he released her teat from his mouth.

"It wasn't me," he protested with an innocent look, then returned to his supper.

The twins were trying not to watch, horrified at the sight of two grown men still feeding from their mother. The huge cat-like woman watched the twins.

"Brother and sister then—twins. Interesting." She paused briefly, slapping the other son around the side of his head. "I have six, you both don't need to fight over one, cut it out."

Her attention turned back to the twins. She was about to speak when she heard a noise, the sound of rubble falling somewhere close. The baying cats which had been drawn to the woman like magnets suddenly began to flee. Her two sons shot up, wiping their mouths clean of their mother's lactating fatty milk. The big woman stood, picked her coat up off the floor and put it on, fastening the buttons.

Marica and Hanisi looked around them. Marica caught sight of a small shadowy figure, creeping up behind the fat feline woman. Five, maybe six, little people. They crept low.

"What is it?" one of the sons whispered.

"Someone or something is out there," said his mother, her eyes darting from side to side, while frantically fastening the final button on her coat.

Unexpectedly, a dozen hands fell over her. She screamed as she fell backwards over the boulder. A bundle of children climbed all over her, punching and kicking.

"Boys help me," she cried from under the bundle of bodies.

Her sons turned to aid her, but just like their mother, dozens of children ran out from every shadow, every hole and dark place, smothering them.

"Mum, help," they yelled as they were dragged to the floor.

⚹

The mother and her two sons lay wrapped from their ankles to their nose in their own parcel tape. Muted moans came from them as they squirmed and wiggled on the floor. The twins had been cut free by a young teenage boy. Hanisi was speaking to him sternly, whilst Marica retrieved their weapons and belongings that the sons had taken from them before their capture.

"What the hell were you thinking, leading them all out here in the open?"

Marica heard her brother raising his voice at the youngster. With all the arrogance of a teenage boy, he answered back in a low voice, with an air of conceited pride.

"Well, you would be dead if I hadn't."

Marica hastily interrupted, knowing her brother too well. He had a short fuse and stubborn pride; this argument would go nowhere.

"Brother please, I'm sure you're grateful, just as I am," she placed a calming hand on his shoulder. Looking at the young man, she spoke to him as an equal. "Connor, what you did was fearless, my brother and I are so grateful for your assistance."

Hanisi was about to speak, but one look from his sister made him stop in an instant. Connor looked pleased with himself and he smiled. He was tall for his age, handsome, but his face was in two halves, with the left half black and the right side white, the skin pigmentation divided by an S shape which wormed all over his body.

"We have been down that hole for weeks now. What's happening?" Connor complained.

Marica spoke, "not for much longer Connor, we are all leaving tomorrow."

Connor smiled at her. Before he could reply, two small girls, filthy and wide-eyed came running up to him, pulling him by his ragged shirt sleeve.

"Quick, you must see this," they shouted in stereo.

"What is it?" Connor looked at them inquisitively.

"Quick, you must come."

They both ran back towards the small van which belonged to the large woman and her sons. The twins and Connor followed.

"Wow," Hanisi whistled, astounded at what he saw.

The vehicle was loaded with ammunition, machine guns, grenades. An arsenal of weapons.

Marica looked to her brother. "We need to get this lot to the Goose, now."

Hanisi nodded. "Connor, hand out the weapons and ammo to those old enough to carry a gun, then take all the children back to the bunker. This bloody time stay down there," he ordered. Connor signalled to another teenager who was nearby, whispering in his ear. The boy nodded and disappeared, shortly he returned with dozens of other young boys and girls. Hanisi and his sister were in the back of the van going through the stash and handing out weapons to the dirt-covered youths. Once everyone was armed, there were still more than fifty machine guns and various other weapons left in the van. The twins looked at the armed motley crew of adolescents nodding their heads approvingly. Connor stood at the front of the gang looking like a natural leader.

"Now get back to the bunker, the lot of you," Marica waved her hand at them.

Pointing at the three figures which still rolled about on the floor. "What shall we do with these three?" Connor asked

Marica looked at her brother with a blank expression.

"Put them in the van. We can't let them go. They'll go straight to Bliksem," Hanisi instructed the youths.

$

The children of Aris returned to the bunker. The feline woman and her sons were loaded onto the back of the van. Hanisi and Marica drove the van to an area of wasteland not far from the arena. They had one last thing to do before going back to The Golden Goose. Three large trucks had been hidden in a dilapidated warehouse, covered over with black tarpaulin which also had been covered in soil and rubble amongst other junk. One-Eyed Alan had brought them here a long time ago. The children would be loaded onto them when the time came.

The vehicles were safe and Hanisi checked their batteries were still working whilst Marica checked the tyre pressures. Everything was in good order. The twins were heading back towards the van when Marica paused in her tracks.

"What's that? Listen," she whispered.

Both strained their ears. In the distance, they could hear a rumbling, crashing noise, followed by desperate screaming and frantic shouting. They took in their surroundings, two large, rusted iron beams which once held up the floors of the warehouse would serve as a viewing-outpost. They ran towards them. Marica removed some binoculars from her rucksack, handing them to Hanisi. They both climbed up the girders with ease, their hands and feet moving up the beam like a rat scurrying up a tree. The metal poles were almost fifty feet tall, but they ascended them with lightning speed.

They looked out over Aris and towards the sound of the chilling screams. Hanisi lifted the binoculars to his eyes, scanning the rooftops and the streets. He paused, focusing in on a green haze which laid over a large part of the metropolis.

"What can you see? What is it?" Marica asked impatiently.

Hanisi remained silent and Marica strained her eyes in the direction Hanisi was looking.

"What is it?" she asked again.

Her brother turned to her. His face was ghostly pale, a fear showed in his eyes which Marica had never seen before. Finally, he spoke.

"We need to find Alan now."

₿

The green haze crept through the streets like ghastly fingers of death. The monsoon rain poured from the cavern ceiling, falling slowly onto the dark streets of Aris. Blood flowed from the dead, washing over cold floors, running down the cracks in the pavement, weaving, twisting, and spinning into the gutters. Flowing towards the bubbling drains blocked with waste, creating a dirty foam of scum. Soggy rats ran about, biting on the hundreds of corpses which littered and lined the streets. Fractured buildings stood like hollowed carcasses of dead beasts.

The thick veil of toxic green gas was released by Bliksem's Chemist, on this already broken and crushed suburb of Aris. Corpses slowly began to twitch and jerk, the sound of bones cracking and snapping like large branches echoed through the streets. The limbs of the poor souls popped back into place, leaving their bodies in grotesque, contorted positions. Rats played with eyeballs, popped from sockets, rolling them around on the floor.

The hollow-eyes of the corpses stirred, rising on new legs of muscle, their skin now a greenish-purple. Hundreds stood in a new foul pose and started to file down the street. Their noses twitched and sniffed at the air as they moved. The rats became easy fodder for the Hollow-Eyes. Drool hung from solid jawbones as they tore into the rodents, forcing the furry animals down their throats. A rat's tail hung from a mouth, wiggling as a Hollow Eye sucked it in. The hunt for flesh had begun and the rank mob flowed from every house, alley and broken doorway. A man-made army of the dead.

If chemical warfare wasn't bad enough, it had just evolved into something truly evil and terrifying. The battalion of death marched hot on the scent of rancid meat. The sound of running engines was their focus of attention.

Like a disorganised band of vile mercenaries, they moved forward as a solid mass. Lights appeared on the rear end of the two lorries, tempting the Hollow-Eyes forward. The back doors swung open by Klóns dressed in protective chemical suits and gasmasks, revealing the source of the smell which now enticed the Hollow-Eyes towards them. Rotting slabs of Vinayaki hung from hooks, fermenting and infested with parasites. The aroma was sweet to the new-born monsters. With astonishing and furious speed, they rampaged up the ramps and into the rear of the two lorries. Faces crazed and grotesque, they crowded around the raw meat, tearing the flesh from bone.

The vehicle's doors closed behind them, trapping the five hundred Hollow-Eyes inside. Slowly the trucks moved off, leaving behind nothing but half-eaten rats on the road.

CHAPTER SEVENTEEN

Adria was surrounded by flames. She had watched the Klón escape through the fire, carrying the man whose legs were left under the iron beam.

"Adria," a small voice screamed out from the other side of the fire.

With squinted eyes, she could see the outline of the older girl through the flames. The smoke cleared for a brief second and Adria could also see the other two men who had been arguing with the legless man before the explosion. One was draped over the other man's shoulder. The man carrying him was holding a hand to his right eye as it wept blood.

A wall crumbled and fell behind her, showing her an exit from the inferno. She began crawling towards it. Again, she heard the older girl frantically calling out her name. A creaking sound warned Adria that the ceiling above was about to cave in. A hot metal pipe spun down dangerously close, almost hitting the older girl in the face. She put her hands up just in time, screaming out in agony as

burning hot metal seared her palms. Suddenly the ceiling above
came crashing down. Dust and rubble filled the lab.

Adria picked her way out of the building. Looking behind her,
she noticed the three figures were gone—buried. She sobbed as she
ran on her tiny legs, leaving behind the burning buildings.

$

Adria woke up crying. Instant fear gripping her, she shot
upright. She was sitting on her bed in the villa, sweat leaking
from every pore. Her hands and feet were no longer bound.
Dread came over her. 'Where was Vasiliy?'

She looked about, uncertain of what to do next. Her body
trembled and ached. 'Was Mikhail here? She hoped so, but
what now? What was to become of her?' She laid back down,
curling up in a ball, shaking nervously as she cried hopelessly
into the pillow. She started to go over the dreams and visions
which invaded her sleep more often. 'Who were the people in
it? What did it mean? Who was the girl?'

Her thoughts were suddenly interrupted as the door to her
bedroom opened. Her heart stopped, terrified it was Vasiliy.
She peered towards the doorway through gaps in her hands.
Standing there silhouetted against the hall light was Mikhail,
Oliver the foul rodent on his shoulder.

"I am so happy to see you," Mikhail said. "It's okay, you're
home now." He moved towards her, sitting next to her on
the bed. Oliver sniffed the air and scurried from shoulder to
shoulder.

Adria looked at Mikhail, tears rolling down her face. She

forced out the words which fell from her lips, "what are you going to do with me?"

Mikhail looked at her, compassion seemed to show on his face. He placed a reassuring hand on her shoulder. She flinched. "What do you mean...do with you? Nothing, you are home. You are safe."

Anger welled up in her stomach and she jumped up from the bed, her legs wobbling as she steadied herself.

"Safe?" she screamed at him. "Your brother raped me, do you know that?"

Frightened by her sudden outburst, Oliver darted into Mikhail's top pocket. Mikhail looked her up and down, trying to look sincere.

"Listen, what Vasiliy did to you was unforgivable. He has been punished, but he is also my brother, what would you have me do?"

Adria was taken aback by the question. She could only stare at Mikhail speechless.

"Come on, you've had a couple of rough days, get some rest and we'll talk later. I have things to sort out."

Adria freaked out. Was he being serious? "A bad couple of days? Don't you dare leave me here alone with Vasiliy, Mikhail, please I beg you." She pressed her palms together, pleading with him.

Mikhail stood up. "He won't hurt you again, believe me. Now I have to go." He began walking towards the door.

"Are you selling me to The Cracker, like the other girls?" she yelled at him.

He turned, watching her for a moment—giving away nothing—then closed the door.

"Mikhail," she howled.

Throwing herself onto the bed, she scrunched the duvet up in her fists. She screamed, punched the bed and head-butted the pillow until her body was exhausted. Then she noticed something on the bed. Mikhail had left a bag of Cane there. She didn't hesitate. It had been forty-eight hours without the drug. Frantically shaking, she began tipping the blue powder onto the back of her hand. So desperate and eager for the drug to take away the pain, she didn't bother to crush up the rocks and chunks to make easy work for her nostrils to snort the drug. She devoured the chemical with a furious appetite. Adria had hoovered all of it up within minutes—her nose bled, but there was no more pain. Her head felt as though it had left her shoulders and was floating away. Her brain was intoxicated in a protective haze, her body was numb. It felt good.

It felt so fucking good.

$

Adria didn't know how much time had passed; could have been hours, or minutes, but the sounds of shouting had made her come out from her Cane cocoon. Gently she slid from her bed, bare feet sunk into the plush carpet underfoot as she tiptoed across the bedroom floor, her body still feeling numb from the drug. Slowly she turned the handle on the door, opening it just a crack and she put her ear out trying to overhear what was happening. The two brothers were shouting, she was sure. But their voices seemed muffled, distant. She realised they were outside, to the rear of the villa. Slowly she edged her way out onto the landing, quietly closing the door behind her. She kept to the wall, creeping around the top of the stairs. The villa was plain with whitewashed walls and no artwork hung from them. There was no clutter, the place was pristine and minimal. The floor was cold marble and Adria wondered for a moment how many times had she polished it on her hands and knees over the years.

Mikhail's bedroom door was open. She made her way to the doorway, keeping her ears wide open. The brothers still squabbled outside. At the far end of his bedroom was a large patio door, which led out onto a balcony. Adria crouched down as she moved out through the doorway and out onto the balcony. The brothers were directly below her, she could clearly hear them arguing. Mikhail was going mental at Vasiliy.

"So, you killed The Hog, but left our fucking money in his pocket, are you thick?"

Vasiliy was silent for a second, then spoke, "I got her back, didn't I?"

"I am amazed you did that without fucking it up," Mikhail said scornfully.

"Is The Cracker coming for her then?" Vasiliy asked.

Mikhail's voice went up another level. "No. You're a dumb fucker. Bliksem wants her, don't ask me why, but he does. I don't want anything to do with that man. He can have her for nothing, this is far bigger than us."

"Shit." Vasiliy sounded confused. "What's so special about her?"

Adria slumped with her back against the patio door. Why would Major Bliksem want her? She shook her head, confused.

"Who am I?" She asked herself as her mind began to wonder.

She brought herself back from her daydreaming and continued to listen. Mikhail, who had now calmed down, was still talking. "There is a case under the stairs with twenty kilos of Cane in it. Bring the gear with Adria to the club in two hours. Get her cleaned up first, and try not to fuck her again. Oh, and don't be late. I am not going to leave Bliksem waiting. I will meet you there, I am going ahead now. The place needs cleaning up."

Vasiliy nodded. He understood. Adria had heard enough. She was creeping back through Mikhail's bedroom when something caught her eye, something which had always been there, but she had never taken much notice of it before.

Hung on the wall, two samurai swords gleamed at her.

Adria's heart sank. Mikhail had been like a father to her, but after hearing the two brothers talking, her heart had broken. Bliksem, the ruler of Aris, now wanted her, but why? Not even the brothers knew. One thing she did know; Bliksem was pure evil, she would rather die than be his slave.

₪

She stood in front of a full-length mirror, steam surrounded her from the hot water coming from the running shower. Still wearing the prison-issue blouse, she pulled it over her head, inspecting her bruised body.

Staring into her reflection, she spoke, "What's the point in living? No one will ever want me now, I am ruined."

She banged her forehead hard against the glass repeatedly.

The thought that Bliksem would now have his way with her made her stomach turn. Her body trembled as she turned away from her reflection, disappearing into the steam. The fresh hot water doused out the scum and fleas which had attached to her body in prison. Her feet were submerged in scummy water. She began washing her body, running her hands through her hair, wincing in pain at the bruises left by Vasiliy and the cut inflicted by Lucia on her shoulder.

The bathroom began taking on a different shape. Adria knew the anger was coming. She tried to control the rage, focus on it. Everything turned black and white, two dimensional. Her fists clenched, knuckles white, as her eyes turned black.

Suddenly a banging came from the door. Then the voice; the voice of Vasiliy. "Adria are you in there?"

This time it wasn't revulsion or fear she felt from hearing his voice. No, it was pure anger, a rising turbulent fury. Slowly she edged out of the shower cubicle, gliding through the steam like an angel emerging from heavenly clouds. She unlocked the door, opening it inwards. The hot moisture escaped the bathroom, leaving her raw naked form standing in front of Vasiliy. She smiled at him, holding out a hand she invited him in. His eyes widened with excitement and he began to unbuckle his trousers, letting them fall to his ankles. He literally tore his shirt off, such was his lustful hunger for her.

Adria grabbed his hand, pulling him towards her.

He staggered in, trousers tangled around his feet. She pressed her naked body up against his. She could feel his hot breath on her neck as he began to grope her body. She pushed the door closed as Vasiliy lashed out his tongue, licking her neck. Taking hold of her breasts, his breathing quickened.

Adria looked over his shoulder. Her body was numb, and so was her heart. Her eyes stared at the wall behind the door.

Two samurai swords gleamed at her.

$

Mikhail was sat on the toilet in the bathroom at the rear of the bar, thinking. 'Why did Bliksem want Adria?' The Cracker had told him the Major was looking for a sixteen-year-old blonde girl. Adria might not be the one he was looking for. Maybe he just liked his women blonde and young. It wasn't for Mikhail to question. What Bliksem wants, Bliksem gets. He did feel sad though, which was confusing him. When they found Adria, it was always their intention to sell her eventually. But truth be told, since the day they had discovered her in the garbage, Mikhail had grown fond of her. He had never really cared for anyone apart from Vasiliy. The sentiment was always lost on him. Of course, there was Oliver, but he was very fond of all animals; they were loyal and trustworthy.

He wasn't going to let it bother him anymore. He had earned enough money over the years, one last big deal today and he could leave Aris with his brother and return to their homes in Iris and live like kings. Mikhail stood up, wiping himself clean as Oliver danced about his feet. The sound of a boat engine pulling into the jetty below alerted him that his brother was here.

"We will be out of this shit hole tomorrow," he said to Oliver.

Twenty minutes later Mikhail was polishing glasses and Oliver was scurrying around the bar looking for crumbs.

Mikhail dug in his pocket. Taking out a small lump of cheese he placed the yellow cube on a small china saucer and laid it on the counter.

"Here, I am going to see what is taking Vasiliy so long."

The rodent nibbled at the small yellow cube.

Mikhail opened the back door which led to the wooden stairs and down to the jetty. The small wooden pier was lit up with oil fed lamps, perched upon tall poles on either side of the gangway. The lake was a torrent of sound whereas usually it was stagnant and still. The rains had come and the torrential downpour bombarded the lake. The noise was deafening, echoing throughout the cavern. Mikhail looked down the pier, his boat was moored to it but there was no Vasiliy or Adria. Something was at the end of the jetty though. A small, black square box. Mikhail went for his gun, but he cursed himself as he remembered he had left the silver revolver in the toilet. He edged closer. The lamp flames flickered in the moist air, shimmering, swaying. One or two went dark, ceasing their dance.

"What the fuck is going on?" he shouted as he realised it was the suitcase containing the Cane. "Vasiliy?"

There was no reply.

He remained still, looking about him. Nothing moved apart from the bats, the lake and the lamps which shimmered. He went for his phone and again cursed himself as he had left it with his gun. Gingerly he carried on until he reached the case. Quickly he picked it up. Glancing into the speedboat, it was clear it was empty. Mikhail's face showed his apprehension as he backed off towards the wooden steps.

Behind the speedboat, a head of blonde hair emerged from the water.

☙

Mikhail placed the suitcase on the bar. Oliver had finished his cheese and was going crazy, frantically sniffing the case, jumping over it and scurrying around on the surface. Mikhail brushed him off to the side. Feeling dejected, the rodent darted down the counter and onto the floor.

Turning the case towards himself, Mikhail flicked open the latches and the lid sprang open. Blood gushed out over the bar, covering his hands, the white cuffs of his smart shirt turning a dark crimson. He stepped back in horror. His face was spasming with shock, as he stared into the dead eyes of his brother. Vasiliy's decapitated head sat in the case, his eyes bulging from their sockets. The final terrifying moment when you realise you were about to die was etched upon his face. Mikhail began to retch and, covering his mouth with his hand, he caught vomit.

"Oh my god. No,' Mikhail screamed out in a furious rage. His bulky frame seemed to double in size as every muscle in his body tensed up.

Madness filled in his eyes. He stared at his blood-covered hands, sobbing. He began pacing back and forth. The Klón doorman—who stood all day and night outside—came in, responding to the screams of anguish. His massive bulk made the room almost shake as he stomped in.

Suddenly the jetty door flung open. Standing there was a demon; Adria was naked and dripping wet, her blonde locks soaked through and hanging down the side of her face. She held a samurai sword in each hand and her black eyes stared into Mikhail's soul.

"Why did you have to kill him?" Mikhail screamed at her. He turned to his Klón. "Kill her," he pointed at Adria.

The huge synthetic man waded towards her, pushing over tables and chairs in his wake. As he reached the bar, Adria had not moved, she just stared at him. The Klón halted in his tracks, confused. He blinked, wiped his eyes, and looked at her again. He then turned to Mikhail puzzled.

"I can't do it, boss."

Mikhail was dumbfounded. "What? Kill her."

"No, I won't." The Klón stood there, staring at Adria in disbelief.

Mikhail suddenly sprang forward. Grabbing a bottle off the bar, he smashed it over the counter and charged towards Adria. But she was too quick. Remarkably quick. She stood to one side and brought down a blade, severing Mikhail's lower left arm. He screamed in agony, lifting the stump to his face. Blood jetted out from the gaping wound, painting the ceiling scarlet. His forearm fell to the floor.

Oliver came out of his hiding place and began gnawing on the protruding white of the elbow bone. Mikhail looked down horrified as his pet ate part of his body. The air left his lungs. Looking down, Adria had thrust the two blades deep into his chest, breaking his ribs. The sharp points exited out of his shoulder blades and struck into the wall behind him. Adria let go of the swords and Mikhail hung in mid-air pinned to the wall.

She looked at him sternly. "This is for all the women you have wronged," slamming her foot down hard on the floor, Mikhail heard something squelch and squeak.

He looked down at Adria's barefoot. Flattened underneath was Oliver, his small eyes hung from their sockets, his guts had blown out of his rear end. Mikhail's head wobbled for a second, then rested on his chest as the last breath left his lips. Adria turned and walked back to the door she had come bursting from, tears rolling down her cheeks.

Turning, she looked at the Klón. "Thank you, you are free now," she said, "you can go."

The Klón stared blankly at her.

"Free?"

CHAPTER EIGHTEEN

The Chemist screamed out with rage, pushing over a table which was covered in petri dishes, filled with Klón embryos. They slid across the white surgical floor. Pacing back and forth, her long thin body moved in circles around the bloodied mess. She was furious. She stamped her foot and her high heel punctured a snotty looking foetus. Her eyes wandered around the vast lab, glaring at row upon row of Klón embryos in various stages of growth, searching for an answer.

"Why won't it work?" she cried, "it makes no sense."

The embryos were hooked up to drips. Needles pierced into the foetuses, feeding them via a tube linked to glass tanks filled with liquid food. The Chemist scraped her heel against a table leg, unsticking the embryo from her shoe. The foetus slipped off onto the floor, lifeless. She looked down at it, turning up her gaunt face in disgust.

Pacing the room again, she watched her scientists working on the Klón production through the glass walls. The growth rate of a Klón was rapid, from embryo to employment within two years. After a year they were almost fully grown. It took another year to train and educate them, brainwash them into obedience. Their IQ was far lower than a human, making them easy to manipulate. Hence, they obeyed the System and would die to protect it. They were slaves just like the Faze addicts.

The Chemist lurched towards her desk, sitting down. Her skinny frame bent as though it might snap in half. In front of her were dozens of papers filled with digits and symbols. Burnt patches and scorched edges had destroyed critical parts of the information.

"What am I missing? Why can't I see it?" She rested her head between her hands.

The papers were headed in bold writing, it read:

Klóns; The Gender Production Program, Female Chromosomal Development.
Professors Alander Saunders and Jon Singleton.

$

"Do you really believe it's him?" Techno looked giddy, his wild eyes bulging from within his goggles. He stared at the photo in Bliksem's hand.

"I believe so, we never found their bodies," he handed the photo to Techno, who lifted the goggles off his eyes, revealing eyelids which had fused to his forehead by fire.

"If he is alive, then they might have all survived," Techno

said, his face lit up excitedly.

"Corporal Adar lost the One-Eye and paid the price for his incompetence," said Bliksem. Techno shuddered, remembering Bliksem sticking the blade through the back of the man's head. "We have a man inside," Bliksem continued. "He has reported dozens of wanted men and women are meeting at The Golden Goose as we speak. The gangs of Aris are planning to revolt."

Techno was beginning to foam at the mouth. Bliksem turned his nose up and stroked his ginger beard.

"Our friend, The Cracker, has informed me he saw a young girl, sixteen or seventeen years old with blonde hair, only two nights ago at Mikhail's club. It might just be a coincidence, but worth checking out."

Techno wiped foaming spittle from his mouth with the back of his hand, smearing the slime down the front of his shirt. "If this One-Eye turns out to be Alander. I want him. He took my fucking legs, I want him to pay," Techno spewed the words out.

"He will be all yours, you have my word, but we need him and the rest of them alive."

Techno shuffled about on the back of his Klón carrier uncomfortably, he was about to speak when the two men were interrupted by a soldier. He informed Bliksem that the Chancellor, ruler of the System, was online, wishing to talk with him.

Bliksem waved Techno and the soldier away and then turned to the monitor in front of him, punching some buttons on the panel awash with flashing lights.

"Father," he spoke into the microphone in a begrudgingly low tone.

His father spoke in a deep voice, "what news from Aris, Major?"

Bliksem reported the shipments of Cane and Faze which were pouring out of the city, as well as Techno's advances in drone technology. He tried to avoid the subject, but he knew this was not what his father wished to discuss.

Cutting him off, his father asked, "The Chemist, has she been successful?"

The Major looked obviously annoyed by the question. "No, they still die in the early stages, but she has made other advances. You will-,"

The Chancellor cut him off again. "I don't care if she has replicated you a million times over. We need female Klóns. We need to start breeding with them—our bloodline will be immortal and live forever. No one will ever extinguish our name, we will rule for eternity. What are her excuses this time?" The Chancellor spoke harshly and with authority.

Bliksem twitched. "She has none, but I have more news. I believe Alander is still alive and in the city."

There was a long silence.

The Chancellor finally spoke. "Are you telling me, that the only man who has the key to the gene program is in Aris?"

He licked his dry lips nervously. "Yes, I am sure of it."

"So, let me get this straight. He has been living under your nose all these years?"

There was a long pause.

"It looks that way," Bliksem mumbled, his right leg shook anxiously under his desk.

"You are a fool. I suggest you find him immediately, then bring him to me, personally!"

"Bring him to you? To Iris?" Bliksem was about to protest.

He hated the journey, it took up to a week to get there.

"Do not argue with me, boy. Find him now. Do not kill him. And do not fail me."

The line went dead.

Bliksem stared at nothing.

He hated his father and his obsession with gaining immortality, but being on the wrong side of him was not an option.

A distant alarm rang out. His mind whirled with anger.

Rising to his feet, he thumped the desk with a fist, shouting at the top of his voice, "Stór!"

$

"Luca," Alan said, answering the call.

"I've found her Alan, she was brought into the prison last night. She should be with Sophia now."

Alan froze, he was speechless for a moment.

"Are you there, Alan?" Luca shouted down the phone.

"Yes, I'm here, are you certain it is her?"

"She is the spitting image. Has to be her. It's Adria."

An alarm sounded in the background.

"I have to go; Alan, I promise I will get her to you safely."

"But, Luca—"

The phone line went dead. Alan looked about in disbelief as a huge smile formed on his face.

$

Alan made a detour after receiving the call. Turning eastwards and away from the direction of The Golden Goose. He had called Jon and informed him of the good news. And once again tried to talk him out of fulfilling his mission, which fell on deaf ears as usual. Then Alan's phone died. That would be the last time they spoke.

Painfully slowly, he crawled and picked his way through the decimated streets and buildings of the underground city. His clothes were stained and made filthy by things he'd rather not know about. His glass eye had become so loose, he had put it away in his long jacket pocket.

Several times, he had ducked into a dark corner or alleyway just in time. Blue had become very useful—growling a warning long before Alan's old ears picked up the sound of nearing drones. Alan decided to attempt and convince more Oddities to join the revolt against Bliksem. So far, leaders from numerous gangs had joined. But the biggest group of them all remained in hiding, and without their numbers the revolt would be a massacre.

Alan now stood in the shadow of an old factory. Before the days of Bliksem the east side of Aris was a vibrant hub of activity. Huge factories and warehouses once churned out fabrics, plastics, metals; all manner of items. Now they were empty, a ghost town, rusted and derelict. The old commercial centre was lifeless, apart from one building which still harboured life.

Hiding, shunned, isolated.

The Tears of Aris was a gang—mainly Oddities—living amongst the wreckage and waste, led by a strange individual. Alan had already tried to convince him to join the cause. He prayed he could persuade the leader this time. It was a stab in the dark, but he had nothing to lose. Alan edged out from the shadows, Blue by his side. Flickering lights from old lamp posts made their movements look disjointed.

They made their way over the deserted street, directly in front of them were two barred metal gates. Blue began growling as they came to a standstill. Alan knelt down beside him, gently petting him.

"It's okay Blue, it's okay," he soothed.

Segments of gravel around them began to rise from the ground; stones and rocks rolled away as six figures arose from the earth. Blue snarled, showing red gums and sharp fangs. Alan whispered into his ear, settling the mutt down again.

"Alander, what brings you here again?" said a shadow.

"I need to see The Crane, urgently."

He stared at the dark outline of the Oddity, but if he was nervous, he didn't show it. The shadow moved forward and Alan removed his torch from a pocket, lighting up the man. It was Tusker, a chunky, short, broad Oddity. His head and face showed no hair, and a big tusk protruded from his bottom lip, which was carried by a square jaw.

"What's changed? We will not join your feeble revolution Alander," Tusker condescended.

Alan's face burned with anger. "Take me to The Crane, I assume he still gives the orders?"

Tusker glared at the One-Eye and his dog. "I asked you a question. What has changed?"

Alan rubbed the sore eye socket, which ached when the glass was removed. Through gritted teeth, he replied, "we have found Adria."

He kept his eyes on Alan, thinking for a moment. "Okay, Alander. But I don't think this will change his mind."

Tusker signalled to one of his men to unlock the gates, then led Alan and Blue through them into a large courtyard. The gates were locked behind them, the five remaining shadows disappeared back into their rubble holes and hid from view.

$

Alan and Blue followed Tusker towards a tall warehouse. A high chimney arose from the centre, disappearing into the cavern ceiling above. Shattered windows scarred the outside walls. On the top two levels, the windows were either battened with plywood or had been painted black where glass survived. Tusker slowed his step. Holding out a hand, he caught a drop of water. He turned to Alan.

"The rains have come."

Alan nodded with a smile as Tusker upped his pace again. They moved around the massive structure until they faced the rear. The muscular arms of the horn-lipped man pushed two giant boulders aside revealing a metal door. They stepped inside, closing the door behind them. They had entered a tiny, wooden, box-like room. A stiff rope hung in the centre and Tusker began to heave on the line, lifting his feet off the floor. Slowly it took his full weight and the room started to move upward. Blue shifted about, whimpering.

Alan was in deep thought. 'How were Hanisi and Marica? Was everything going to plan with Luca? And Sophia, his daughter?' He silently prayed she was with Adria, and they were both safe.

Tusker gave out a grunted sigh as the lift finally came to a standstill. The elevator sat at the end of the large building, a vast open room was in front of them. Bedding covered the floor and Alan could smell food. He was hungry. Blue ran ahead, sniffing out its source as armed guards moved aside allowing them to pass. One of them had a forked tongue which zipped out of her mouth and back in again.

He looked side to side as they moved up the centre of the room. Sick Oddities laid upon the floor with filthy blankets, coughing and spluttering. Others were obviously suffering from malnutrition. He had never seen The Tears of Aris in such a terrible way. The gang of Oddities were resourceful, surviving in a large tribe for many years. They moved from one site to another if the System and Bliksem's men came too close. So far, they had remained undetected. But lately their numbers had swelled; it would only be a matter of time before they were found out.

Alan always marvelled at people's creativity to make the most out of the few things they own. A man with no arms sat on a crudely made rocking chair. It rocked on two halves of a tyre attached to the bottom of a legless seat. Long tubes made from aluminium cans snaked across the floor, welded into the massive chimney which rose in the centre of the room and up into the ceiling. What little food the Oddities had was cooked at the end of these tin can vents. He looked at three women, who were in the process of roasting a rat on a stick, their heads turned towards him as he passed. All three had fused skin growing over their eyes, making them blind. Cheese graters were used as lanterns and hung from a string in mid-air, wax dripping from their centres.

Tusker led Alan around the chimney. Blue had reappeared by Alan's feet, licking his lips.

"What have you been eating?" Alan asked, then decided he didn't want to know.

He estimated there were over five hundred Oddities in the great room, some played games with carved wooden figures, others slept. A few watched through peepholes in the wall and windows, keeping an ever-watchful eye for Klóns and drones. A mother bathed a new-born child in a wheelbarrow.

Finally, they came to a round table entirely made of motherboards and circuits from the electrical goods which were once produced here. The table was surrounded by a dozen chairs all made from old tyres, except one. The Crane, leader of The Tears of Aris, reclined in a chair made from old books and papers. As Alan and Tusker approached, he sat up. The other eleven Oddities sat around the table, either half-asleep or murmuring, turned and looked at Alan and his dog.

"Crane," Alan nodded a smile at the Oddity.

Crane said nothing as he slowly stood. Alan had never stopped being surprised by the man's height. The Crane, as his name suggested, was nine feet tall. He was not broad or skinny, he was lean muscle. His dark hair which had never been cut, coiled around his neck and torso like a snake, and ended abruptly just below his buttocks. He looked at Alan with deep blue eyes.

"Alander, Alan, or One-Eyed Al today? Which do you prefer?"

"It makes no difference to me," Alan replied, "I don't have time for niceties today Crane, I have come to ask you one last time. Will you join us?"

"My people are sick and hungry, we don't wish to play in your silly game of war. I have told you this before, have I not?" The Crane spoke as he walked around the table and came to a halt in front of Alan.

Blue pissed himself at the sheer height of the lanky Oddity, a yellow puddle trailed behind him as he backed off behind Alan's legs.

"Your dog has pissed on my floor," The Crane shook his head and tutted his disapproval. The others around the table chuckled.

"Are you surprised?" Alan replied. "I think I shat myself the first time I saw you."

The surrounding men laughed louder. The Crane stared them down.

"So, One-Eye, what can you tell me that will make me lead my people to certain death in your pop gun revolt? What could it possibly be?" he grinned at Alan.

Alan grinned back wider. "We have found her, we have found Adria."

The Crane stopped smiling.

$

The Chemist looked across the lab floor. Her mind churned repeatedly. She had tried and failed countless times to create a female Klón. She knew Bliksem's patience would run out and she was close to despair.

Then something caught her eye amongst the dead foetuses on the floor. She blinked, unsure if her eyes were deceiving her. Something moved, she was sure of it, just a brief movement. Gradually she eased her spindly form out from behind her desk. Her long, bony legs moved across the floor, avoiding the sickening mess. Standing in the centre of the lab surrounded by the small lifeless forms, she crouched down, brushing away a few of the dead new-borns. Reaching out with elongated fingers she lifted a foetus from the bloody mess. Holding the embryo in her palms, she studied the foetus intently.

Several minutes had passed and the foetus still hadn't moved. Her patience had run out. She lifted the minuscule Klón into the air, about to launch it into the nearest wall when she froze, looking towards her hand. The Chemist felt the pulse of a tiny heartbeat. An under-formed leg twitched. The Chemist began to laugh and cried hysterically as a siren sounded in the distance.

CHAPTER NINETEEN

This Morning

Jon remained still in his wheelchair for several hours after Alan had left him. He had even fallen asleep for a while, until he was woken by Alan's call informing him that Adria had been discovered.

His body was dying, rotting from the inside. He never fully recovered from that fire the day he escaped Bliksem's labs. Alan had carried him out from the rubble to safety. Although that was twelve years ago now, it only seemed like yesterday. Jon could count on two hands the number of times he had left his damp-smelling flat since that day. Alan brought him supplies every month and tried to convince him to leave his hovel and move to The Golden Goose, but Jon always declined. He didn't wish to be any more of a burden than he already was.

Wheezing, Jon forced his hands to push the wheels on his chair, edging towards a full-length mirror propped up at an angle against the wall. Parking in front of it, he looked at himself and didn't like what he saw. Pale, deathly white, heavy bags sagged under his eyes. He had gained a lot of weight and lost all his hair. Laughing to himself, he said out loud, "I look like a fat, rotting egg."

His eyes scoured the room, the mess disgusted him. Empty bottles of alcohol made a small mountain in one corner. Ashtrays overflowed with extinguished roll-ups. The ripped and tattered carpet underfoot was alive with fleas and other bugs. The walls were almost black from damp, fungi grew in one corner; the spores added more misery to Jon's long-suffering lungs. Blood-stained tissues and rags made a horrible heap next to where his chair had been parked by the balcony door overlooking the lonely street below. Jon however, had some peace of mind from the news that Luca had found Adria. It brought him some happiness in his gloomy world, his only regret was that he wouldn't be there at the end.

Reaching into a pocket stitched into the side of his chair, he pulled out an envelope and opened it up. He took out a pinch of dark, dry tobacco and a cigarette paper. Hands shaking uncontrollably he struggled to roll up the dried leaf. Licking the gummed edge, his tongue showed blood which came up from his scarred lungs. He placed the crinkled, bent smoke between his dry lips, lit it and took a long drag, blowing the smoke into the mirror. He watched the smoke slowly disperse until it revealed his rounded face, then he took another drag, repeating the process. After three pulls, his lungs began to scream at him to stop. He didn't. He coughed uncontrollably to the bitter end of the roll-up, then threw the butt onto the rank carpet. Turning his chair he wheeled towards the balcony door.

His hands were filthy from the muck on the carpet which clung to the rubber tyres. He edged the chair out onto the balcony. The wall designed to stop anyone falling to their deaths had crumbled and plunged into the street years ago. If he lost control of his chair, death was inevitable. Jon could hear the distant ring of a siren coming from the direction of the prison and the lab sector. Moist air left his bald scalp wet and he smiled broadly knowing the rains had come, everything was going to plan.

Above him hung a cable tied into a neat noose. Reaching up he pulled the wire down and working the knot, he unfastened four hooked ends. He attached the four hooks to his chair, struggling with the two that hooked behind him. It was a task his lungs didn't approve of, wheezing and coughing until he finally attached them. One remaining cable hung from the pulley. First, he belted himself tight into the chair, then grabbing the wire with both hands he moved to the edge of the balcony. He hated heights and sweat showed in patches on his shirt. Looking down, he couldn't see the pavement. The small lights in his room offered little to the balcony and he knew once he was over the edge, he would be in darkness. There was a torch attached to the arm of his chair, but it would be too dangerous to turn on at this height; drones would easily pick him up and come nosing. The chair hung over the edge.

Closing his eyes, he rolled forward, his heart leaping into his mouth. He held the cable firmly with all the strength his dying body could offer. The chair violently swung out too far and coming back on itself he crashed into the wall, his knee cracked against the hard-concrete tower block, tearing a hole in his trousers and the skin on his knee.

"Fuck."

He moaned in pain, forcing him to open his eyes, hanging on for grim life as he and the wheelchair swung back and forth. After what seemed like hours, the chair finally settled in mid-air. Jon began to lower himself, white bone protruded through bloodstained trousers. He had no feeling in the other leg.

"Why was it the good leg?" he mumbled under his breath.

Looking out into the darkness, he continued moving down the levels of the dirty high rise. Eventually, the wheels touched down on the gravel. He sighed in relief and rapidly unattached the hooks. Jon turned on the flashlight, lighting up the main doors to the tower block. The path was covered in rubble, taking some time for him to manoeuvre his chair into the lobby. He cursed Alan.

"Could have bloody swept up," he smiled, thinking of his old friend, then shook the thought from his mind.

Rolling into the corner, he found the large rucksack which Alan had planted there earlier. Under his chair was a rack where he placed the bag gently down.

Jon looked down at his hands, now covered in small cuts from the grit and broken glass littering the floor which his wheels had picked up. Spitting on them he rubbed them together, removing the particles and grime. Spinning the wheelchair around, he rolled out from the lobby, back onto the street. Looking north towards the main entrance of the city.

He smiled and set off.

$

Jon passed dozens of addicts lying in doorways or moving on the pathways like zombies. A Klón patrol had gone by him and luckily they didn't stop to pick him up. They tended to leave people in wheelchairs alone. They were banned from the Baráttan pits. It was deemed too unsporting. The last time a disabled person in a chair fought in the pits, she had rolled into a den with a snow bear. She survived apparently, sadly the bear lost all his teeth trying to eat the chair.

Jon's hands were now bleeding badly, he had been rolling the wheels for an hour over the broken streets. He was nearing the entrance to Aris. The long road led from the desert plain above, straight through the middle of the city, passing the square where The Golden Goose sat and eventually leading up to the gates of the prison and lab sector.

He could make out a queue of traffic leaving the city, traders with armoured trucks loaded with Faze, weapons, Vinayaki meat, and Cane. The large wall which blocked the entrance towered above and climbed so high it joined the wet cavern ceiling. The gate was heavily guarded by Klóns and Bliksem's soldiers.

Pausing on the road which rose towards the outside world, Jon looked back at the metropolis which spread out as far as the eye could see. The bright lights which hung above the lab sector seemed more brilliant than usual, lighting up the grim grey city. The prison siren still rang out. The city looked lifeless, like a rotting carcass on the desert plain—hollow, and somewhat sad. Jon remembered the day he and Alan were sent here by the Chancellor to do his dirty work. The city then was alive, buzzing with all walks of life. People were happy. Jon would leave this world and Aris in a far worse place than when he arrived, but his end would be significant.

His time had come and this would give the people of Aris the chance to escape. Through tears he smiled. Turning his chair, he continued.

"Papers?" said a tall soldier, protected by two Klóns shadowing him.

Jon had wheeled his way up to the entrance gate. Vehicles were busily being searched by Bliksem's men, turrets of heavy guns peered from large slits in the wall. Jon could smell the damp air coming in from the monsoon rains which pelted the desert plain beyond the wall.

"Oh yes, papers." Jon acted absentmindedly as he searched himself, patting his pockets.

"Hurry up, retard," the soldier growled at him.

"One second, how silly of me, they are in my bag."

Reaching down, Jon slid out the rucksack and lifted it onto his lap, he unfastened the zip. The soldier looked down at the open bag and his jaw dropped.

Jon smiled up at him as he pushed a bloodied finger down on the detonator.

CHAPTER TWENTY

Sophia and Zarrah had covered some ground between themselves and the prison. On several occasions they needed to avoid bumping into Klón patrols. They decided to take the fastest route Sophia knew, but it was the most dangerous one.

The Kanani ghetto was utterly lawless and no cameras filmed the streets here. No patrols hunted for Oddities or the young. Kanani was inhabited by the Yamyam gang. Very few people who came across them lived to tell the tale. Sophia had heard rumours, stories, and urban myths of cannibalism and human sacrifices.

They had to move fast, but with caution. Leaving the main street, which now flowed with filthy water, they entered a tall grey tower block and climbed a few levels. The addicts were home and it appeared to the girls that a comatose body was slumped in every corridor they went through.

Finally, Sophia pushed open a door into an apartment and the musty air filled their lungs. Zarrah was shaking with cold, still dressed only in her damp prison blouse. Going through a bundle of old clothes Sophia tried to find something more suitable for her to wear—wading through lice-ridden rags was not an easy task. Used needles tainted with addict blood were scattered around the room carelessly. Eventually she found some trousers and a black jumper and she handed them to Zarrah. They were filthy but it was better than freezing.

Groaning, snoring, and the hacking coughs of sleeping addicts resounded through the block. Zarrah turned her back on Sophia, pulling the sodden blouse over her head. Sophia observed tiny scales, which had only recently emerged from Zarrah's spine, poking out from her dark skin.

"What happened to your parents?" Sophia ventured, unsure if the teenager would answer.

Zarrah pulled on the stinking garments, still shivering from the cold, damp air. A light flickered on the ceiling, making the room shimmer. Sophia saw a movement in the corner of her eye and noticed a rat scurrying amongst the rubble and waste.

"I never knew my father; my mother is probably dead by now. We were taken over a year ago. They took mum straight to the pits," Zarrah's voice wobbled with emotion.

"So, your mother was not an addict?" Sophia quizzed her further.

"No, my grandparents were brought here from Iris."

Sophia nodded, deciding to leave the conversation there, deducing a none-of-your-business tone in the young girl's voice.

"Come on, let's get out of this stinking hole," Sophia motioned with her head towards the door.

Zarrah stood still inspecting Sophia's face. "You look older than Adria and your hair is different, but you look similar.

Are you related?" the youngster asked.

"That is a very long story and we need to move," brushing the question away, Sophia left the room followed by the teenager.

The two of them picked their way through the wasted bodies of Faze addicts sprawled out, covering the cold corridor floors, moaning in their drugged, comatose state. Flickering lights made the passageways even eerier. The smell of something foul forced them to cover their nose and mouths. Sophia recognised the odour of a rotting corpse, which added a further foul stench to the waft of human waste that also plagued the tower block. Their eyes watered and at one-point Zarrah heaved and retched.

They were heading to an old fire exit, at the rear of the block. It would only be another five minutes on foot from there to the villa, where Sophia hoped Vasiliy had taken Adria.

They turned a corner into darkness, forcing Sophia to turn on her flashlight. The sudden brightness shining down the passageway made the floor move. An intrusion of cockroaches—panicked by the sudden light—scattered and crawled up the walls, up onto the damp, dripping ceiling above their heads.

"Quick," Sophia reached out her hand and took Zarrah's, leading her down the corridor with haste.

The cockroaches seemed to grow in number as they moved until they were almost ankle-deep. Zarrah began crying.

"They are crawling up my trousers," she sobbed.

Sophia turned to her. "We're nearly there."

The roaches were falling from the ceiling onto their heads. One landed on Sophia's neck and crawled down the back of her top, investigating her body. She tried to block out the feeling of the spindly legs tickling her skin. Sophia could hear

Zarrah coughing and spitting and she grimaced, aware that she had probably sucked one into her mouth. Her hair moved with dozens of the insects. Staring ahead, she made out a door at the end of the corridor. She moved her feet as fast as possible, cursing herself for not leaving the tower block the way they had come in.

They finally reached the door, Zarrah was in obvious distress as she swatted helplessly at the roaches that were still growing in number. Sophia turned the handle. The door didn't move, it was locked.

"Shit." Sophia began kicking at the door, Zarrah squeezed in beside her and joined in, both hitting out in a frenzy. Sophia turned around, lighting up the way they had just come. Her eyes widened with horror as a massive wave of cockroaches swam towards them. The ceiling above their heads began to sag, floorboards split and cracked, and thousands of the insects fell on them.

"Keep your eyes and mouth shut," she shouted at the younger girl, who immediately obeyed.

They could no longer kick at the door, waist-deep in an insect tsunami. Sophia banged her fists on the door screaming for help. The ceiling finally gave way, the intrusion rolled over them and they both disappeared under the wriggling mass.

Darkness was created by the thousands of roaches covering Sophia, making her lose her sense of direction. In a desperate attempt to cover her face she had dropped the flashlight. Kicking it by mistake, it rolled out of reach. Holding out a hand, she caught hold of Zarrah. The sound of the cockroaches wriggling all around them was deafening. They crushed them underfoot, adding to the skin-crawling noise.

Sophia heard a crack or a crunch and realised someone was

unlocking the door in front of them. Pushing her arms up through the throng, she waved her hands frantically about. The level of roaches slowly began to fall and Sophia was able to push her head out from the wave of bugs. The door opened outward, allowing the cockroaches to thin out. A dim light lit the figure of a person silhouetted in the doorway. She couldn't make out who it was.

Suddenly Zarrah's head erupted out of the swarm, gasping for air, her face blotched with tiny bites. The level of the roaches fell rapidly. The two girls held on to each other, Zarrah looking at Sophia teary-eyed. "What the fuck just happened?"

Wriggling about, Zarrah was pulling insects out from her trousers whilst Sophia untangled a couple from her dreadlocks. Kneeling, she retrieved her flashlight from the escaping bugs and turned the beam towards the doorway. Her face turned a deathly white.

Zarrah saw the horror on her face and asked, "What is it?"

"Run," Sophia pulled Zarrah by the scruff of her neck and began to run back down the corridor, back the way they had come.

The flashlight danced up the walls as they ran, creating crazy shadows. Sophia urgently tried to find an escape route. She was dragging Zarrah who was sobbing.

"What is it?" Zarrah cried out again.

Sophia came to a sudden halt. Staring wide-eyed down the corridor, she reached for her handgun. It wasn't there.

"No! Fuck it."

She must have dropped it in the swarm. Zarrah could hear footsteps coming from behind them and in front of them. She grabbed hold of Sophia's hand tightly and they both shook nervously. Coming out from the darkness in front of them was a man. His skin was brownish orange. He wore no shirt and around his neck hung a necklace of human teeth. His long, matted hair was decorated with the rib bones of infant children. Long sharp nails scratched at his own skin in a manic way. He wore rings on every finger embedded with human eyes, some were decomposing, one or two still looked fresh and seemed to stare at Sophia, as if some hint of life might still be in them. Zarrah gasped at the sight.

Sophia moved forward and the Yamyam stepped to meet her. Showing his sharp, blood-stained teeth, his fingers still scratched frantically at his chest. Sophia eyed him up. She was around the same height as the man, but he was more muscular. She tried to make out if he carried a weapon of any kind.

Suddenly Zarrah screamed causing Sophia to turn around. Zarrah lay on the floor, tangled up in a net unconscious. Standing over her, two more of the cannibal Yamyam people. Sophia heard the blow, but she didn't feel it. Blood ran over her eyes blurring her vision. As she fell to her knees a net was cast over her and she was kicked to the floor. The mad chatter of the Yamyams spoke in a hastened, crazy tongue.

"Bitings, bitings, bitings."

The three figures repeated the word to each other while continuing to kick Sophia until her body no longer moved.

CHAPTER TWENTY-ONE

Adria stood on the bank of Lake Aris. Staring out over the water which rippled with the monsoon rains filtering through the rock above. The bats fluttered down and drank from the rank water.

She was looking at the club which stood on the other side of the water, where not long ago she had killed Mikhail. She was thinking about the Klón and why he disobeyed Mikhail. 'Why didn't he kill her?'

She wished he had.

Tears rolled down her face, the harsh reality of the last few days kicking in. Looking down at her blood-stained hands she fell to her knees, covering her face with them as if she could block out the world and all the horrors. It felt like she had killed her father. She had loved Mikhail. But now she could see it all so clearly. Both brothers were greedy. They had no feelings for anyone, just money and reputation.

She sat for some time, thinking of the past. Mikhail taught

her to speak correctly and he read to her. 'How could someone be so devious, so evil?' She felt stupid at how easily she had been manipulated and fooled for most of her life. Her heart, body, and mind were broken beyond repair.

She moved a hand between her legs—which was still painful—but the real damage was more psychological, emotional and internal.

Vasiliy had not only violated her physically, but he had also scarred her mentally. She tried not to think about the three sisters and what they had done to her as well. Every time she did, it made her sick.

"Why did you do this to me, why? Fuck you, you bastards," she screamed across the lake, pulling at her hair. "I'm a dirty addict, a murderer. I've killed four people." She began laughing at herself insanely.

Only two days ago, Adria would not have thought about killing anyone. Now she had killed four people and the horrid rodent—which didn't worry her too much. She had made up her mind earlier in the shower; after killing the brothers, she would kill herself. She had nothing now, nothing to live for.

She thought briefly about the man, Luca, who had helped her escape from prison. 'And who was this Sophia? Why did they want to help me?' Nothing mattered now. She had longed to see the outside world. Stories of stars and the moon, trees of green, tales she had heard from the punters that came to the club. She would never get to see any of it, she had given up.

Finally rising to her feet, she staggered up to the villa. She had left all the lights on, and they lit up the path from the jetty. Every step seemed to take an eternity. The cravings for Cane were coming, creeping back again, which was how she intended to leave this fucked up world. This is how she would end it all, on a fucking big high.

Adria walked through the villa, up the stairs and into her bedroom. On the white plush carpet lay the bags of Cane she removed from the suitcase to replace with Vasiliy's head. She noticed the carpet underneath was turning red from the blood seeping out from under the shower room door. Pushing it open, it revealed the headless corpse of Vasiliy. Staring at the headless man she showed no emotion.

Moving away from the door, she reached down, picking up a bag of the blue stimulant and crashed onto her bed. The addict took over as she tore at the plastic bag like a possessed animal, taking great handfuls of the drug. She shoved the powder into her face, licking and snorting repeatedly. Her nose eventually began to run with blood, her eyes almost bursting from their sockets. Adria's heart raced so hard, her head felt like it would explode at any minute. Crazed, she kept going, her whole body paled and shook, sweat dripped from every pore.

"I don't want to live anymore," she screamed. She banged her head violently into the mattress. Adria tried to stand, but her legs had no feeling. Collapsing back onto the bed, she pushed herself across the top of the sheets until she hung over the edge of the bed. She frantically grabbed another bag, tearing it open with her mouth. She began lapping up the sour powder, gagging. She continued. The whites of her eyes turned brutally red; finally, she was violently sick over the remaining bags and the blood-stained carpet. Adria's head slumped forward. Her body was limp, blood and vomit dripping from her face.

℔

The sound of something popping caused Sophia to stir. Spitting, hissing, and crackling from a burning fire made her wake. The smell of roasting meat crept up her nose. Painfully she opened her eyes, one swollen from being kicked in the face and the other eye stuck together from the dried blood from the blow to the head. Her head throbbed as she tried to move, but her hands and feet had been bound with rope. The floor was cold and hard and jagged stones which had come loose from the concrete stabbed into her ribs.

Lifting her head, she strained to see where she was. Her face was red with dry blood and she could feel the heat from the spitting fire in front of her. Roasting on a spit, the source of the hissing and popping was a human torso. "Oh, no."

The torso was that of a young woman. Looking to her left Sophia noticed a bundle of dirty clothes, the same clothes she had dug out from the filthy heap for Zarrah to wear not long ago. Sophia lowered her head, resting her forehead on the floor.

"This is all my fault," she said to herself.

Sophia decided to lay still, aware that no one had noticed her stir. She sensed there were at least five Yamyams around the room. She heard one move towards the fire. Keeping one eye slightly open, she watched as he came up to the roasting body with a large sharp carving knife and began sawing at the corpse. The scuffle of more feet moved towards the fire. The cook was joined by four more of the foul cannibals, their fang-like teeth gleamed in the firelight, making their already jaundiced-coloured skin turn a brighter orange. Their heads bobbed like pigeons, all chattering eagerly and excitedly. They all spoke the same word with open palms held out towards the cook.

"Bitings, bitings," they repeated, "bitings, bitings."

The cook handed them all a fresh slice of human meat. A tear ran from Sophia's eye, she didn't know the young girl well, but to die in such a vile way made her heart sink—and after all, Sophia had led them down that passageway. She turned her face away, she couldn't watch anymore.

While the man-eaters ate, their backs towards Sophia, she managed to wiggle herself back a few feet, finding a large, jagged stone protruding from the ground. She began rubbing the rope which bound her wrists. Suddenly one of the Yamyams rose to his feet, shouting at the cook, "more, more, bitings, bitings."

The others joined in moaning at the cook. Sliding the leftover torso off the spit, he added what remained into a massive pot of thick stew. The diners started pointing to a dark corner. Sophia couldn't see what they were looking at through the smoke emanating from the fire. The cook groaned and trudged into the darkness, re-emerging with a young naked girl, dragging her by the scruff of her neck. Her body was bloodied and bruised but her dark skin shimmered in the firelight.

Sophia's heart leapt into her mouth, it was Zarrah.

She tried to resist as the Yamyam pulled her towards the fire, a filthy rag was stuffed in her mouth as a gag. Shaking with fear, the heat from the fire made her skin glisten. The waiting cannibals bounced around on the floor, eagerly waiting for the fresh meat. Zarrah tried to pull away from the orange looking cook, he was the ugly man who had stood in their path earlier. His eyeball-ringed hand held her arm just above the elbow. Forcing her to the ground, Zarrah cried, moaning through the gag. Her hands and feet were also bound with rope. She attempted to wiggle away, only to be punched in the back of the head causing the room to spin and making her eyes go blurry. The evil faces of the Yamyams circled around her as they laughed and dribbled. The chef inserted the spit through the ropes which bound her, then with an old brush, began basting her in oil. He cackled and hummed a tune as he applied the fat to Zarrah's naked form.

Sophia looked on from a distance, horrified. Frantically she filed the rope faster on the jagged stone, when she noticed her handgun was on the floor behind Zarrah's clothes. One of the cannibals must have found the revolver amongst the cockroaches.

"More bitings, more bitings," the four Yamyam diners continued, scratching at their skin with rank talon-like nails.

She watched them, praying none of them would turn and notice her. Finally, the rope snapped. Curling herself up in a ball, she began working the knot at her feet. One of the men stood and walked over to the cook, taking hold of the spit. Together they threaded the pole through Zarrah's feet and wrists, lifting her off the floor, holding the spit at both ends.

Squirming, Zarrah desperately tried to free herself as they heaved her over the fire. They were about to rest her onto the posts which held the spit, when an ear-shattering bang echoed in the room, followed by a second. The two Yamyams holding the spit fell backwards, a single bullet hole to both their foreheads. The spit fell only inches from the fire, Zarrah rolled away, looking back to see Sophia standing behind the remaining diners. Before they knew what was happening, she had executed all three of them. They slumped forward and their heads landed in the fire. The smell of burning hair soon filled the room.

Zarrah studied Sophia who seemed to be in some sort of trance. Her body looked paler than before, her eyes dark and hollow, reminding her of Adria in the polytunnel. Abruptly Sophia snapped out of her daze and ran over to Zarrah. Removing the gag from her mouth, she began untying her from the spit.

"Thank you," Zarrah began.

Sophia cut her off. "No time to talk, get dressed quickly, there are more of these sick bastards around here. They would have heard the gunshots."

Frantically Sophia removed the rope. Zarrah dashed to the bundle of clothes, getting dressed as fast as she could. She ignored the pain from the bumps and bruises she had received, her oiled body helped slide the rank garments back on.

Sophia grabbed a burning log from the fire, her torch nowhere to be seen. She had no idea where they were now. Brandishing the flame around the room, she noticed there were no visible doors or windows. Zarrah pointed to the ceiling where a considerable hole exposed the cavern roof hundreds of feet above the tower block. The end of the ladder hung over its edge, Sophia was able to jump up and grip the rung, pulling it down. The two girls immediately climbed up onto the rooftop. Sophia ran to the edge, looking out over Aris as she tried to get her bearings.

Zarrah called out to her, "can you hear that?"

Sophia strained her ears. Footsteps. Hundreds of footsteps, bare feet slapping on a cold floor, getting closer and closer. The chattering of sharp teeth, lots of voices repeating the same word.

"Bitings, bitings, bitings."

Sophia knew where they were from looking over the edge of the tower block; they only had to cross one street to safety. The Yamyams would not follow them over the road. They would be back in Bliksem's territory and wouldn't risk being captured and taken to the pits or slaughterhouses. Sophia could also make out the lake and roughly where the villa sat—where they would hopefully find Adria. The Yamyams had brought them closer to their destination, but they were thirty storeys up now. She was thinking fast, scanning the rooftop. 'Two doors at either end would lead back down the levels. But which one would be safest?' This question was answered for her immediately. The door on the southside of the roof burst open, dozens of Yamyams bundled out, brandishing crude weapons crafted from human bone; sharpened ribs were attached to poles like massive forks, arm and leg bones were made into small sharp spikes. The dirty, orange-bodied freaks ran at them chattering insanely.

"Bitings, bitings, bitings."

"This way," Sophia cried out. They fled towards the north door, Sophia still holding the burning log.

The footsteps grew louder behind them as more and more of the hunters appeared from the stairwell door. Sophia reached the exit first and her mind flashed back to the previously locked door and the cockroach intrusion. Thankfully, the door swung open and she was hit with the foulest smell ever to creep into a person's sinuses. Poking the burning log into the darkness, a million flies buzzed through the air. The stairwell was awash with maggots and other parasites which fed on the Yamyams dumping ground. Rotting human carcasses littered the way, but they had no choice. They fled down the stairs, their feet squelching on rotting innards. Bones cracked underfoot. They did not stop to look. Down and down they went. At one point something stuck to Sophia's foot. Kicking it off, a skull filled with rotting mush smashed against the wall.

"Bitings, bitings."

The chatter chased them, echoing down the stairs.

Zarrah was lagging and exhausted. She cried, "I can't go on."

Sophia turned back, grabbing the girl by the scruff of the neck.

"Come on," she screamed at her. Zarrah felt Sophia's strength and was taken aback by the power she possessed. Footsteps were gaining on them, but the remains of the eaten began to dwindle underfoot, making their progress more manageable. They passed several addicts who blindly walked past them. Their screams shortly followed. Sophia threw the burning torch over the edge of the stairwell and watched the light fall, only two more flights. Looking back upstairs, the torch lights of the Yamyams were on the level above. "Come on," she screamed at Zarrah again. "We're almost there."

They gave it all they had. Their lungs screamed for oxygen, their bodies ached. Zarrah was close to passing out with fatigue. Finally reaching the ground floor, Sophia flung open the fire exit, leading out onto the street.

Laying on the floor just outside the door, two addicts sat up, disturbed from their drugged coma. They looked confused as the door burst open and the two girls ran across the street in front of them, panting with panicked faces. Sophia looked back over her shoulder just in time to see the two addicts being dragged back into the doorway. The door slammed shut, muffling their screams.

A hundred voices spoke through chattering razor teeth, "Bitings."

CHAPTER TWENTY-TWO

Sophia watched the road from the window of a building. She and Zarrah had rested here, briefly regaining some energy after their flight from the Yamyams.

"I need a shower," Zarrah complained about her oily skin. She sighed, hugging herself cross-legged on the floor. Sophia ignored her. Across the road in front of them was the villa. The high walls which surrounded the house were dotted with cameras. A lone Klón guarded the main gate. The area was well lit and the road was maintained here. Large screens which dotted the city showed a curfew was now in place. The siren from the jail seemed to have grown louder, tannoy speakers had also been utilised with a monotone voice repeating itself over and over again.

"Curfew in place, remain indoors," the speakers bellowed across the city.

Zarrah rose to her feet and joined Sophia at the window. Looking out, she said, "do you think Adria is in there?"

"I hope so." Sophia's eyes remained on the gate.

"How will we get past the Klón?" Zarrah asked, attempting to wipe grease from her dark face.

"The Klón? I am not worried about him, it's the two brothers who concern me." She spat on the floor. Her mouth was dry and she was thirsty and hungry. "Stay here, but if I'm not back in an hour, you must leave. Go to the wastelands, the old stadium, do you know it?"

Zarrah nodded.

"When you arrive there, hide and wait for the signal."

Zarrah looked up at Sophia, confused. "What signal?"

"You will know when it's time," Sophia placed a reassuring hand on the young girl's shoulder and she jumped out of the window onto the road.

The teenager watched as Sophia walked casually up to the gate. The Klón began to raise his machine gun which hung from his shoulder, but something stopped him from pointing the barrel at her. Sophia was talking to him but Zarrah couldn't hear what she was saying. The dull tones coming from the tannoy speakers muted their conversation. The Klón had a confused look on his face. He released his grip on the machine gun and opened the gate, allowing Sophia to just walk straight into the villa's compound unhindered. The gate closed behind her and Sophia could feel the confused red eyes of the Klón staring into her back as she walked up the gravel driveway leading to the villa's entrance. Garden statues lit the path. She looked at them in silent wonder as she crept forward, beautiful carvings of naked men and women, unknown beasts and creatures with cruel faces, the likes of which she had never seen.

Sophia had spent her whole life in Aris scraping by in

poverty. She had never seen the sky, the sun, or the stars, and she longed for things she had yet to experience.

On approaching the villa she removed her handgun from the holster, checking the mag—only one bullet. Her lips tightened and she cursed herself for not bringing extra ammo. Vasiliy's car sat outside the front door and a huge fountain with a carved fish blew water from its mouth in the centre. Sophia hadn't seen anything like it.

Creeping up to the car she peered over the bonnet, looking in through the lit windows. Why they even bothered putting windows into the buildings she was not sure—they let in some fresh air when the cavern became hot, but most of the time it was mild. If you were lucky to live close to, or in the lab sector, you benefited from the artificial lights. The villa was silent. There was no movement inside, no sign of life, no sound at all. Sophia kept low. Edging out from the car, she scurried across the drive and up to the main door. She noticed it had been left ajar. Very gently, Sophia pushed the door open, the bright open space of the hallway almost overwhelming her. The neatness and the décor took her breath away and for a second, she was lost in awe. Shaking her head, she refocused on her mission. She knew about the brothers, their reputation preceded them. They were violent, vicious thugs.

Sophia tiptoed across the hall and slipped into the lounge. Although the room was clear of clutter it was still a sight of wonder to Sophia. Silk-covered chairs, plush carpets and leather sofas. The sitting room opened into a vast kitchen. Two large patio doors at the rear looked out towards Lake Aris.

Once she was satisfied no one was on the ground level, she made her way up the stairs. Her handgun held out in front of her, eyes darting between the three open doorways on the landing above. She peered into the first bedroom, which was in darkness and the bed was empty. Reaching the second door, a sick feeling began to rise in her stomach, as though sensing someone was in this room.

The light was on in here. Sophia spun into the room, keeping her back to the wall. Immediately she dropped the gun onto the carpet and sprinted towards the bed, she grabbed Adria's shoulders and rolled her over onto her back. Her face was pale, purple veins mapping the skin. Blood and sick hung from her chin, her blonde hair was clumped and matted. Her naked body caked in dry blood.

"No," Sophia cried, rocking her. "Wake up, please."

She screamed at Adria, tears flowing from her eyes. She placed two fingers on her neck, probing for a pulse. Feeling a very faint beat, Sophia wrapped her arms under Adria's armpits and heaved her off the bed, towards the en-suite shower room. She ignored the headless corpse of a man and the blood-splattered walls.

"Come on, don't die on me now, please." Sophia was beside herself. She managed to drag Adria's zombie-like body into the shower, slumping her body against the tiled wall and turned on the shower, spraying Adria with cold water. Vomit and bile leaked from her blue lips.

She left her under the shower and ran down to the kitchen, manically rummaging through the cupboards, pulling out their contents, spilling cereals, flour, and sugars amongst other things onto the floor. Finally, she found what she was looking for. She grabbed a large bag of salt. Seeing a considerable-sized jug, she filled half of it up with salt then added water from the luxurious taps.

Adria was still unconscious, her body looking even paler by the time Sophia returned. She knelt next to her, barely noticing that she was also getting wet. Pulling Adria's head back, she forced the girl's mouth open and poured the saltwater into her throat, a little at a time. "Come on," Sophia screamed at her, shaking her, pleading with her to survive. Again she poured the saltwater down her throat.

Suddenly Adria's body began to jerk and spasm violently. Sophia stepped back watching helplessly as she wiggled around the shower floor. Projectile vomit, stained blue from the Cane, erupted out of Adria's mouth. Her eyelids began to flutter as more bile escaped from her mouth and nostrils, causing her to cough harshly. She was fitting. Sophia knelt next to her again trying to calm her, holding her close and firm, attempting to stop her from banging her head and doing more injury to herself.

$ \mathcal{S} $

Adria was dying, her mind was awash with visions and dreams.

The man holding a bleeding eye socket.

Biting into the rat by the rubbish mound, starving.

The fire, the fire. The ceiling falling.

The strange man losing his legs.

The rank faces of the three sisters. Vasiliy throwing dirty rags at her.

"Clean yourself up," he grinned at her.

The hot metal pole falling from the ceiling, the girl catching it, screaming as it burnt the flesh of her palms. Adria looked into the girl's eyes, her face, it was her own face.

The cold prison shower, the prison officer hosing her down as she huddled in a corner, shivering.

The water-filled her lungs. She gasped for air, vomit rose from her stomach.

The taste of salt stung her lips.

℔

Her eyes sprung wide open; another torrent of vomit left her mouth.

"Adria can you hear me? Say something please," said a soft voice.

Adria looked up through the showering water. A figure stood over her. She tried to see who it was, but her vision was a blur.

Sophia carried Adria back into the bedroom, laying her gently on the bed. They were both dripping with cold water. Sophia was shaking, and with trembling hands she rubbed a towel over Adria. Her breathing had steadied, so had her heartbeat, but she was unconscious again.

"Come on, you can do this," Sophia whispered in her ear, "please wake up."

Once Adria was dry, Sophia wrapped her up in a duvet and found some spare clothes. She dried herself and changed into them. She paced the bedroom for some time, thinking to herself anxiously, wondering who the headless man on the bathroom floor was. It was one of the brothers—that much she was sure—but she had no idea which one lay there dead. Sophia was on edge; the surviving brother could return any minute. She moved towards the window, which looked out towards the main gate. The Klón still stood on guard obediently. She was aware she had been gone well over an hour and hoped that young Zarrah had listened to her and headed towards the old stadium.

The hairs on the back of Sophia's neck suddenly rose, quickly she spun around. A cold hand grabbed her by the throat. A demonic-looking Adria lifted her off the floor. Sophia tried to speak, but Adria's grip was so tight.

"What do you want with me? Who are you?" she screamed at Sophia, whose face was turning purple.

She tried to prize Adria's hand from around her neck, but her grip tightened. Sophia lashed out with a hefty kick, her boot connecting with Adria's stomach. Groaning from the blow Adria loosened her grip for a brief second. This was all the time Sophia needed. Quickly she pushed down on Adria's elbows, ducking down she ran forward into Adria's torso and threw her over her shoulder. Sophia flung her onto the bed.

"Adria, stop it," she cried, "I am trying to help you."

She leapt onto Adria, attempting to restrain her. A flailing fist caught her in the right eye. Sophia grabbed Adria's wrists and forced her body weight down on her.

"Who are you?" Adria cried.

"A friend," Sophia said. "Don't you recognise me?" She sat back, feeling the fight had gone from Adria.

Adria studied her face, confusion and horror setting in. "Why do you look like me?" she screamed and lashed out again.

Sophia caught her wrists. This was when Adria noticed the scars on Sophia's palms, scorched by fire. She relaxed. Sophia let go of her wrists and crumbled onto the bed next to Adria. Both women were exhausted and they stared at the ceiling.

"You were in my dreams, you were in the fire?" she mumbled exhausted; but she still looked angry and full of rage. Turning her head she faced the slightly older woman. "Who are you? Why do you look like me?"

Sophia held Adria's hand and softly said, "I am you."

CHAPTER TWENTY-THREE

Luca made his way back to the ground floor level of the prison. The siren was still ringing loudly. All the inmates were behind locked cell doors and the officers were checking to make sure everyone was accounted for. It wouldn't be long before they discovered Adria was missing.

He made his way through the maze of corridors until he eventually approached two steel doors. They were padlocked with a large chain around the handles. Luca fumbled in his pocket, taking out a key. Looking back over his shoulder, he made sure he was alone before unlocking the chain.

Entering the darkness, he turned on his flashlight, revealing a vast storeroom. He walked straight into a giant cobweb which brushed his lips. He spat and wiped the silk net from his face. Shining his torch down the gangway, he noticed the large shelves on either side housing boxes of paperwork, tools, light bulbs, and all kinds of junk which the prison maintenance team had stored here over the years. The room was thick with dust and stank of damp, causing Luca to cough as he walked down the aisle. The maintenance room went on for what seemed an age, the muffled sound of the siren still sounded above.

Finally, he reached the far wall. To his right was a stack of boxes as tall as himself, filled with old chains, manacles, and locks. Quickly Luca heaved the boxes off each other, stacking them behind him, creating a false wall. Against the wall where the boxes had stood was a tiny metal door, just big enough for Luca to climb through. He pulled at the old, rusted door and with an ear-piercing screech it opened. Shining the torch revealed stone steps which disappeared down into the darkness. Luca crawled through with a groan.

$

The Boss-man played with the unlocked chain of the maintenance room. Standing in front of him were two young human officers eagerly awaiting their orders, panting like excited puppies being let off their leash for the first time.

The Boss-man gestured with a nod towards the door. "Find out what he is up to, then bring him back to me, alive."

The two clean-faced rookies pulled their telescopic truncheons from their belts, flicking them out to their full length. The ends glowed and fizzed with an electric charge that would stun their victim. They both disappeared into the dark. The Boss-man grinned, stroking his big beard.

℔

Luca crawled down the stairs until he reached a point where he could stand upright, just before the stairs began to curl into a spiral carved into the natural rock of the prison's foundations. Reaching the final step, Luca flashed the torch about. He was standing in a vast void, an ancient catacomb which spread out underground from the main entrance to Aris and deep into the lab sector. He had spent a lot of time over the last year down here. No one knew the catacombs existed other than One-Eyed Alan, who had given him the task of planting the explosives.

Luca recently checked that they had not been damaged by rats chewing through the dozens of wires which zig-zagged across the floor, or that damp had wetted the charges. They might have been discovered at any time, but everything still looked the way he had left it. Behind the bottom of the spiral steps was a pile of rubble. Luca began moving the broken rocks and stones he had placed there previously. He reached into the rubble and pulled out a timer. A wire ran off into the darkness and linked up to the detonator and the hundreds of plastic explosives which were dotted in strategic positions. The blast would bring the lab sector and the prison down.

Luca flicked the switch on the timer and pressed a few buttons before the terminal lit up. He punched in some digits and his finger hovered over a green button. The display screen read twenty-five minutes. That's all the time he had to get out of the lab sector unhindered. He held his breath for a second, then hit the green button. The timer beeped and the digits began to fall. Luca rested the timer back on the rubble, turned

215

around, and climbed the steps with speed, until finally, he was forced to crawl on his hands and knees again.

He pushed his way back out through the tiny doorway, not bothering to shut it. Pushing the boxes out of the way, Luca began to make his way up the long aisle. He was halfway along when the silhouette of a man stood in front of him. He halted in his tracks. Slowly he moved his hand to his inside pocket and began to pull out his gun.

Suddenly there was a crash. The second young officer had pushed over one of the towering racks, just missing Luca, who sidestepped out of the way. A flash of blue light whizzed past his eyes, just missing him. The rookie swung his electric stun truncheon in the air. Luca had withdrawn his gun but he dared not fire the weapon, the whole prison would be down here and it would all be over. The rookie lost his footing and tripped. Luca caught him by the collar and pistol-whipped him around the back of his head. The man slumped and he let him fall to the floor.

Swiftly, he retrieved the truncheon from the unconscious man. He looked up as the other officer came charging towards him. Luca was faster and stronger than the youngster. He easily dodged another blow. The man tumbled past him and Luca stabbed the truncheon into the back of his skull. The hiss and smell of burning hair turned Luca's stomach and the man fell to the floor, jerking in agony.

Luca knew he had been sniffed out and that The Boss-man would be waiting for him beyond the doors. He looked at his watch. Eighteen minutes to go. It looked like he would be going down with this shitty city.

♭

Olaf gave up his struggle with The Cracker's two thugs and slumped onto the floor of the cage, the trailer rocking back and forth. The Vinayaki was still thrashing about, the siren causing the bull distress. The horrible midget whipped at the beast repeatedly, cackling abuse at the sad creature. The gate swung open and Courtauld, still without his artificial leg, was tossed in. He landed with a crash at Olaf's feet before looking up at his hairy friend and winking.

"Well, guess you're stuck with me," he grinned.

Olaf raised his eyebrows, shrugging his shoulders. "I have been stuck with worse," he moaned, turning his attention back to The Cracker who was now walking around the large trailer, checking the beast hadn't broken anything.

The Cracker's two men were busy tightening the chains and poles which attached the Vinayaki to the cage. The animal had settled down, allowing one of the men to put blinkers back over his eyes. The Vinayaki made a low growl, his body bled from the new whip lashes.

Olaf's face twisted angrily. "If I could get my hands on that little shit, I would crush his skull."

"I wouldn't bet against it," replied Courtauld, who was nursing his wounded arm.

"Look," Courtauld continued. The one-legged man pointed to his elbow, which was pouring blood. He poked the wound with his finger and laughed.

"Look, I can see my elbow bone."

Olaf looked taken back by the funny man's comment and found it strange that the wound didn't seem to hurt or bother

217

him. "Doesn't that hurt?" Olaf quizzed him.

"Yeah, fucking kills," Courtauld smiled mischievously.

It left Olaf looking totally perplexed, and he shook his head in disbelief. Casting his eyes around to their fellow captives, he realised Courtauld and himself were the only men on board. The women and children had moved into a corner, huddled up, fear in their eyes. Olaf stood tall, his muscular body half covered in black fur. He walked towards the terrified group. One of the children's mouths fell open, in awe of his size. Others turned away, fear of being raped, beaten, or both, apparent horror showing on their faces.

"We won't hurt you, I promise," Olaf gestured with open hands.

Courtauld was giggling behind him.

Olaf looked at him. "What is so funny?"

"You, you great oaf. Do you have any idea how intimidating you look?"

He looked pained as he looked back at the shaking, petrified slaves. Mumbling to himself, he slumped back on the cage floor. Courtauld continued to probe his elbow.

$

Luca crouched by the doors craning his ear towards it. He could hear the impatient pacing of feet treading the polished corridor floor on the other side. Luca could only assume it was the Boss-man. He checked his watch. Fifteen minutes.

"Shit," he cursed under his breath. "Come on," he whispered, praying the senior officer would lose patience and enter the dark room.

He retrieved the second truncheon, replacing his handgun back inside his prison jacket. The footsteps stopped, and ever so slowly the doors began to creak open. The light from the corridor flooded in, followed by a large boot. Luca held his breath as the Boss-man stepped into the room.

Lighting up the aisle with a torch, the Boss-man could just make out the unconscious bodies of his officers amongst the fallen racks. He stepped forward again. The doors swung closed behind him. A sudden harsh flash of blue drilled into his skull. Luca leapt up from his hiding place, brandishing the two truncheons. He stuck the two high voltage clubs into the Boss-man's temples. His body wriggled and spasmed, but he did not fall. Luca pushed harder on the truncheons and The Boss-man turned to face him, the blue light lit up crazy eyes, which were almost hidden by his beard. He released the batons, whipping the Boss-man to the ground. He grimaced hearing the man's skull crack open. His body instantly went limp.

Luca stood frozen for a moment. He had never killed a living thing before. He trembled, nerves getting the better of him. In a panic, he dropped the truncheons, flung open the door and ran down the corridor. He risked a quick glance at his watch. Ten minutes.

He still had one thing to do. He ran through the corridors, sweat trickling down his tanned face and ruining his neat hair.

Turning into a passage, he came into the central part of the prison. This was the main terminal and a solitary guard was watching monitors from a chair. He turned and saw Luca running towards him. Before he could open his mouth, Luca was on him. The guard fell from his chair and he used the heel of his gun to knock the officer unconscious. Quickly he turned, looking at a large panel of buttons and switches in front of him. He began punching some keys, then he hit a large red knob. More alarms sounded and every cell door in the jail sprung open. Confused inmates peered out from their cells. Guards who were still checking the levels looked in horror as the main gates to the prison wings opened.

Someone shouted out, "the gates are open!"

Then all hell broke loose. Male and female inmates armed themselves with whatever could be used as a weapon. One officer was caught out on the fourth floor of the women's wing. He was thrown over the balcony screaming.

Luca ran out from the main gate of the jail. Reaching the courtyard, gunshots rang out. Hundreds of inmates came piling out behind him. He didn't dare look at his watch. The main gate to the lab sector was swarming with armed guards. The inmates charged at them and a battle pursued. Luca turned his attention to a trumpeting roar. Turning, he saw the Vinayaki slave cart which he had seen earlier from the window. The two thugs were standing in front of the bull, again trying to calm it down. The Cracker was high up on his seat, thrashing at the creature with his whip. The slaves on the trailer were rolling about and being thrown from one side to the other. The Vinayaki rose on his two back legs, causing The Cracker to fall from his seat. The small slave trader crashed to the floor. He looked up with an angry frown, but before he could stand, the huge Vinayaki moved, stomping backwards. The midget screamed in horror as a giant hoof fell on him, crushing him into the floor. A bloodied hand grasping a whip was all that remained visible. Some inmates who had been brought to the jail by the Cracker recognised his thugs and piled on them. Their screams were short-lived.

Luca rushed towards the beast. He had an idea.

"Let us out of here," a bellowing voice called from the cage.

Luca looked up, a giant of a man was rattling the bars. Looking at him it was clear he wanted to help. He looked at his watch. Four minutes. Only four minutes left.

They were all going to die.

CHAPTER TWENTY-FOUR

Stór studied the bloody mess of Mikhail impaled to the wall by two swords. With sick admiration, a rare smile appeared on his face. His attention turned towards the Klón doorman who sat nearby. Stór sauntered purposely across the room, standing over the security guard. His huge shadow covered him like the cloak of the grim reaper.

"Who did this?" growled Stór.

"The girl, the blonde girl, Adria. She did it, then went back to the villa, I think?" He looked up at the bigger Klón with confused eyes.

Stór removed a radio from his belt.

"Mikhail is dead. The girl is called Adria," he spoke into the radio.

There was a brief silence, then Bliksem replied, "where is she?"

"The villa. I'm leaving now."

There was no reply, Stór returned the radio.

"You are coming with me," he motioned to the doorman to follow him out of the club.

"But I am free now, she told me. I am free."

Stór stopped in his tracks.

He turned and stared at the doorman with dark, menacing eyes. "No one is free in Aris," he snapped.

$

"I am you." Sophia looked into Adria's eyes.

Adria did not reply. Her eyes were vague, void of anything. They rolled back into her head. Sophia reached out a hand and gently moved a wisp of curly blonde hair which had fallen over her youthful face. Tears rolled down Sophia's cheeks.

"What have they done to you?" She studied Adria's pale body. A cut on her shoulder, inflicted in the fight with Lucia in the polytunnel, was turning septic and bruises dotted her body. Sophia sat up on the bed, tenderly rubbing Adria's arm.

"Wake up, please," she begged her, wiping a tear from her eye.

Adria stirred. Her eyes rolled back into place, flinching at Sophia's touch.

"I won't hurt you, don't be scared," Sophia tried to reassure her.

"I don't understand how you can be me?" Adria mumbled through vomit-tainted lips.

"There is a lot to explain, but we don't have time now." Sophia was concerned that the missing brother would return anytime. "Where is the other brother?" She looked at Adria with worry etched on her face.

"They are both dead," Adria's voice wobbled with a note of sadness.

Sophia was relieved. "Where is the body?"

Adria began coughing and spluttered her reply, "at the club."

Sophia tried not to show her concern. "Then we must leave now, someone will find him soon. They will come here first."

She faded away again and groaned incoherently. Sophia grabbed her hands and pulled her up.

Vomit ran from Adria's mouth as she protested, "where are we going?"

"Somewhere safe. Can you stand?" Sophia helped her rise to her feet.

Adria wobbled as the room span about her. She was still heavily intoxicated. She questioned whether the girl holding her up was even real. Sophia wiped her body down with a towel; she found some suitable clothes and helped her dress. Then she pulled a blanket from the bed and wrapped it around her, covering her head. Adria's shaking hands held the sheet around her face. Sophia helped her towards the door.

Adria suddenly froze, rigid. "I can't leave without that; I cannot live without it," she pointed to the bags of blue Cane on the floor.

"You don't need that shit anymore. I am taking you away from this life." Sophia tried to move them both forward.

Adria fell to her knees. "No, I won't go, you can't make me. Don't tell me what to do. Why the fuck do you want to look after me? Why didn't you let me die?"

She became hysterical. Sophia looked angry. There was no time to argue and too much to explain. Quickly she picked up two bags of stimulant and pushed them into her top.

"Come on! We don't have time to argue," she pulled Adria up off the floor. As they left the room Adria glanced at the headless corpse in the bathroom with emotionless eyes.

♄

Bliksem put down the radio, a rare smile threatened to crack his red face. Adria was alive, and this meant the One-Eyed Man must be Alander. The blank monitor in front of him made a crackling sound; the gaunt face of The Chemist appeared.

"I have great news for you, sir," The Chemist backed away from the screen. Her body moved like a robotic locust, Bliksem thought. She held a tiny living thing, the limbs moved about slowly in The Chemist's palm. Her face was lit up like a new mother holding her first child.

"I have broken Alander's code. I've done it, we have a girl, at last."

Bliksem's rare smile widened even more. "I congratulate you. My father will be pleased, as I am. But there is something you should know."

The Chemist moved closer to the screen.

"Adria is alive." Bliksem was not sure how the Chemist would respond.

"She's alive?" The Chemist paused for a moment, digesting the news. "If she survived, did Alander and Sophia as well?"

"Yes, they are both alive. Alander will pay for what he did to you; you have my word." He continued, "We no longer need him alive."

225

The Chemist began to sob in a way which disgruntled him. He turned off the monitor and rising from his chair he thumbed the machete hilt at his belt. It was time to visit The Golden Goose.

CHAPTER TWENTY-FIVE

Now

The sudden noise of armoured vehicles screeching to a halt alerted the gang members in The Golden Goose; they got to their feet, weapons raised. Sophia pulled her handgun from the holster. She had led Adria back to the pub slowly - they had to avoid two drones on their way back through the streets of Aris. The teenager, Zarrah, had vanished by the time they left the villa. She could only hope the youngster had taken her advice and was making her way to the wastelands.

Shortly after leaving the villa, Sophia had heard armoured cars roaring towards the building. She had been right. If they had waited any longer... Sophia didn't want to dwell on it. She turned to Steev, the hairy, foul man who always gave her unwanted advances.

"Go down to the basement and warn the others," she ordered him.

He did not argue, but a lingering look made her skin crawl

as he disappeared below the bar. Ratty, the pointy faced man, was busy loading shotguns on the bar. The crowd of gang leaders, Oddities and humans alike checked their weapons. The fierce woman who had shouted at the screen not long ago was weighed down with bullet belts crisscrossing her chest. She was looking out the window as Bliksem was busy beating an addict's head in. What remained of the body was grossly incorporated into the radiator of the vehicle.

"Bliksem!" she yelled over her shoulder.

The crowd began to turn over tables and took up their positions, aiming their weapons at the door.

"Where's my dad?" Sophia had not been able to contact the one-eyed professor and she needed him now, more than ever.

"They're coming," the woman shouted.

Sophia jumped behind the bar and standing next to Ratty, they prepared for the attack.

$

Bliksem and twelve Klóns walked up to the door of The Golden Goose. There was a trail of blood from the severed head of the addict, which he held in his hand by the hair. He scanned the building. The pub was small compared to the high tower blocks which surrounded it. Four floors high, the windows were mainly blacked out. The filthy painted sign of The Golden Goose was lit by a dim light and the filtered rain which fell on Aris seemed to sparkle in its glow. The distant alarm of the prison still rang out and if anything, it had gone up in volume. He gestured to the Klóns to go in first. They readied themselves, armed with heavy machine guns and the electric cobra snares which were attached to their belts. They began to steamroll towards the door.

Suddenly there was a huge bright flash of light which blinded Bliksem. The whole city shook with the explosion. He fell to the floor, covering his head. The Klóns halted in their tracks, looking towards the great cavern entrance a few miles away, where a massive ball of fire lit up the cavern ceiling and the city.

Bliksem crawled back up onto his feet. Dust clouds now hampered his vision. Attempting to focus through the haze, he followed the Klóns' line of sight. His face turned red with rage. Before he could speak, the sound of smashing glass made him turn his attention back to the pub. The windows broke from the inside on all four floors. Glass shattered, raining down onto the street. The orange fire of a dozen blasting gun-barrels erupted within. He turned and ran back to his armoured car. The Klóns were pinned down by an avalanche of bullets which sprayed their bodies. Bliksem didn't wait; he sped back towards the lab sector, glancing in the rear-view mirror as he drove away, watching the Klóns fall one by one.

$

Alan paced back and forth outside the old derelict warehouse, aimlessly kicking small stones. His face was foreboding.

Thousands would die today: the addicts of Aris would all be lost. He could not save them all, not today. But the uprising would be the chance he needed to make the world a better place.

He polished his glass eye with a tissue. Blue followed him back and forth, occasionally looking up at his master; wondering what was happening. Alan had spoken at length with The Crane, who in turn was talking to The Oddities about joining the fight. Alan's phone was dead and he had lost track of time. He had to go and he had to go now; he couldn't wait any longer. Turning his back on the old warehouse, he began to head home. A door opened behind him, and crouching as he came through the doorway, the lanky Crane walked over to him with a grim look. He was about to speak when a massive explosion shook the ground. Alan looked towards the cavern entrance miles away; a bright orange haze glowed over the city. He closed his eyes and thought about Jon for a moment, a bitter smile on his face. There was no time to mourn.

$

Hanisi and Marica had driven out of the wastelands. They had attempted to call Alan, but the signals were down. The streets which were usually lifeless in this part of the city were busy, Oddities and humans, both young and old, were heading towards the stadium. The gangs of Aris had sent out the word. The battle was about to begin. Hanisi was at the wheel and he pushed his foot to the metal. Moaning muffled voices and pained groans came from the rear of the van as it bumped up and down over potholes. The guns and ammo in the back moved about, bruising the three taped-up bodies.

Marica turned to her brother, half smiling, "what are we

going to do with them?"

Hanisi smiled back, "I have no idea."

A giant fireball lit up the city. Smiles left their faces.

⅋

Adria stirred from her coma-like sleep. Her body ached: every bone, every muscle throbbed. Her brain felt as though it would burst from her ears.

The building seemed to rock and she looked about curiously. She was laid on a makeshift bed, surrounded by beer kegs. "What was that? An earthquake?"

She tried to stand, but her legs gave in and she almost vomited again. Fear gripped her, not fear of where she was, not fear for her life; it was the fear of losing her only friend. 'Where was it?' She needed her friend to stop the pain. To block out the visions, the dreams. 'Where was the Cane?' That's what mattered, that's all she could think of; all the fucked-up shit going on was cast aside, rational thinking lost. Only the buzz, only the high, that's all she wanted.

"Where are you?" she cried out.

⅋

Sophia burst out from the main door of The Golden Goose with Ratty by her side and the overladen woman who was brandishing the largest heavy machine gun Sophia had ever seen. Bullet casings flew as she pulled on the trigger, riddling the Klóns with holes. Sophia watched as the Klóns fell, a strange sadness in her eyes. Behind her, in the distance, the giant ball of fire lashed at the wet rock walls and ceiling. Tears welled up in her eyes as she knew Jon was dead, sacrificing his own life for the people of Aris. It was bittersweet, in the end, which is how he wanted it.

The battle for freedom. The struggle of Aris had begun.

CHAPTER TWENTY-SIX

Bliksem drove several blocks away, before turning a corner and pulling up onto the pavement. He left the vehicle running. In front of him was his army standing to attention, row upon row of Klón and human soldiers. Six moles, the deadly drilling machines, sat in front of the parade. Hovering above their heads were the newly developed Dragonfly drones. Their synthetic wings hummed, as they flapped faster than the eye could see.

Bliksem spoke into his radio. "Techno, we are ready."

"Yes, sir," answered the enthusiastic cripple from the comms room. He would be of little use on the ground when the fighting began. But in the comms room he would be Bliksem's eyes and ears. He had sent scout drones to the main entrance of Aris. "The wall has fallen," he said nervously.

Bliksem did not reply.

Instead his face began to turn purple, veins started to bulge in his neck. Spitting on the floor angrily, he looked up. A set of lights from a moving vehicle came into view, heading straight towards him. He didn't flinch. He watched the truck approaching until it halted in front of him.

Stór jumped out of the vehicle. "She was not there; she must be with the rest of the scum."

Bliksem replied coldly, "tell the men to kill everyone, but not the women. I want those two girls alive."

"What about Alander?" Stór quizzed him.

"The Chemist has finally deciphered the DNA code. He dies."

Stór nodded and joined the ranks, passing on Bliksem's orders which slowly filtered through the army.

Bliksem spoke into his radio, "now."

The Moles' engines started up. The drills began to rotate, the machines tipped forward, grinding and boring into the road. Concrete and rock cracked as they drilled into the hard ground, slowly vanishing into the earth. Bliksem pulled his machete from the sheath, signalling for the army to move north. Three thousand soldiers turned on their heels in unison and began to filter through the ghetto.

The Dragonflies followed, buzzing overhead.

$

Adria hid under the blanket. The sound of gunfire above hurt her ears, frightening her. She could hear the scurrying of feet and voices. Peeking over the blanket, a man appeared from behind the beer kegs, followed by another man and another.

They were all armed as they ascended the ladder up to the bar. More and more people came out from the floor. Adria watched in disbelief as a never-ending file of armed men and women continued to pour out from the basement.

$

"Where's your dad?" Ratty asked, looking down his long, pointy nose at Sophia.

"I don't know," she snapped. "He'll be here, I know it."

Ratty looked at Sophia with obvious affection in his eyes. He put his arms around her. "You're right. He'll be okay. I love you."

Sophia smiled at him affectionately. Her gaze wandered into the surrounding tower blocks looking for her father. A long line of armed rebels began filing out of the pub and onto the street, they mingled, talked, but were ever watchful. They look scared, Sophia thought. Throughout the ghetto, the gangs of Aris mobilised and began to pour into the main square. Sophia started talking to the leaders, reassuring them that Alan would be here soon. She urged them to take up positions in the surrounding tower blocks. No one was listening; it was chaos. She began to panic, shouting louder for everyone to hear. Her voice was still drowned out by their chatter.

"Will you all calm down and shut the fuck up," came a bellowing voice.

Heads turned and voices hushed. The large woman with the necklace of bullet belts had spoken. Tara was her name. She was respected and feared just as much as the bravest of men.

"Sophia is speaking. Listen up."

Sophia acknowledged the woman with a smile and a nod and then raised her voice. The crowd, which now numbered around two thousand, listened.

"Alan has not returned. I don't know where he is. But we cannot wait for him. Bliksem is coming, the wall has fallen. Your children will be free if we can hold here." Her voice faltered. She didn't know what else to say. Moans and groans came from the crowd and they began talking amongst themselves again.

Tara stepped up next to her. "You heard the girl, Bliksem is coming. Get into your positions. Now!" she screamed her authority.

The gangs of Aris—some only armed with basic hand weapons—began to move into the surrounding tower blocks. Gun barrels poked through a hundred windows. Sophia was alone standing with her back towards The Golden Goose. 'Where was he? And, Luca, Hanisi and Marica? Why were none of them here?' A hand clasped her shoulder.

"Don't worry. He'll be back." It was Steev.

Sophia flinched but thanked him.

The doors of The Golden Goose flung open, Sophia turned to see Adria staggering out and onto the road. Steev quickly walked away.

$

A voice spoke to Bliksem on his radio.

CHAPTER TWENTY-SIX

"The girls are both here, no sign of One-Eye yet."

"Keep me updated. We're en route. You have my orders."

Bliksem returned the radio to his pocket, picking his way through the rubble. Now and then he would pass an addict huddled in a corner or curled up on the floor. The addicts would wake from their comas soon and head to the lab sector for their daily fix. The army moved speedily and stealth-like as they crept towards The Golden Goose.

$

Sophia ran towards Adria, catching her just before she fell.

"Help me," Adria cried. "Where is the Cane, where is it?"

This was the last thing Sophia needed.

The roar of an approaching van hurtling towards her distracted her from replying. She was about to reach for her handgun when she heard Hanisi calling from the driver's window not to fire. Ratty was nearby and he ran into the empty street, waving and shouting for everyone to hold fire. The van came to a halt a few feet from the pub. Marica leapt out of the cab and ran towards Sophia and Adria. She threw her arms around Sophia. "Sorry, we were held up."

"You're here now," Sophia smiled.

Marica looked at Adria, then back at Sophia. "You found her," she said, a big smile on Marica's face. "If it weren't for your hair, I wouldn't be able to tell you both apart. What's wrong with her? She looks sick."

"Cane," Sophia said through gritted teeth.

"Oh," Marica, looked at Adria again. She was swaying,

purple veins in her cheeks seemed to pull at her eyelids, showing the red flesh underneath.

"She cannot stay here, Bliksem is coming. Take her back to the stadium. Please." Sophia begged her friend. "It is what my father would want."

Marica hesitated, she wanted to stay for the fight and she was about to refuse, but studying Adria again, she said, "you must leave as well Sophia."

She was about to protest but Marica cut her of mid-sentence. "If Alan is not here now, it might be too late. You are both too important to die here and there is something evil coming, Sophia. Bliksem has created monsters far worse than the Klóns. They are coming."

Sophia thought for a moment; she knew her friend was right. Solemnly she nodded in agreement. Adria began groaning at her again. Then rested her head on Sophia's shoulder.

Tara joined the three women. "Leave, now, all of you, go! They're here." She pointed above the tower blocks. Coming into view were six lights which hummed in the darkness.

Marica reached out and took Sophia and Adria's hand and led them towards the van. Ratty was busy unloading the vehicle with Hanisi passing out the extra guns and ammo to the gangs.

"Who you got wrapped up in there?" Ratty asked, gesturing towards the three bundles.

Hanisi smiled back at him. "It's a long story."

The van emptied of the military hardware, he slammed the doors on the three bundles as Marica and Sophia helped Adria into the cab and squeezed in next to her.

"Hanisi, come on," Marica shouted out of the window.

Sophia watched the drones; their lights were growing ever

closer. Hanisi appeared at the open window. He grabbed his sister's hand.

"I'm staying here," he said.

"Oh no, you're not," Marica scorned him.

"I am. Someone has to tell Alan you are all safe and what we have seen. We're outnumbered, they need me here. Now go." He leaned in and kissed his sister.

She held him tight; her bottom lip began to tremble. "Please survive, don't die. Find us," she sobbed.

"Get back to the stadium and move everyone out of there. Head to The Core as Alan planned."

There was another massive explosion followed by another and another. The rebels hung out of windows, looking towards the southern end of the city. Cheering and shouting broke out.

Hanisi looked towards the lab sector; buildings were burning. "Luca," he said out loud and smiled. "Now go." He pulled away from his sister. Marica was reluctant to let go. She watched him walk away and disappear into The Golden Goose, then moved into the driver's seat. Adria was in between her and Sophia, unconscious.

Ratty stood in front of the van as it reversed back up the road. He mouthed, "I love you," at Sophia. She fondly smiled back at him.

$

Techno danced about in his crate. He watched his Dragonflies hover into the main square on screens in front of him. Dribble swung from his chin. He had created a system which he could control from his seat on the Klón's back. A small keyboard in front of him, he began manically punching buttons and keys. He armed the Dragonflies with their heat-seeking missiles and they were ready to fire, targeting The Golden Goose. A small joystick was in his right hand and he moved it around until the crosshair was on target on the screens in front. His finger hovered over the trigger, awaiting Bliksem's orders.

There was a huge bang and the comms room shook. The Klón carrying Techno stumbled as another explosion ripped through the lab sector.

"Noooo," Techno cried as the power went down.

The screens went blank, the lights went out: darkness. Huge cracks tore through the corridors. Scientists fell through holes which opened in the floor. Electrical equipment burst into flames. Glass shattered and cracked. Rubble fell from above. Screams for help echoed throughout the lab sector.

Aris was falling.

CHAPTER TWENTY-SEVEN

The Chemist held onto the tiny foetus, keeping the embryo tight against her flat bosom. She had connected tubes onto her breast, attached to the embryo's mouth. The Chemist had crafted a medicine from female hormones, allowing her to produce breast milk. The foetus being undeveloped, needed a tremendous amount of nourishment, draining her energy.

The laboratory rocked and shuddered. Emergency lighting flashed on and off sporadically, causing mayhem. Launching towards the desk, the Chemist scooped up a handful of papers with her free hand. She stuffed them into the pocket of her long white lab jacket. She then reached for her radio.

"Techno, can you hear me? Techno?"

The radio crackled and for a moment there was silence. A huge crack appeared in the floor and began to branch out until a huge hole opened. The large tank which fed the foetuses slid towards the gap, dragging with it monitors and other electrical machines, which then burst into flame.

"Yes," Techno finally replied.

"What's happening?" The Chemist screamed down the radio. Another explosion knocked her off her feet, but she caught herself with her elbows on the desk.

"The wall is down, the whole sector is down; Aris is falling. The rebel gangs have destroyed everything," Techno shouted into the radio.

"Head to the escape shaft. Meet me there." The Chemist had to shout above the noise of falling rubble and spitting fires which broke out around her.

"What about Bliksem?" Techno yelled back.

"Fuck Bliksem. I have what the Chancellor wanted. We must get to Iris."

$

The bloodthirsty crowd were shouting excitedly in the Baráttan pit arena when the floor caved in. The whole angry mob and desperate contestants were sucked into the void. The prison crumbled and the courtyard was a large smoking hole. Many of the inmates escaped. Word was spreading that the wall to the outside world had fallen and that an uprising had begun. Many were willing to join the fight, arming themselves with crude weapons; bricks, metal bars, anything they could find.

Faze addicts waking from their drug-induced comas began their regular procession towards the main entrance to the lab sector. But it was now rubble. Thousands of the addicted stood there in bewilderment, their minds no longer their own.

It would not compute; they would not get the fix they needed to stay alive. Their bodies would give up. There would be no handouts today or tomorrow; they would all die. They remained though, staring blankly into the burning lab sector, like brain-dead zombies, expectantly waiting for the Faze rations.

They were not coming.

$

The van drove away from the main square. The three women were silent apart from Adria's occasional groan.

Finally, Marica spoke, "how did Adria react to the news?"

"I haven't told her yet," Sophia shrugged her shoulders. "How can I? Look at the mess she's in. She killed those two brothers. They've messed her up."

Marica looked impressed Adria had killed Vasiliy and Mikhail. "She's got your DNA alright. Wait until she finds out that you are both the same person, give or take a couple of years—that's going to mess her up." Marica turned the wheel as she spoke and pulled onto the straight road which would take them into the wastelands.

"How do I even tell her what we are? Where do I start?" Sophia looked confused.

Marica looked to her oldest and dearest friend. "How did Alan tell you?"

Sophia thought about it; she couldn't remember. "I worked most of it out myself, I think."

"Well, we need to get out of Aris alive first and somehow

wean her off that blue shit. After all, it's not every day you get told you're a female Klón."

She nodded grimly.

Sophia rested her eyes and laid her head on top of Adria's. Her thoughts took her back to her childhood. She was eight years of age when she escaped the lab sector with her father and Jon. She remembered crying, clawing at Alan's hand to return for Adria, but the fire was too fierce. They sought refuge with the Tears of Aris. The Crane saw to it that Alan and Jon received medical attention. Jon's spine was broken, her father had lost his eye and his right leg was damaged.

Alan, of course, was not Sophia's biological father. Professor Alander was one of the greatest minds in the System, brought to Aris for his knowledge of artificial intelligence and his ground-breaking DNA reform program. Initially, the Klóns were being tested as labourers, to work the farms and slaughterhouses. But their sheer size and strength, as well as minds which were easy to manipulate, made them far better soldiers. Faze was then brought to Aris to subdue the human workforce. Alander was openly against its use and distanced himself from the experiment. The Chemist led the Faze program.

Pressure from The Chancellor and his son Bliksem to create a stronger, even more robust Klón, was placed on Alander's shoulders and after some years he had a breakthrough. Stór was born, stronger and more intelligent than the Klóns before him.

The Chancellor still wanted more; he wanted female Klóns, so he and Bliksem could breed with them in order to create a superhuman, forging a bloodline which would live forever. Alan refused to continue his work, and for his disobedience he was met with blackmail. His wife and children, who still resided in Iris, were threatened with death. Alander succumbed to their threats and he continued his work. After many failings, Sophia was finally born. Healthy and beautiful, unlike the Klóns before her. Her body grew at the same rate as a human, and to make the situation worse for the fate of Alander's family, Sophia did not produce a womb. They murdered Alan's wife and his children were forced into slavery—or so he was told. Alander broke for some time and he refused to eat, or work, but in time he eventually returned to the lab. He had Sophia to raise now.

Four years later, he successfully produced another female Klón. He named her Adria. More years passed and Alander watched the city of Aris slowly fall apart. He mourned helplessly for the people he loved who were turned into brain dead addicts. Adria, just like Sophia, grew like a human. Their DNA came from the same woman. Adria and Sophia were almost identical, but Adria would be able to carry children. Her DNA had been modified in the same way as Stór's: she would be as strong as him and even more intelligent in time. The Chancellor and Bliksem were still not happy, as they wanted Klóns they could breed with immediately.

Deceived, Alan learned his children had been executed by family on their mother's side. He knew time was running out. He had brought up the two girls as his own and he would not see them turned into whores for Bliksem and his twisted father. Alander attempted to destroy all his work and take his new daughters to freedom. After he blew the lab up alongside his work colleague, Jon, they hid under the nose of the System in plain sight. But Alander had never given up on finding Adria.

Sophia had a gut-wrenching feeling that she would never

see her father again. He had taught her so much. He would sit her upon his knee, then pretend to sneeze making his glass eye pop out. Sophia was fascinated with the eye—she would sometimes hide it from Alander. He would hold the eye up to the light and Sophia thought the colours inside were almost fluid-like. Alander would give her maths or science tests and when she was stuck on a question he would roll the eye across the desk and say, "the answer is staring you in the face," then laughing, pop it back into the socket.

The van jolted to a stop, waking Sophia from her thoughts. She looked up and out of the windscreen. They were at the stadium. A young teenager stood in front of the van, the beam from the headlights lighting her up. She had a big smile on her face.

"Who's that?" Marica said.

"It's Zarrah," Sophia smiled back at her.

$

Bliksem's forces had taken up position around The Golden Goose. He had climbed ten flights of stairs and now looked down into the main square with Stór by his side. Bliksem held out a hand and Stór handed him a set of binoculars. A multitude of explosions from the lab sector echoed through Aris and he helplessly watched as the Dragonflies hovering overhead came crashing to the ground. All the drones throughout the city lost power and fell. The thousands of screens and cameras which littered the streets ceased to operate. Bliksem screamed, "fuck this, what's happened now?"

A human officer came running into the room behind them, red-faced and panting. "Sir," he said breathlessly.

"What is it now?" He turned on the officer with purple-faced fury.

"The lab sector, the prison," the officer stuttered, "it's gone."

"Gone… Gone where? My arsehole?" Bliksem lurched forward, squaring up in the man's face.

"The gangs, they have blown the whole lot up… Sir."

He grabbed the officer by the collar and spun him around, throwing him through the glass window. The officer screamed as he plummeted to the earth. Bliksem turned on Stór. "Kill them all, women and children. Leave none alive."

Stór left the room.

Bliksem looked back through his binoculars. 'Where was One-Eye?' The Major bit his lip. His father would kill him for this—he would be disowned by his family. Returning to Iris a disgrace was not an option. Alander. This was all his fault. He looked through the binoculars at The Golden Goose. A vision of how he would kill Alander painted a pretty picture in his mind. He left the room to join his men.

$

Tara had taken control of the gangs and along with Hanisi they attempted to form some order. They split their forces into four. Tara would protect the pub. Hanisi was setting up a defensive position to defend the square from a tower block to the right of the pub. Ratty would take a quarter of the of the gangs and would build a barricade in the centre of the square, using a line of rusted cars and debris from buildings. Anything they could find was added to the blockade: doors, window frames, tables, and chairs were dragged out from the pub. The remaining militia was held back a few hundred yards down the road. Steev was amongst them. Most of the people here were armed with simple weapons: hammers, rakes, bricks, baseball bats with twelve-inch nails embedded in them. They would add support if the Klóns breached the blockade.

$

A thousand pairs of red dot eyes came out from the darkness. The human soldiers were shadowed by the Klóns who were all armed with high-powered machine guns. They marched in perfect timing. Bliksem led the line, his face twisted in determined rage. Meanwhile, Stór had climbed to the very top of a high-rise tower block. He positioned himself in a corner overlooking the whole scene. On his back he carried a sniper rifle. Pulling the strap off his shoulder, he pointed the gun towards The Golden Goose. His sights fell on an Oddity who was peeking through a first-floor window. Stór settled the gun, slowly putting pressure on the trigger.

Bang. The Oddity took the bullet in the forehead, his head rocking back and forth. Slumping forward, he fell from the window. Both armies came to a standstill, watching the Oddity fall through the air in silent slow motion. A surreal, eerie silence spread across the battlefield.

Then the floor began to rumble.

CHAPTER TWENTY-EIGHT

The Oddity lay on the path outside the entrance of The Golden Goose, blood trickled from the hole in his forehead. The gangs of Aris opened fire, orange muzzles blasted from open windows and framed broken glass.

Klóns were pebble-dashed with bullets but somehow, they kept moving along the wet ground. One Klón was hit a dozen times before a shot took him in the face and he stumbled to the floor, his eyes turning to grey.

Bliksem had moved to the rear of the ranks. The road in between his forces and the angry gangs of Aris began to crack. Tarmac and concrete bulged, swelling up in mounds. Puddles which were still growing from the monsoon rain disappeared into the earth as the grinding of drills erupted from the ground. Techno had been able to send a program out to the Moles before the power cut off. The six deadly corkscrew-like drills wheeled out from the ground on their tracks. The metal spines opened outward like a clam's shell, revealing their deadly payload. Bullets bounced off them like hail on a tin roof, not inflicting any damage. Hanisi watched from a window, high up in the tower block which sat next to the pub. "Quick bring me the rocket launcher," he called to one of the Oddities stood around him.

A small pudgy man with more chins than you could count answered him. The tiniest of legs carried his large body as he waddled over to Hanisi, passing him the missile launcher. They only had four missiles so each one needed to count. There was no better shot than Hanisi or his sister. Marica crossed his mind and he prayed silently to himself that she would make it out of Aris safely.

The Moles opened fire before Hanisi even had a chance to load the rocket launcher, armed with heat-seeking missiles which whizzed with a screeching sound through the cavern air. Twelve rockets slammed into The Golden Goose, exploding on impact. Body parts, rubble, and splintered wood flew into the air amidst desperate screams for help from within the pursuing inferno.

Hanisi looked down on the destruction and grimaced. People were launching themselves from high windows, their clothes on fire. The terrifying screams of a woman jumping from a top window engulfed in flames ended with her body breaking on the road below. More people jumped from the top of The Golden Goose, attempting to escape the blaze, only to die on hard concrete.

Hanisi aimed.

The funny-looking man placed a rocket into the rear of the launcher. "Loaded," he said.

Hanisi lined up the nearest Mole. The mechanised arms had

retracted back into the metal shell, reloading. He closed his eyes. Taking a deep breath, he reopened them and pulled on the trigger. The missile whistled towards its target, exploding on impact. The rocket left an empty crater where the Mole had sat.

Stór was busy taking out burning bodies who rolled about, desperately trying to extinguish the flames which melted their skin. He performed his task with deadly accuracy. He didn't see where the rocket Hanisi had fired came from. He combed the high rises with his red eyes, intently searching for the source.

"Loaded," shouted the little man again.

Hanisi pulled the trigger, taking out a second Mole which burst into flames. The remaining Moles continued bombing the pub. A handful of people bundled out of the front door, Tara being one of them. She looked towards Ratty. His men were pinned down behind the barricade whilst the advancing army blasted holes in their defences. The bullets were coming too quickly for the gang members to respond. They huddled and cowed, desperately trying to avoid the shower of bullets. The weapons the Klóns carried were too powerful. The rounds punctured the barricades, splintering wood, leaving large holes in metal. Dozens had fallen; men, women, human and Oddity.

A loud crack sounded as the beams gave way. The sound of the dying building echoed about the square. The fighting almost came to a standstill as the two armies watched the roof of The Golden Goose collapse in on itself. The walls fell outward, crushing burning bodies. A vast blanket of dusty smoke blew across the battlefield, giving the rebels a chance to fight back through the grey mist.

Tara had just managed to move away from the falling debris. She ran towards Ratty, her foot stepped over the old pub sign which lay scorched on the floor.

"We're fucked," she screamed at him over the ricochet of bullets which rattled onto the old car they were hiding behind.

"Should I call a retreat?" Ratty looked at her.

"Retreat to where? There is nowhere to go; we need to buy the others enough time to get the children out of this shit hole." Tara rose to her feet, brandishing her heavy machine gun, a bullet belt hung from the weapon. She screamed at the gang members hiding behind the makeshift wall. "Come on."

The dust was beginning to settle as she climbed up onto a car, standing on the roof. She let the bullets fly into the faces of Bliksem's approaching men; they were only yards away from the barricades. Ratty signalled for reinforcements to join the line.

Steev shouted out, "now."

The five hundred strong, poorly armed regiment charged to the wall of death. The gangs of Aris clambered out from behind the barricade, desperate and brave. They fell in scores to the ground. Mad, red-eyed Klóns shot them down mercilessly.

Hanisi had watched The Golden Goose crumble and the charge of reinforcements. The Moles were empty of ammo and sat idle. Bliksem's forces were too close to the barricade for him and his men to lay down fire. He couldn't risk hitting his people. Hanisi turned. "Nothing we can do here now, boys," he motioned for his small force to follow him.

A bullet whistled past his ear, striking the little man in the back of the head. Hanisi instinctively fell to the floor. Keeping low, he crawled towards the doorway.

☙

Hanisi and his men ran out from the ground floor of the tower block, with the aim of circling Bliksem's forces. Another man took a sniper's bullet to the chest. They upped the pace, but Stór was picking them off one by one. Hanisi watched the rooftops until he finally spotted a blast from the sniper's rifle.

He shouted over his shoulder, "join the fight. I'm going to get him." He pointed up to the rooftop, as he veered south towards the tower block which Stór was firing from.

His men continued forward and opened fire onto the rear of Bliksem's forces.

Tara was still standing atop the car screaming with fury. Bliksem had gone back into the cover of a high rise behind him where half his force hid, waiting impatiently to join the fight. He waved his machete forward and they ran out from the shadows.

Hanisi's men had no chance; suddenly, they were sur-rounded and massacred. Klóns pulled limbs from the sockets, twisted necks, and crushed bodies underfoot. The surprise attack took down every single one of them. Bliksem's forces pushed forward.

"Take her down,'" Bliksem pointed at Tara.

A human soldier aimed from a distance, letting a bullet fly. It got Tara in the shoulder and she fell back over the barricade. Bliksem's men pressed on. The gangs of Aris were outnumbered and the blockade crumbled.

The battle was lost.

֍

Around fifty rebels knelt on the floor with their hands behind their heads, surrounded by Bliksem's men. Guns hovered over them, smoke drifting from hot barrels. Bliksem stood on the car; Tara was now on her knees, with her back to his legs. His machete was tight against her neck. She grimaced in pain as blood soaked through her top from the bullet hole in her shoulder.

"Where is One-Eye?" Bliksem glared at the desperate men lined up on the floor in front of him. "Where is he?"

No one spoke, at first.

Then Ratty responded, "he was in the pub; he didn't come out."

Bliksem eyed the pointy man's face. "Are you lying to me, boy?" Bliksem sneered at him angrily.

Tara tried to move and Bliksem applied more pressure with his blade, slicing the skin on her neck just enough to make her keep still.

"Where are the two girls?" he continued, agitated.

Tara shouted out, "Fuck you Blik-,"

Her throat spat out blood and spots splashed Bliksem's crazed face.

His eyes searched the prisoners for another victim. A ruckus had started in the ranks way back behind him. Turning, he tried to make out what was happening. Loud voices and shouting turned to screams of horror as the sound of bullets being fired rang out. The floor trembled and his army parted like a wave in front of him. The unmistakable roar of a Vinayaki bellowed. Bliksem watched wide-eyed as it thundered towards him. Riding on the Vinayaki's back were three figures. He recognised one of them. His champion of the Baráttan pits, Olaf.

Bliksem's jaw went slack.

The Vinayaki charged towards him and thrust his massive skull into Bliksem's chest, throwing him through the air like a rag doll. He landed with a back-breaking crunch.

Bliksem's army became overrun as Luca led the army of angry prisoners with him. Olaf and Luca leapt from the beast. Courtauld held onto the bull's reins as the creature continued to crush and head butt the enemy. Swinging his deadly tail, the Vinayaki broke any Klóns within reach with its mighty power.

Bliksem's body lay smashed. He was going to die, but not before his broken hand reached for the radio. He spoke softly into it, "Release them."

$

Several blocks away two lorries revved their engines and began to crawl towards the main square. The trailers' walls were being hammered on from within.

The Hollow Eyes were hungry.

$

Hanisi was nearing the top floor. He glanced out of a window, smiling as he saw Luca riding in on a Vinayaki. But Bliksem's forces still outnumbered them five to one. Hanisi carried on up the steps, sweat pouring from his face. The tattoo of the tiger on his brow looked fierce in the dim light of the stairwell.

$

Bliksem's army regrouped, as did the gangs of Aris. They stood facing each other over the road. Thousands of dead and dying bodies lined the street between them. Courtauld still sat upon the Vinayaki, although it was severely injured now. Bullet holes leaked blood from all over the bull's tough skin.

Bliksem was crawling away, coughing blood. He dragged himself to the street corner where he could watch the final battle. The two factions eyed each other as the city around them burned. Faze addicts ran about the streets; lost—brains scatty and confused.

Olaf stood in front of the rebel line, his muscular, hairy arms pulsated with adrenaline, eyeing up the Klóns. He was about to charge across the street when two sets of headlights came into view. Everyone paused on both sides. Suddenly Bliksem's army began to run back into the high rise tower block behind them. The Vinayaki became unsettled and began to thrash around nervously. The gangs of Aris stepped back as the two lorries pulled up in front of them. Their heavy wheels crushed the remaining life out of any survivors on the blood-soaked street. Bliksem looked up, blood showing on his white teeth in a sinister smile.

The rear doors of the trucks opened, slowly lowering down

a ramp. The gangs readied themselves. A shot rang out and another man fell from Stor's rifle. A strange noise came from the rear of the vehicles. A terrifying, hollow screech. Sniffing hungrily at the air, a tall woman stepped out onto the ramp, her body unnaturally hunched. Her empty eye sockets, black and hollow, made her look demented. Her nose twitched, her head turning towards them. She shrieked and leapt towards the rebels. Hundreds of the Hollow Eyes followed her out of the trailers, sensing fresh meat. They moved at such a speed that they were all over the gangs in seconds.

Men and women dropped their weapons and fled. The Vinayaki turned in sudden panic and threw Courtauld off his back, but before the sad beast could run, the Hollow Eyes were on him. They ripped into his flesh, tearing chunks from the animal's legs. The bull stumbled and fell. Courtauld crawled away horrified.

Olaf had dropped onto the ground and was holding off a Hollow-Eyed woman, his hands around her neck. She pecked at him with razor-sharp teeth which chomped and snapped. He slammed a massive fist into the side of her head repeatedly with all his power, but the thing would not budge. Luca ran up behind the Hollowed-Eyed woman, putting a bullet in her brain. No blood came from the wound, but she flopped to the side, dead.

"Did you see that I hit her twenty times and she didn't move once?" Olaf looked around.

The gangs of Aris were becoming dinner for the Hollow Eyes. Prisoners and gang members ran for their lives. Some fell and were torn to pieces, horrifying screams filling the air. The Vinayaki lay lifeless on the floor; half a dozen Hollow Eyes had gnawed into his stomach and were feasting on the bull's innards.

Luca looked around him. "Shoot them in the brain," he shouted.

The one saving grace was this: once the Hollow Eyes tasted flesh they carried on eating their victim, blind to the world about them.

Another man fell from the sniper shooting from above.

Olaf looked up towards the source of the shot, "Bastard."

He spotted the heavy machine gun which Tara had been carrying laid next to her pale corpse and ran towards it. His huge fists knocked the heads of Hollow Eyes who leapt at him. One grabbed onto his foot, sinking sharp teeth into his calf muscle, forcing him to stop. He slammed a huge foot down on the monster's head, making a surprising sound. There was no cracking or snapping of bone—it sounded like their whole bodies were hollow, not only their eye sockets. He carried on limping until he reached the machine gun and threw the heavy gun's strap over his shoulder. Ripping the last bullet belt from Tara's torso, he loaded the gun.

"Duck! Get fucking down," his voice thundered.

The gang members and prisoners leapt for cover. Olaf opened fire, roaring in triumph as the bullet shells spun into the air and the Hollow Eyes fell. Some of them looked up from their bloody dinner to a bullet in the brain. It was easy pickings for Olaf.

Luca was busy executing the Hollow Eyes, who were preoccupied eating the dead. The machine gun roared until Olaf was surrounded by smoke and empty shells. He threw the smoking gun to the floor and looked about him. Courtauld had crawled to his side and Luca was to his right. A dozen other men, a few Oddities, and inmates stood with them. The smoke cleared.

The Hollow Eyes were dead. But from across the road, the red eyes of the Klóns re-emerged from the shadows.

"A hundred to one. I've had worse odds," Olaf laughed.

Luca looked at the hefty man and smiled grimly.

⚡

Bliksem watched on as his army returned to the battlefield. The sound of approaching vehicles from the east made him turn his head. Dozens of headlights appeared down the road tearing towards Bliksem's army. Gunshots rang out from the moving cars. The human soldiers in his army dropped their weapons and ran. He cursed them as he slowly pushed his shattered body up the wall until he was upright. There were at least twenty vehicles which pulled up in front of the Klóns, guns blazing.

A dog was running behind the cars, barking, a blue handkerchief fell from his neck and turned red from the blood-soaked streets. Bliksem watched the dog run up to a bald one-eyed man as he stepped out from a car.

"Alander," Bliksem spat the words out loud enough for him to hear.

Alander turned, his one eye meeting Bliksem for the first time in twelve years.

CHAPTER TWENTY-NINE

Hanisi reached the top floor of the tower block but Stór had blocked the door to the rooftop. He needed the advantage of surprise, so smashing the door down was not an option. He moved back down a level, creeping through the dank building. Inside the smell of gun smoke and the burning buildings of Aris overtook the damp odour. He looked out of a broken window at the small courtyard fifty floors below. A group of odd-looking half-naked men and women sat around a fire. Two more men were dragging a corpse towards them. Hanisi thought the dead body looked like one of Bliksem's men. He could smell burning flesh in the air.

He climbed out onto the ledge. The stonework was falling apart and although dangerous, this gave him a foothold to ascend the outer wall. Slowly, he crawled spider-like up the decaying brickwork, up and over onto the roof. He looked around. Tucked up in the corner he saw the sniper. Hanisi gulped when he realised it was Stór. The strongest and fiercest of all Klóns.

℥

Alander, The Crane, and Tusker moved towards Bliksem. He tried to speak but coughed blood. Tusker grabbed him by his collar and Alander signalled with a nod to follow him.

The Tears of Aris had come to the fight and formed a line with the few survivors. Bliksem's army was now outnumbered and the Klóns looked at their enemy, confused. A pile of their dead lay in the middle of the road. Alander and The Crane walked up to the mound. Tusker followed, dragging Bliksem by his crazy red hair. He threw the Major to the floor. The Klóns grew restless seeing their master treated this way.

Alander looked towards the Klóns. "You need not fight anymore," he shouted across the road, then he looked down at Bliksem. "Tell them to stand down. This is over."

Bliksem spat at him. His face was ghostly white.

"Kill them all. I order you," Bliksem cried.

The Klóns moved forward as one. Alan turned to the Tears of Aris as Blue growled by his feet at the oncoming Klóns. The crowd gathered in front of Alander had known him for twelve years.

He looked at Luca and nodded. "Sophia, Adria?" he asked.

Luca looked to Ratty. He was injured and covered in blood.

"They left before the fighting started," Ratty said.

Relief showed on Alander's face.

The Klóns were cautiously advancing.

Alander raised his voice to the gangs of Aris. "Our fortune is like the moon some of you have never seen; we are changeable, ever waxing and waning. This is a hateful life. First, it oppresses and then soothes as the fancy takes it. Poverty, power—it melts like ice. Fate is monstrous and empty. We are a malevolent whirling wheel. Well-being is vain and fades to nothing."

Alan's face was full of emotion as he spoke and the gangs of Aris took in every word as he bellowed out the words with passion.

"Shadowed and veiled, it plagues us all now through this game." Alan ripped his shirt from his body, revealing his torso, scarred and burnt by fire. "I bring my bare back to their vanity, to their villainy. Fate is again health and virtue. Drive on, weighted, always enslaved. So, at this hour and without delay, pluck the vibrating strings, since fate strikes down the strong man. Weep with me, fight with me."

The gangs of Aris roared with new energy.

Courtauld looked up at Olaf, who was raring for the fight. "You didn't understand a word of that, did you?"

"No, but he sounded fucking good," laughed Olaf and he charged forward.

Luca looked up at Alan, standing tall on top of a mound of dead Klóns as Bliksem lay dying at his feet. There was not a man or woman amongst them who would not give their life for Alander. And they all charged forward, waving, firing, and shooting their weapons, screaming furiously. Luca met Alander. He was about to reassure him his girls would be safe when blood suddenly splattered over Luca's face.

Alander fell forward and Luca caught his body, a sniper's bullet in his back.

"No," Luca cried.

☱

Adria stumbled out of the van, catching sight of Zarrah, the young girl who had saved her life in the polytunnel. Her stomach groaned with cramps, and buckling over, she vomited a pale blue liquid. Sophia placed an arm around her, holding back Adria's hair.

"It is going to be okay. It will be out of your system soon," Sophia spoke gently.

All Adria wanted to do was curl up in a ball and hide away. She tried to speak, but the taste of chemicals ravaged her tongue and she retched again, making her eyes stream. The blue Cane that washed around in her body also dripped from her stuffy nostrils.

Coughing, she wiped the rank taste off her lips before asking Sophia, "where are we? Where are we going?"

"We are at the old stadium. We are all leaving Aris and heading to The Core."

Adria looked up from her hunched position, confusion showed on her pale face. "Leaving Aris? The Core? Where is that? Why?"

"The Core is north from here; it will take months to get there. It is beyond the System's reach and our father has friends there which can help us all start a new life," Sophia tried to explain.

Adria stood upright and stared into her sister's eyes. "Father? I have no father," Adria sounded bitter; her pale face began to turn red.

"You do and he loves you. Please understand there is so much you don't know and you are not well enough to take it all in right now," Sophia replied.

"I'm fine. I just need another blast of Cane. That's all I need," Adria grew angrier.

Sophia was about to reply when Zarrah walked over to them both. Adria calmed down, seeing the youngster approach. Meanwhile, Marica stood at the back of the van talking to Connor, the two-toned young man who had saved her and Hanisi from the gun traffickers. They were discussing what to do with the three bundles which still rolled about groaning in the back.

"Cut them free," Marica told Connor.

Connor pulled a large knife from his belt and went about cutting the tape. The fat feline mother stretched and growled her disapproval at being tied up.

She stared at Marica with her yellow dot eyes. "I always remember a face," she hissed at her.

Marica smiled back, "so do I."

The feline's sons were cut free and immediately they began harassing their mother for milk.

"Not now," she howled at them. They lowered their faces avoiding their mother's scornful look. "Come, we need to go," she slapped both her sons around the ear and they darted off in the direction of the main entrance. The large mother gave one last lingering look at Marica, before vanishing out of sight.

Marica had a feeling their paths would cross again.

A series of explosions rocked the floor. The children and elderly who had hidden underground emerged from darkness, their scared faces glowed in the fires burning throughout the city. Marica looked towards the lab sector as more blasts continued. She hoped Luca was safe.

The explosions frightened Adria. The noise from the bombs

vibrated around her head, making her feel disorientated. Her eyes felt heavy—she was about to collapse. Sophia and Zarrah caught her just in time. Together they laid her in the cab of the van. Adria slept.

Sophia, Marica, and Connor went about organising the crowd which now gathered around them. Connor picked two men from the group who he knew could drive, and they set off with Marica towards the hidden lorries which were not far away.

"There are too many people back there," Connor looked at Marica concerned.

"We will fit them all on, even if they have to sit on the roof," Marica snapped back.

It was unusual for her to speak that way, Connor thought. "Where is Hanisi?" he dared to ask.

Tight-lipped, trying not to show any emotion, she mumbled, "he will be here soon."

She doubted her own words and her stomach churned nervously.

$

Hanisi kept low to the floor, Stór almost in reach. The Klón looked through the sights of his rifle, watching as Tusker threw Bliksem to the ground. First, he targeted Tusker, then, his sights fell over Alander. But a shadow caught his eye.

A sharp pain ripped into his back just under the rib cage. Stór pulled the trigger and Alander fell. Stór turned on Hanisi, who had sprung back a few yards, took another shot, the gun clicked empty. He cursed his luck and removed his bow from his back and before Stór could rise to his feet an arrow took him in the chest, followed by another. The huge Klón didn't flinch and began steaming towards Hanisi. He managed to release another arrow which punctured Stór's stomach. It didn't slow him down. His large hand grabbed Hanisi by the neck and he began to squeeze it tightly, lifting him off the floor. Hanisi kicked out frantically, clawing at the Klón's vice-like grip. Stór stomped over to the edge of the rooftop and dangled Hanisi over the street below. He was losing consciousness and Stór became a giant blur.

Able to pull an arrow from his quiver, he brought it down with as much strength as he could muster. Stór cried out, the arrow protruding from his right eye socket. Stór roared and launched Hanisi into the air. Hanisi's body fell a hundred feet down without making a sound.

Stór crumpled to his knees. He pulled the arrows from his body, plucking the one from his now dull red eye socket. His face twisted as he tried to stand up. Banging came from the rooftop door which he had barred from the outside. A dozen fists seemed to be hitting at the door, and the weight of whatever was behind it made the door buckle as it swung open when the hinges shattered.

The pitter-patter of bare feet ran towards him. Stór looked up in horror.

"Bitings, bitings, bitings."

CHAPTER THIRTY

The battle was over. Bliksem lay dead from his wounds, blood curdled around his purple lips. Alander's head lay upon Luca's lap as Blue licked at Alander's hands. The Tears of Aris had decimated the remaining Klóns.

The city was burning. Rocks were beginning to fall from above, crashing into buildings and rooftops, smashing roads, crushing people who fled in the mayhem. The air was thick with dust and smoke. Waves of bats flew out of the underground city, seeking a new home. The victors surrounded Alander. Olaf was there, Courtauld leaned on a makeshift crutch, Steev standing beside them. They were blackened and bruised. Tusker was organising the Tears of Aris, seeing to the wounded and loading them onto their vehicles. They also picked weapons off the dead Klóns and searched the dead for anything of use.

The Crane bent over, like a sighing tree bowing under the weight of summer leaves. "Alander, you did it, we've won," he said. Holding out a hand, he gripped Alander's.

Alander smiled. "Pass me that will you?" he pointed to his handkerchief, which had fallen from Blue's neck.

The Crane passed it to him.

"Luca, in my pocket," he struggled for air as he spoke.

He reached into Alander's trouser pocket and pulled out his glass eye. Alander took the cloth from him and wrapped it in the fabric.

The sound of falling rubble signalled time was running out.

"What are you waiting for," he coughed blood. "Let's get out of here."

Luca patted Olaf on the back and gestured for him to help Alander. The huge man lifted Alander, who groaned in agony, off the floor and carried him to one of the waiting vehicles, which were full of survivors. Alander lay on the rear seat of an open-topped car. He sat up briefly, just in time to see a considerable chunk of the rock fall from above and crash onto the burnt sign of The Golden Goose. He sighed with a bitter smile and lay down.

The Tears of Aris moved out of the square. All around them, people were fleeing. Disoriented Faze addicts darted back and forth trying to find cover, military men and prison wardens had ditched their uniforms and were making a break for freedom. As more and more debris fell, a wave of dust followed the convoy as the whole lab sector collapsed in on itself. A section of the cavern ceiling fell, crashing into the stagnant lake. And for the first time, stars looked down on the crumbling city of Aris.

Tusker drove at the head of the convoy. As they pulled away from the square, a voice cried out to wait. Coming out from the dust was Ratty. He was holding a lifeless body in his arms.

He passed the dead body of Hanisi onto the rear of a truck and jumped on board, his pointed face grim. Tears had left tracks on his dusty cheeks.

Coming in from a side road, Tusker noticed the headlights of three lorries. He put his foot on the brake and waited. The leading truck pulled out in front of them. Hanging off the sides, sat on the roofs and crammed into the open back, the children of Aris clung on.

A van followed the three lorries. Sophia was at the wheel. They could not stop, not here; the whole cavern was on the verge of collapse. She looked out the window, hoping to see Alander. But the visibility was getting worse. The convoy crawled up the hill to where the wall and entrance to Aris once was, now nothing but a decimated pile of metal and rubble twisted amongst burning timber. Sophia's eyes fixed on two metal handles of a wheelchair which protruded through the ruins.

Tears formed in her eyes as she slowly drove by.

$

"Come on. You're a fucking idiot," Techno moaned at the Klón who struggled with his massive frame in the small tunnel.

Following them were a few armed men and sandwiched between them was The Chemist, holding her baby under her coat. Her lanky legs struggled to find footholds as she moved. They had been in the darkness for an hour and the tunnel had got steeper and steeper.

Techno tried to look over the Klón's shoulder. He spotted a

light briefly. "We are almost there, come on," he pushed his carrier.

Finally, they crawled out from under the ground and found they were standing on top of the rocky mountain. Smoke filled the air as it escaped through the entrance to Aris. In front of them was a fortified hangar. A dozen Klóns patrolled the area. They recognised Techno and looked at him dumbly.

"Quickly open the doors," he looked up at the night sky, the moon full and bright. The doors opened and just inside the hangar, dozens of dune buggies were lined up.

The Chemist began barking orders. "Fill them with fuel, all of them," she yelled, pointing at the cars.

The Klóns dutifully complied. Techno steered his Klón towards a small office and The Chemist followed behind. Inside was a single monitor, a desk littered with buttons and knobs. Techno began flicking some switches and turning dials. Machines under the office desk began to beep and the screen hissed with interference.

"Everything is still working," He jumped about excitedly. His scarred face was covered in filth which stuck to his greasy skin.

Suddenly a voice came over The Chemist's radio. "Anyone there?" the voice asked.

"This is the Chemist," she spoke slowly.

"Bliksem is dead. Alander is dying. He won't last long."

Awkwardly the Chemist tried to balance the growing foetus in one hand and the radio in another. Techno reached out offering to take the new-born.

"Don't you dare touch my baby with those festering fingers," she snapped at the legless man. Techno sat back shocked, rejection showed on his face.

The Chemist spoke into the radio again. "Where are Adria and Sophia?" she questioned the voice.

There was a brief silence. The Chemist became visibly agitated by the pause. "Well?" she snapped again.

"Your children are still alive. They are heading to The Core," came the reply.

The Chemist smiled and stroked the pink jelly-like flesh of her new-born, which was feeding furiously from her bosom.

℥

The convoy rolled out from the smoking cavern entrance. The overloaded trucks slid on the desert floor now moist and coming alive with vegetation from the monsoon rains. Vinayaki wandered on the plains, grunting warnings in the moonlight. Bats flapped blindly above and the air was warm.

Sophia looked towards Adria sat up next to her. She was shaking—craving—and had begun to cry, not because her body needed drugs, not because she had been raped and hurt.

She cried because, for the first time in her life, she could see the moon and stars.

Sophia and Zarrah also sobbed. For them, the night sky was something they could only imagine, until now. The lack of light pollution out on the plains allowed the stars to come out and they hung above a cloudless sky.

"I never knew it would look so beautiful," Sophia said.

"Look at the moon," Zarrah pointed up at the night sky, her mouth ajar, her eyes filled with wonder and excitement.

Adria remained speechless, but her face said everything.

271

Sophia noticed colour appear in her cheeks.

They drove on for what seemed an age. Marica led the convoy up a mountain pass. It plateaued at the top and she brought the vehicles to a halt. Marica leapt from her seat, desperate to find her brother, as was Sophia desperate to find her father. Her eyes searched the crowd as the men, women, children, and Oddities left the vehicles. The majority had never left Aris, wide-eyed they stared up to the heavens. Marica caught sight of Ratty standing at the rear of a buggy.

"Ratty, where's my brother?" she cried out.

He didn't need to speak. Slowly she walked towards him. Laying on the back of the vehicle was her twin brother. His body still, blood dried around his lips.

"No, no, no," Marica fell on his body and clasped her arms around him, she held him tight and begged him to breathe.

But Hanisi was gone.

$

"Sophia," Luca spotted her amongst the crowd. "Come quickly, where is Adria?" he asked. Sophia looked behind her. Adria was following, Zarrah helping her walk.

"She's here."

"Follow me," said the ex-prison officer.

Adria caught sight of the man who had led her from the prison and she quickened her step. They moved between several trucks, where a small group of people huddled around a figure, propped up against a makeshift pillow of coats. Sophia pushed through the throng.

She fell to her knees. Reaching out she grabbed her father's hand.

"Sophia," he coughed, "we made it, girl."

Sophia smiled at him; she looked to his chest, blood oozed from the exit wound. She began to shake and cry.

"There is no time for tears, my love, where is your sister?"

"She's coming. Adria," she called.

The surrounding group moved aside, allowing Zarrah to come through them with Adria. Alander burst into tears, seeing the girl he had lost twelve years ago.

Adria knelt beside the man. "I remember you, now I see you." Adria suddenly remembered things which had been locked away for so long; stories he would read her at night-time, being thrown up in the air. A wave of mixed emotions hit her.

"I am sorry I lost you. I never gave up trying to find you. Please, forgive me," Alander spoke slowly, pausing to catch his breath between words.

Adria didn't know what to say, this was all too much. She nodded and looked at the dying man with confused affection.

"Can everyone give me some space with my daughters?" Alander looked around at his old friends and they politely moved away.

"Luca," Sophia said, "can you look after Zarrah for me?"

He nodded.

Olaf was nearby and heard Sophia say the girl's name. The big man took one look at Zarrah and knew instantly. She had to be Inyoni's daughter; he had found his Wild Woman's little girl. He went to speak but then it hit him. How do you tell a child their mother is dead? Olaf went numb.

Courtauld was standing nearby. He looked up at his big

friend, as if reading Olaf's mind.

"I will do it," he said, patting the big man on the back and they followed Luca and Zarrah.

"Zarrah, that's a lovely name," said Courtauld.

$

"My girls, back together at last," Alander held their hands. Blue was still sat by Alander's feet, forever watching him. "I don't have much time and there is so much I want to say."

His teeth were bloodstained and his skin was turning paler by the second. His hands grew cold, but he continued. "I'm sorry I brought you into this world. I'm sorry I lost you, Adria. But you are in this world, I believe, for a reason. You are stronger than you know, and you will grow even stronger in time." Alander's face turned grim. "The Chemist will not give up trying to find you."

"The Chemist?" Adria looked even more perplexed.

Alander lips tightened. "You and your sister came from her DNA; she was a mother to you both. In the beginning she fed you from her own breast. But she is evil and obsessed with pleasing The Chancellor. She must be stopped from creating more children. She will turn them into fighting machines with no morals."

"She might have died in the lab sector?" Sophia looked at her dad.

"True." Alander's words began to slur. "We can hope. But if not, The Chemist will come looking and neither of you is ready to fight the System. Thousands of Faze addicts have perished today. I could not save the addicts of Aris. But you two have the power and a way to cure the millions of addicts in the System." He paused for air.

Sophia wiped fresh blood from his mouth.

"I don't understand. How can we save all those people?" Sophia tilted her head.

"Head north, leave the System. find Jeptoo, he lives at The Core."

"Who's Jeptoo?" Adria replied. Alander removed a bloodied rag from his pocket. Grabbing hold of Sophia's hand, he placed it in her palm. She felt something hard and round inside it. Alander held their hands tight, his fingers began to tremble. "Jeptoo taught me everything I know. Now remember girls, the answer is staring you in the face."

Alander's head fell forward as his last breath left his lungs.

Sophia and Adria did not move. Their bodies trembled with sorrow as Blue began to howl at the moon.

CHAPTER THIRTY-ONE

"Chancellor, some unsavoury characters are calling from Aris. They are demanding to speak with you. They are on-screen now, should I put them through?"

The ultraviolet lights made Claytus' skin look wet in the round hall. Long, thin tubes of low-pressure mercury vapour ran around the circular room. A few feet in front of the Chancellor's secretary was a spiral tower of cables and wires, which rose to a point like a pine tree. The tip met a large, blue, disc-shaped solar panel in the ceiling.

Multiple humming machines and computers surrounded them at the base. Claytus waited patiently for a reply, sweat leaking from his disfigured, bald, pink scalp. Claytus came from the far south of the System's reach. Growing up, he belonged to a nomadic people who lived in the frozen desert. The tribe known as the Borghild practised artificial cranial deformation. Claytus had two pink ram-like horns protruding from the back of his head, which were injected with steroids until he was sixteen years old. Elongated and packed with muscle, they curled at angles down his back. They curved under his arms by his elbows and, coming to a point, they jutted out in front of him level with his navel. From within the spiral maze of electric cables and wires, a bright blue hexagonal light emerged. Heavy breathing emanated from within the mass of electrical branches, and a harsh voice sounded.

"Is it my son? Is it Bliksem?"

"No, my lord, it's the disgusting engineer and The Chemist. They tell me Aris has fallen." The hexagonal blue light grew larger and brighter. Claytus spoke with a calmness which hid his fear.

"Put them through," said the rasping voice of the Chancellor.

"My lord," Claytus bowed and turned. A pink tail of spikes trailed behind him as he left the round chamber.

A few seconds later, a large screen ascended from the floor where Claytus had just stood. The screen crackled with interference, then hissed and flickered for a moment. The features of Techno and The Chemist appeared in front of him.

"My Chancellor," they both said simultaneously, then bowed their heads. All they could see was the hexagonal shaped light.

"Go on. What of Aris?" the Chancellor asked.

The Chemist spoke, "my lord, it is with great sadness... I am afraid to tell you–" she paused. "Your son is dead, Aris is in ruins. The gangs, they rose up and-,"

"Silence," the Chancellor snapped.

Techno averted his eyes from the screen like a scared child.

"My son was weak, Aris can be and will be rebuilt. We have other ways of producing Faze for now. What news on Alander? And your children? This is my only concern."

277

The Chemist swallowed deeply. "Alander is also dead. Sophia and Adria have fled," she coughed nervously then continued, "our informant tells us they are heading north."

The cables and wires which made up the tree-like cocoon began to spark and glow red, as if the Chancellor's anger transmitted through them. His voice bellowed at the screen. "I wanted Alander alive; he is the only one with the knowledge I want. We will track down the girls, but I want them alive. Do you hear me? Alive. Do you know how long I have waited for–," The Chancellor's voice stopped dead.

The Chemist was holding something up to the screen. A fleshy form wriggled in her palms, no bigger than a loaf of bread. A tube ran into the embryo's mouth, filled with mother's milk.

"I have broken the code," The Chemist smiled broadly.

"Is it female?" The Chancellor questioned her.

"Yes and she is strong, she grows by the day, quicker than any before her."

"Then bring her to me now."

"My lord," they both replied again. The screen went dead.

Claytus waited outside the chamber door, listening. The Chancellor's voice spoke in his ear, Claytus raising a hand to the earpiece which he always wore.

"Find Pizda and Kusse and tell them to report to me. And let them know their brother is dead. Immediately."

Claytus turned away from the door.

$

Adria stared at the gaping cave mouth of Aris. Thick grey smoke billowed out from the city. Now and then, a loud crash would sound as more of the cavern roof caved in. From high on the plateau, in the failing moonlight she could make out a mass of people still escaping from the city. She felt a pang of sadness in the knowledge that most of them would be Faze addicts, and without the drug and no known cure they would be dead by this time tomorrow.

Adria's mind was beginning to feel clearer. The overdose she had taken still made her feel sick, her body felt feeble and weak, but her mind was coming back to some form of reality. Behind her a makeshift camp had been erected, screams of the dying and injured sending shivers down her spine. She felt angry, sad, hopeful, and confused all at the same time. She was beginning to remember more about Sophia and Alander; playing with toys in their bedroom, bath times, Alander and Jon reading her stories. Adria was overwhelmed with her conflicting emotions. She had so many unanswered questions. But Sophia was beside herself. After losing her father, she had discovered her dear friend Hanisi had also died. Sophia and Marica now comforted each other.

Adria had seen the young girl Zarrah running off sobbing, an odd-looking couple of men followed her. Adria thought best to stay away. She should be sad, she should be doing something to help, but as the Cane slowly left her system, the urge for more was growing.

She attempted to put it to the back of her mind, but it nagged at her, it spoke to her. It will take away the pain; it will take away the self-loathing.

She argued back silently with the voices in her head. 'Fuck off, leave me alone'.

The voice disappeared, and then seconds later it snuck back. Just one more line, that's all, no more after that. She promised the voice, one more, but later. She was interrupted from her internal argument by a thin man with a pointed, rodent-like face. "Hi, I am Ratty. I knew your father very well."

"He was not my father," she snapped back at him, unsure why she felt so angry by his comment.

"I understand," Ratty replied. "But I can assure you, he never stopped loving you. Alander never gave up trying to find you."

"So why the fuck didn't he then?" Adria's eyes darkened.

Ratty took a step back and held out his palms. "Sorry, I know this must be all very confusing for you."

"Confusing? Confusing? it's a total head fuck," Adria began to shake, her fists clenched white.

"Please, let me tell you what I know. It might help," Ratty pleaded with her.

Adria took a deep breath and seemed to relax her body. "Okay. It is a mess in here," she pointed to her head.

"It's okay, I understand. Sophia can tell you a lot more than I can. But I will tell you what I know. Alander and Jon were both seriously hurt in the fire. Alander blew up the lab deliberately to get you and Sophia away from Bliksem. You see, they had plans for you. You were to be sent to Iris to be used as a breeding machine for The Chancellor. Are you aware how unique you and Sophia are?"

"Not really. So you are telling me I was created in some fucking lab to be someone's whore?"

"I wouldn't put it so harshly, but yes I guess so." Ratty's face turned red. This wasn't going the way he hoped.

Adria looked back at the harsh black smoke which she could taste on her lips. She remained silent for a while, computing her thoughts. "So Alander's plan backfired, and I was still basically used as a whore, imprisoned, raped, bruised, scarred. Where was my saviour when I had to eat rats and festering garbage to survive?"

Adria's voice raised, but she kept her temper under control, allowing Ratty to continue.

"Alander and Jon were so badly injured; most people would have not even tried to find you. The fire was so intense. It took years for Jon and Alander to get back to health. They hid with The Tears of Aris while they were on the mend. Alander changed both his and Sophia's appearance. They could have escaped Aris, but instead, they remained for one reason and one reason only, which was you." Ratty tried to gauge a reaction.

Before she could reply, the brawny form of Tusker emerged from the darkness. "There is a meeting now; I was asked to find you. Follow me."

Tusker held back the flap to a large tent. The Tears of Aris were used to upping sticks and moving from place to place at the last minute, and this time it was no different. They had a makeshift kitchen and they were cooking pots of Vinayaki broth in one tent, where an orderly queue of hundreds of children waited to be served. Adria followed Ratty into the round tent, Tusker following them in too. Sitting at the head of the congregation, was The Crane. He talked with his long thin arms. Adria had never seen a man so tall. His hair which twisted around his body, although looking odd, was fascinating.

Adria spotted Zarrah. The teenager sat on the floor, her head was resting on Olaf's shoulder. Next to her was the one-legged man. Tusker took a seat to the right of The Crane.

To his left sat Sophia and Marica, their faces full of sorrow, holding hands. Ratty joined them and followed by Adria, they all sat cross-legged on the floor, apart from The Crane who sat on his throne of books which were melded together, making an impressive throne-like armchair.

Adria parked herself next to an extremely hairy man giving off a bad odour. He apologised and moved over so Adria could fit in. "Hi, my name's Steev," his breath stank like a rotting corpse. Adria noticed Sophia glaring at him. He pretended not to notice and began talking to the man on his right. Adria listened in. There were many gang leaders here—Oddities and human—but none wielded more power than The Tears of Aris.

The Crane spoke up, "we will be heading east," he said in a deep voice. "It will be a long journey, but it is the best place for the children to go."

A man with three eyes—the third on the bridge of his nose—came forward. "The city of Krak?" he said this with an air of scorn. "It's just a rumour. And anyway it would take months to get there, mountains to cross, rivers. And we would remain in the System's reach for half of the journey. The children won't make it. They would be in Baráttan pits or the slaughterhouses before we knew it. This is crazy talk."

There were a few grunts of approval.

The Crane looked directly into the man's eyes. "Krak is no rumour, my friend, I sent men there, a long time ago now. One returned; he is here." He turned to Tusker, who struggled to smile with the weight of the horn on his bottom lip. This, unfortunately, made him always look miserable.

"Krak is real, I know a safe way there. It will be hard to navigate in a vehicle, and we would eventually have to travel by foot. Krak is a land, not just a city. Everyone there is one of us, spawn from the Faze generations. We can be free. I tell you, brothers, it is real."

The three-eyed man knew Tusker well and respected his word; there was no other choice. "Then, I agree," he said, and he stepped back.

"But my father, he wanted us to travel to The Core, to the north." Sophia joined in the conversation.

Luca had been standing in the shadows; he stepped into the light. "Sophia is right, Alander wished us to go to The Core. We cannot change his plans, not now."

"Friend," said The Crane. "You know as well as I do, that journey is for Adria and Sophia. The Tears of Aris have played their part in this war. We have been labelled Oddities and lived in squalor like rats for far too long. We will go to Krak. And from this day on we are no longer Oddities, we are human just like the rest of you."

The Oddities in the room cheered. The Crane nodded in agreement.

Sophia seemed to be in a different world, deep in thought. She idly played with Alander's glass eye, still wrapped in the bloodied cloth. Finally, she spoke again. "You are right, Crane," she began. "We all have our destinies to fulfil. I am sure I speak for everyone in this room when I say if it weren't for you and your men joining the struggle, well, we would not be here now."

Luca raised an eyebrow at her. Sophia nodded at him, encouraging him to agree.

"So, it's settled, The Tears of Aris will take the children east."

"I will go with Sophia and Adria to The Core. Who will come with us?" Luca asked.

The teenager Zarrah stood up first. "I am different, I am the granddaughter of the Faze generation. But I have no wish to go to Krak. I will follow you."

Olaf stood, his head almost touched the top of the tent. "Where you go, I follow. Your mother wouldn't forgive me if I left you now."

A small voice perked up. "Excuse me if I don't stand, but I am coming too," Courtauld waved a hand in the air.

Ratty, Steev and Connor, the two-toned young man, would also follow, along with Marica.

"Then it is agreed," Luca confirmed.

"You didn't have much choice," The Crane laughed.

Suddenly Adria shot up. "Krak? The Core? What are you all talking about? I am not going fucking anywhere."

Adria stomped out of the tent. Luca turned to follow her, but Sophia's hand was on his shoulder. "It's okay. I'll go." She followed her sister.

"Adria," Sophia called out, running after her.

Adria carried on walking until she arrived back at the cliff edge overlooking the smoking cave mouth. Tears poured down her cheeks and sitting down, she hugged her knees close to her body and rocked herself gently back and forth. Sophia sat down quietly next to her.

"I'm going mad," Adria cried, "please, I don't understand any of this. Tell me, tell me everything I beg you."

Sophia looked at her. Adria looked terribly ill—she didn't want to make things any worse, but she could see it was killing her. She could see it in her face. She had to tell her.

"Okay," Sophia agreed. "I can only tell you what I know. A lot of this is still a mystery to me."

Adria listened intently.

"Alander and Jon were brought to Aris under orders of The Chancellor, to create the Klóns. They've made hundreds of thousands of them, sent to every corner of the System, used as fighters or slaves. These were type one Klóns. Soon they discovered they could not reproduce blood cells and their eyesight was terrible. The blood changed to synthetic blood—which would last—and their eyes needed replacing with mechanical ones."

Adria nodded, remaining silent.

Sophia fumbled with the glass eye in her fingers and continued. "Alander was forced to improve the Klón, but the type two Klón was all but a failure; only one ever survived, he was stronger. Deadlier. Hopefully, he died there," she pointed to the smoking hole. "His name was Stór. The Chancellor held Alander's family, under the threat of death. Alander was tasked with creating a female Klón, one which could reproduce with humans. The Chancellor is obsessed with creating a superhuman, a bloodline which will last forever. It took time—years—but finally I was born from out of the test tube—a type three. The first female. Hundreds were born but they all died within days," she shrugged. "But for some reason, I survived. Alander's family would be free and I would be sent to Iris to be a breeding mule for the Chancellor and his sons."

Adria looked at Sophia wide-eyed, hanging onto every word.

"But I didn't form a womb, and when Alander told the Chancellor he had failed they slaughtered his family. He refused to work for a while, but his love for me kept him going and eventually, he created the Type four Klón. Again, only one survived. She had the same DNA as me but altered with Stór's, making type four the strongest and most powerful, and with what the Chancellor wanted: a womb. You are a

Klón, Adria. We are both unique, and Alander loved us. You would have been tied to a bed all your life if we hadn't escaped."

Adria was silent. Then she began to laugh. "I am a Klón? Is this why Mikhail's Klón didn't attack me, why they always stared at me?"

"Yes," Sophia replied, "although they have their faults, Klóns will not kill their own."

Slowly things started to make some sense. A weight seemed to lift off her shoulders. Adria began laughing nervously. She hadn't laughed in a long time; the feeling was weird. Sudden memories of playing with Sophia came back to her. She looked at Sophia.

"I do remember you." A vague memory came back to her, playing and messing about in the lab where Alander worked. "Why did he give you that horrible glass eye?" Adria asked.

Sophia shook her head. Opening the cloth, she took out the eye and held the glass ball up to the moonlight. The girls looked through the glass, the green colour glistening almost fluid-like. The two young women turned and looked at each other with raised eyebrows. Adria then noticed black ink, written on the cloth. It was barely legible.

"What does that say?"

"I hadn't noticed this," Sophia spread out the old hanky. Scrawled across in black capital letters it read.

THE ANSWER IS STARING YOU IN THE FACE.
FOR THE MILLIONS.

"Give me your gun, quickly."

Sophia handed Adria over the handgun, taking the glass eye

she laid it on a stone. Although the girls were eager to see what their father had hidden from them all this time, Adria slowly chipped away at the glass with the gun's handle

Finally, the glass broke apart. In the centre was a tiny piece of paper and a small vial of green liquid. The note was tightly rolled up. Sophia unravelled it; she had to find a torch to read the tiny scribble upon it.

It read:

FAZE, ANTIDOTE.

℥

The Tears of Aris and the children left before sunrise. A solitary truck sat on the plateau. Ratty, Connor, Steev, and Luca were busy loading supplies which The Crane and his men had left them. Olaf and Courtauld were checking the engine, topping it up with water and oil. Adria, Sophia, Zarrah, and Marica stood hand in hand overlooking the plain. Behind them to the north the monsoon rains were approaching again, thick clouds creeping towards them across the sky. In front of the girls, freshly dug mounds were decorated with small rocks.

Alander and Hanisi were laid to rest. Blue sat by Alander's grave; no one could move him.

To the south the sun began to climb. Sunlight shone on the women for the first time in their lives. The youngest of the four had lost a mother, the oldest had lost a brother.

Adria and Sophia had lost a father. Together they were

sisters, united, bound together by grief. It would make them stronger in time.

A long road lay ahead of them.

An even longer one faced Adria; the road of recovery, self-healing, and discovering who she truly was.

Alander had told Sophia, if they made it out of Aris, The Core would be their destination. Once there, they were to seek out Jeptoo, Alander's mentor. Sophia assumed he would hold the key. The key to opening the ingredients of the antidote—and they were going to need a lot of it. If together, they were going to free the System and the millions of those in slavery and addicted to....

FAZE.

To be continued...

About the Author

Martin White was born in Southampton in 1975 and is frankly amazed to still be alive today. He did not do well at school, dyslexia and immaturity played their part. After leaving school he spent far too much time dancing to rave music in fields, and after a few brushes with the law, he finally fell into the catering industry and worked as a chef, a private security guard and drug worker.

He hung up his chef's knives in 2017 and went back into full-time education and is currently studying Creative Writing at the University of Winchester. His work is inspired by his own life events, that are at times unsettling.

Martin White lives in North Hampshire with his partner Lyndsay and three stepsons, and their dog Maggie. He says writing is the best job in the world.

You can connect with me on:

- https://authormjwhite.wordpress.com
- https://twitter.com/AuthorM_White
- https://www.facebook.com/AuthorMJWhite